A LIVING
HELL

A LIVING HELL

WYATT WILKINSON

urlink
PRINT & MEDIA

INTRODUCTION

The events in this book are fictional. The names of the people involved are fictional as well as the location. People do nasty things everywhere. It is a story of a small town filled with nasty little secrets, if by chance any of the events strike close to home it is strictly coincidental.

To anyone who has been the butt end of a practical joke, the subject of ridicule, or disrespect- This one's for you. It does get better. I will tackle bullying, homophobia, judgmental religious bigots, hate of all kinds, and backstabbing. Some incidents are vile and despicable as well as offensive. These incidents are not intended to give you "good ideas" to torment someone. Please hold the judgment. They have a purpose. I wanted to make it as real as possible. The nasty things we do holds no bounds and neither did I in the following pages.

The day will come when you are exonerated and sweet revenge can be yours. However, never act out in violence. Cuts and bruises heal. The fact that you have overcome and have risen to the top lasts a life time. Success is the weapon of choice. Use it wisely.

Keep in mind that even the most foul and putrid water becomes drinkable. People do change over time. The biggest twat you know may become a friend one day. If you are an asshole, you may become a better person too. We have all made mistakes and done nasty things to one another. We are in one point of view all assholes to someone.

Nasty deeds can cause resentment, anger, hatred, and even worse: suicide or murder. It is unhealthy to dwell on them. You are not a defense attorney that will use past problems to justify the way you treat others. It is never an excuse and the pity party has to end sometime. The sooner, the better. Let them go. I will give the way I apologize and the meaning behind it in time. I know it is easier said than done. Some cuts are deeper than others but they heal all the same. It may just take longer but the scar remains.

The scar is the memory of what happened and the lesson learned. Will you ever trust or talk to the person who inflicted it on you again? It is possible but not always likely. This is not intended to be a fantasy world where we all hold hands and sing songs together. That is just a lie and I won't waste your time trying to feed it you. Use your better judgment. We have all had enemies that became friends and others remain enemies or better yet, forgotten. Left to the side of the road like road kill. Life is a highway, right?

I wrote this book to be a guide. Imagine a new puppy, how do you want it to grow up and behave? Do you want it to be nasty and vicious? Easy way to do that isn't it? Beat it, mistreat it, starve it, yell, swear and torment it. You'll have your wish. I hope you have a kennel and sleep with one eye open. If you don't, it will turn on you. Do you want it to be loving, loyal and great to be around? Train it, feed it regularly, give it a attention and reinforce the positive behaviors with rewards and you will have your wish.

We get angry towards bad pet owners for raising vicious dogs and want to help every time an animal is mistreated. However humans are the same. It's amazing how many times we turn a blind eye to a child being excessively punished in public or worse. It's none of our business. We even do it ourselves to each other and wonder why the guy in the office snapped one day. How did you treat him? Did you stop others from mistreating him?

Have you ever bullied someone in school or at work? The kid that gets cornered and beat up at lunch because he is a little different can grow up and becomes hateful and wants revenge just like the puppy. Is he/ she going to get it whether it's through passive aggressive ways like losing your mortgage paperwork, giving the job your more qualified for to someone else, or setting you up for failure? Or even worse yet, an act of violence? They may even commit suicide. Or is he/ she going to move past it? Are you?

This book is filled with incidents of bullying and revenge whether it is violent or passive aggressive behavior. However, human nature is hard to predict. "Blame the deed, not the breed" is what we say for animals labeled as dangerous such as pit bulls. What do we say for the bullied when they lash out? They were odd, a loner, psycho and didn't fit in. I've always wondered how they got there. Bullying and the way there were raised and treated? The fact is, they haven't learned to get past it. How to move on.

Remember: How do you want the puppy to behave? Better yet, How do you want others to treat you?

CHAPTER 1

• • • • • • ● • • • • • • •

Derry is your typical small town of 3,000 souls or less. A one traffic light town with a down town core that stretches 3 to 4 blocks in either direction. It will have a small hardware store, a couple of convenience stores, a library, a grocery store, three or four restaurants, a small furniture store, a bank, a mechanic, a gas station or two a coffee shop and of course a liquor store. It will have two schools with one being in town and the other just on the outskirts and of course three or four churches. Industry is usually small, perhaps a mill and maybe a fishery or two and maybe even a small factory.

It's a place where everyone waves and knows everyone else. They always seem to give off the "Happiest place to be" persona and are depicted as such in the movies. If you believe that, you probably believe in Santa and the Easter bunny too. Not everyone is going to like everyone just because you happen to live in a small place.

Nestled on the North Shore of Lake McLaughlin, this quaint little town of 3,000 lives to boast itself as the "Greatest Place To Be". With its nice beaches, great fishing, hiking trails, community boat ramp and nearby camping, it's the Greatest Place To Be.

I have so many memories of this place, it's hard to know where to begin. Well, let's start with me. I have the pleasure of being the dreaded middle child. Born in the mid 70's in this sleepy dead end town. John Cougar Mellencamp always makes these places sound great. I still don't get it but anyway ...

We lived by the water on the opposite side of the street. My name is Justin Williamson. Like I said I am the middle child and man does it suck. The stereotypical middle child according to assortment says that the middle child typically feels neglected, insecure, and like to go with the flow. They are loners and have trouble with relationships and have trouble keeping them due to lack of interest. They are not over achievers and like to just get by typically in school and career. They are artistic and creative but don't work well under pressure. They will start many projects but rarely keep enough focus to finish. A career in writing, journalism and creative out leads are the best career options. Anything with flexible hours and constant project changes are ideal for middle children. relationships are not always the best but however a last born maybe a good match.

Ok I did the cliff notes version but now it's time to tear it apart since it is placing everyone in one basket that happens to be a middle child. Let's look at what is right in my case and my case only. Everyone is different so fortune cookie assessments aren't always accurate. Ok neglected, insecure- yes. Go with the flow depends on the situation. I like to lead too. The loner part- please, this is strictly based on your environment and the lack of others your age and interest similarities in the immediate demographic.

As for relationships, my current is 12 years and still going. Vague generalizations don't really stand up, maybe the ones that were interviewed for the study (if one even took place) fit that category but then again not everyone is the same. I got by in some subjects in school that were mandatory but didn't keep my interest. Everyone does that. Forget the generalizations.

The creativity comment is a generalization that applies to everyone. Everyone has creative tendencies and abilities. As for pressure, there are lots of people who don't like working under pressure. It depends what I am doing and what the pressure is. I know lots of people who stat projects and don't always finish. Sometimes your interests change or your career and family take focus away from the projects. It's based on priority. Your children and family should take precedence over finishing a bookshelf in your woodshop.

* * *

I remember taking the bus at a young age where I had a large fat kid and neighbor who used to take his lunch in a picnic basket every day. I dreaded getting an aisle seat. Within a few hundred yards of my bus stop, he'd get on. He's waddle down the aisle with his picnic basket held out in front of him huffing and puffing all the way to the back of the bus bumping his fat ass into everyone who had the unfortunate aisle seat. Those ham hocks for legs and that fat ass stampeding down the aisle every damn day picnic basket in hand and there was always a smell that followed him. A lovely mixture of sweat and flatulence. Luckily for me, this was only for a year.

Don't get me wrong, some of my friends were considered fat and to get the record perfectly straight, I don't have a problem with people being overweight. Sometimes they can't help it whether it's a glandular abnormality or a slow metabolism. There are those out there who don't know how to cook other than premade, processed foods. There's an array of issues. I may bring it into an argument or disagreement just as easily as a skinny person being an anorexic bitch. We all know the words and insults and have used them so spare me the judgment.

Anyway, I didn't have much interaction with him other than having his fat ass in my face every morning. Our dads didn't get along from when they were kids and they still manage to hate each other to this day. I've always loved how parents tell their kids to get along with others when they are just as bad at holding a grudge. Life is full of hypocrisies and double standards, get used to it.

We had a black lab and one day she was gone after more than 7 years of ownership. I was 12 years old at the time. I was walking down the street the one day and fat ass's dad stopped me on the street.

"Hey kid, come here, "he said from the edge of his yard. I went over. He was fatter than his son. The whole family was fat.

"Hi," I said

"I just wanted to let you know I shot your dog," he said smugly.

"No, she died in the field, she was old." I responded. That's what dad told me anyway.

"Your dad told you that, didn't he? That's bullshit. I shot it." he said menacingly.

"No, you didn't," I said giving him a nasty look. The nerve of some people. The gal to say that to a kid.

"Oh but I did and if I had my rifle now I would shoot you too. You better hope I don't see you alone like you usually are. You probably will grow up to be a loser like your dad anyway<" he said with a menacing grin.

"I'd rather be loser than a fat pig like you!" I shot back fighting back I was scared. The look of shock on his face was priceless. I would have been in so much trouble to talk to an adult like that but in this case there would have been an acceptation.

"Oh you have a big mouth for a little twerp and it's going to get you in trouble now run home before I go and get my gun," he said bent over to look me in the face. with a soft, menacing tone. It was creepy. He stood up and sneered and shouted. "Go!! Get out of here!!" I ran. There was no way that sack of shit could catch up to me without his truck.

Now if that were today, things would get really ugly. After I punch him in the face and kick him in the gut on the way down. I'd push him over backwards to see if he would be helpless like a turtle on his back. Then the insults. "Mission Impossible: Finding your penis. Isn't that right fat ass?" Kick him while he's down and then punch him in the face again. "Here I thought fat people were supposed to jolly." Another blow to the face.

"Now I know why you have such a long face. Your wife has to lift more than 100 pounds of fat just to find something the size of a pimple. You're a fat piece of shit!" I would punch his face a few more times and remind him next time will be worse. "Now if I throw a twinky, will you leave?" Follow with another blow to the face. Yes, I have anger issues. He shot my dog and rubbed it in my face. The fact is he picked on a kid because he didn't have the guts to do it to an adult. The jerk off deserves to bleed and have bruises. Today, this is the type of spineless loser who would hide behind a computer and post nasty stuff online.

I of course went home and told him what fat ass told me. He was pissed right off. It was true. Dad retaliated by shooting his 2 dogs. One messed up neighborhood. Luckily that dispute was over and I was never approached by the swine again.

I have an older brother, Anthony, and a younger sister Kelly. We live on one of the most boring roads in North America. Nowhere near anything remotely exciting. There was a small woodlot at the end of the road across from my best friend's house. We'll call her Michelle. The woodlot was used mostly for the older kids to go in and smoke and drink behind their parents backs. There really isn't much to do in a small town other than smoking and drinking. Yes, smoking implies cigarettes and weed. Sadly, substance abuse will grace the following pages on numerous occasions. It seems to be a trend in small towns. It's really expected in large cities. I'll blame the movies for that. Let it be a wakeup call for you. It's everywhere.

Inside the woodlot there were poorly constructed forts, lean-tos and make shift camping areas where you could set up a tent and party the weekend away. It's a small town and there's usually one or two cops maximum. In our case, there was one. The concern was mainly the downtown area and he worked days. There were patrols downtown on the weekend. They really didn't bother with the rural areas. Nothing happens in the rural areas or at least it isn't reported.

I can remember growing up with these people and I didn't really fit in with anyone other than Michelle, her twin brother Mike and older brother Alex. I'd go down to their house to play while my brother would hang out with his friends and my sister with hers. There were times I did hang out with my brother's friends, that usually ended with me being the 5th wheel and then the subject of ridicule or some sort of practical joke or prank. If I didn't go along with it, it was usually "Justin, go home!" I always shrugged and said, "See ya." Jerks.

You know that hollow, sinking feeling in the middle of your chest when nobody cares or you feel you aren't wanted? That got to be my best friend. I think I know that feeling more than anyone. Every time I was victim to a mean spirited practical joke or prank. Every time I got made fun of for one reason or another. My little black hole would show up right on time and suck every ounce of happiness out of my life with every nasty comment, prank and rude gesture I got. Maybe if I had someone stand up for me once in a while, it wouldn't have been so bad. When you get picked on or humiliated, it's always a group effort.

I fought with one of my brother's friends little brothers on my front lawn. For clarity there's only two years difference. He knocked me down and pinned me and rubbed me in the grass. That's when I found out I was allergic. There were no punches exchanged or if there was it wasn't hard. The itching from the grass was nasty.

Give me a potato peeler and I would have peeled the skin off for some relief. Man the itching, then the bumps started forming on my arms. I bucked him off and ran in the house. Of course they started to tell everyone at school I ran in bawling. It was to clean up and stop the damn itching. Of course nobody believed me when I mentioned the itching and reaction. Forget the fact there wasn't a bump or bruise anywhere on my body from the little skirmish. I got my ass kicked by someone's baby brother. Isn't it funny how stories change or are made up along the way. I still get the bumps on my arms after I cut the grass. Just follow the trail of clothing to the bathroom when I'm done.

When I hung out with my sister's friends, it was even worse. Dolls, makeovers and some other lame ass crap for a boy to do. You know who got the makeover. Yup, then the jokes. I just have one question. What the hell was I thinking? Yup, that's one for the therapists.

The other kids in my class at my elementary school were complete jerks. I didn't want to hang with them at all. Mean sons of bitches would be putting it mildly. They were your typical white middle class blue collar working class offspring.

The teachers had their favorites too. For gym class, the most athletic boys and girls were always elected as captains and rarely was it rotated to be fair. Usually within the same 6 people, class after class. They'd pick their friends and then work their way down the class and size selections of the class. Athletic boys first, the odd athletic girl followed by the fat kid, someone of another race or origin, the skinny kids and by the 6th and 7th grade, me. Dead last. I was the smallest boy by that time. Isn't that just terrific? My attitude was if you are picked last, they really don't want you to play anyway. Screw them, I didn't. I spent my class warming up the bench. I had a gym teacher who hated me. They say they don't hate any of their students. That's a lie. Satan's mistress hated my guts.

There was a class where she set up the high jump and another student, Mike, went and jumped over the bar. She looked at him and smiled. Then the pressure was on for me to go. I ran jumped and of course knocked over the bar. She glared at me.

"Did I say it was ok to go?!" she screamed at me in front of the whole class.

"They told me to go after Mike," I responded.

"I'll tell you when to go! Get back in line and wait until I give the instructions!!" she yelled.

"Cunt" I said under my breath, rolled my eyes and went and sat on bench.

For the record, this word is not only used as a vulgar description of female genitalia but also means "an unpleasant or stupid person" by Wikipedia. A contemptible person by another. Can't Understand Normal Thinking as an acronym. A meaning I enjoy is for a mean or obnoxious person for whom you have contempt. Another definition is a person so vile without any redeeming features. Yes she is. Case Closed. I will limit the use of that word. If it ever loses its power we are all screwed. It is a show stopper.

When you use the word, it has the genuine power of shock. Mostly everyone will stop dead in their tracks and stop whatever they are doing. One can hear a pin drop after its use. I love it. Now you have the their full, undivided attention. What you should have had in the first place before pulling out such a word. When it's effects are non-existent, we are screwed.

I have used it to describe gay males and it is held in high regard in that circle. I sometimes will offer the twat waffle (in lieu of the other word) answer to a question. Let's face it, it will be sarcastic, condescending or brutally honest and you probably don't want to hear it. It is a very useful word like fuck. I have friends where we call each other a cunt and it is a pleasurable. Seriously people need to stop being so sensitive. I worked with sisters who would call each other that word for no reason. I am not offended. Keep in mind in places like Australia, the word is used frequently and the most offensive word you can say there is mother fucker. They take it literally- you fuck your mother. For this you will die.

My friends couldn't believe it. What a bitch. She smiles at Mike and yells at me and berates me in front of the whole class. Satan's mistress it is. Medusa would be jealous. My friends complained to the principal afterwards. I went home and told my dad. It turns out that Mrs. Winter's husband worked with his and was a known stool pigeon and whiner and they didn't get along at all. Now it makes sense. Can't get even with dad, have the wife take it out on his kid. What a vindictive, spineless whore.

This is where I think my behavior problems began. That bitch was rude, disrespectful and just plain mean. I should have called her that just to see the reaction and watch the fireworks. I have no respect for people like that and never will. I wouldn't take her crap any more. I was a good kid until that point. Game on. I had one other altercation with her and this time I turned around and called her a fat, stupid pig right to her face. Disrespect me again. I was sent to the office and explained what I did and why. This is a behavior I still do to this day. I despise rude people especially if it isn't called for. I am rude only when someone is rude first. Game on ass-hat.

A meeting was set up and of course my dad went to it and laid it on the table on how she was just plain disrespectful and rude to me for sport. How he works with Mr. Winters and how they have their differences. I didn't get anything for discipline. I think my dad was proud of me for standing up for myself. I didn't really do that much. I was a doormat as a kid. It felt good telling her off. I did better in grade 8, we'll get to that soon enough. Let's just say it's worth the wait.

I can give instances when we were in grade 6 and if you stood up in class and gave a piece of news from current events, you could tell a joke. Clean of course, this is elementary school. I would flip through our English book because it had jokes in the bottom of the page in small print and use one of those. Cheesy but to a grade 6 kid, a little funny. I'd give the news and then deliver my joke. They didn't find it funny or get it. The funniest part is, a couple of weeks later we got to it. The teacher read it from the bottom.

"Why do firefighter wear suspenders?" "To keep their pants up."

It's from a children's grade 6 English book. The funniest part was it had to be explained to these idiots. The teacher at the time said it was funny because you are looking for a funny answer and there isn't one. When he read, he laughed. It only took two weeks too. When I read it, he didn't get it. Two weeks later, it's funny. I wonder how long it'll take for the dullards to clue in who I am really talking about. At the rate of memory loss and the rate of aging, I should be in a wheel chair and in a nursing home or dead before it clues in. By then they'll forget it five minutes later or be on their death bed anyway. Let's face it, I am safe either way.

I am going to jab several insults at these people throughout this book, and I am not going to dummy it down so they get it. It's more fun keeping the dimwitted in suspense. The vacant expressions followed by the feeble attempts to get the insult and by the time they do, you are already gone. Isn't it fun to let them stew on it?

I know I am being hypocritical when it comes to these people, however, I do have my reasons. They were mean spirited and cruel to whoever didn't fit in with them or who they thought to be worthy. There was a girl we went to school with throughout and I didn't get to know her until grade 8 when she was 15. Let's call her Kathy. Kathy was from Mexico and immigrated to America with her family I n grade 3, I think. She didn't speak much English at the time and was instantly a 2nd or 3rd class citizen according to the children of privilege. I was quiet and kept to myself and most certainly didn't join in on the taunting, teasing and downright disrespectful treatment she got. I told them to leave her alone a few times but was ignored.

They would purposely pick her last for sports, ignore her, isolate her from group events, taunt, tease, and flat out disrespect her. I can remember one lunch period where these assholes were smacking flies with their rulers and placing them in her hair. She did nothing to deserve it, nor did she fight back. She sat there at her desk, eating her sandwich while these pricks were putting dead flies in her hair. Of course they were laughing and making fun of her. I would have lost it and went on a violent tirade. The lunch monitor came around from classroom to classroom and finally put an end to it and picked the dead flies from her hair and them gave the class proper Hell for it too.

I have utmost respect for Kathy, she took it in style. When I got to know her in grade 8, she told me what she really thought of them. Rotten twats. No class quiffs. She even said she wished that their kids are treated even worse. Then they'll know what kind of people they were, when their kids come home bruised, crying and not wanting to go back to school. See it first hand and then see how funny it is. Makes you think, doesn't it?

I regret not getting to know her sooner, she was really cool and would have been a great friend throughout. I am grateful for getting to know her for the last year before we all went our separate ways. I really hope she grew up to be a knockout, beautiful woman and I wish her a lifetime of happiness. I hope our paths cross one day and I get to see it for myself.

Most importantly in this case, I really hope those who took part in the way Kathy was treated has changed their ways and actually stands up for someone being bullied. Adults do it too. Sometimes they never grow up. I know this behavior happens everywhere, this story takes place along the north shore of Lake McLaughlin. It could be Texas, Florida, British Columbia, Cambodia or anywhere else.

Bullying is mean, hurtful, immoral. Nobody has the right to disrespect anyone. Picking on someone smaller than you makes you a jerk off. If you're doing it to be the big man, you aren't. I look at you with contempt and look down on you. You are a despicable, no class, waste of skin.

I can assure you, even a sibling will do it so the rest of their peers like them. I wish I could count the bloody, fat lips, the bruises, cuts and scrapes I got from my brother and his friends. Picking on Justin is fun. I even got cut to the bone on a piece of pipe from being pushed on it because it was fun. There was a lot of blood. I have a scar above my right eye from stitches at 3 years old because I got my head smashed into the corner of a coffee table from the kids my mother was watching at the time. They were conveniently my dad's friend's kids. Thankfully that came to an end after I got my eye stitched up.

CHAPTER 2

•••••••••●•••••••

I can't remember how old I was, I was young maybe 5 or 6. We had a cold winter and dad liked to do his ice fishing. I hated going, it's too damn cold and I never catch anything but a cold. He 'd build a new ice shanty every couple of years. He was very good at building things. He built his shed or workshop depending on what you want to call it.

This year he leaned the ice shanty up against the big maple tree we had in the back yard. It didn't have skis on it yet. Just some boards for them to be bolted to were there along with the collapsible frame. It had two wooden ends to it and a heavy blue tarp for the walls that would extend as you stood it up and slid the ends apart.

Anthony and I were outside playing and we got close to it. There was a bit of a breeze coming from the back field and of course it was to the back of the ice shanty. One gust caught it and down it came. Anthony got out of the way but I didn't move in time. It pinned me right to the ground with the wood back pushing down on my nose. I managed to turn my head to the side so I could breathe. It was very tight underneath it and it was hard to breathe. I screamed for him to pick it off of me. He couldn't, it was really heavy. I tried to push with the very limited space I had, I could only turn my hands upward and push. I pushed hard and I could hear Anthony trying to pick it up. It was no use.

"Go get mom," I yelled. It was really getting hard to breathe and it was getting hot under there.

Mom came running out in her night gown, it was an early Saturday morning. As kids we know how it goes, it's hard to get up for school but so easy to get up and play or watch cartoons on a Saturday morning.

"Justin, are you ok?!" she asked in a frantic.

"Yeah. It's hard to breathe under here!" I yelled back. It really was getting hard to breathe. I was starting to struggle.

"Take small breaths. We 're going to lift. I need you to push." she said loudly.

I pushed with all I could and she lifted. I saw a crack of light and then darkness again. Another try. A smaller crack of light and then darkness again. It was just too heavy. I hated every minute under there. It was dark, hard to breathe and I don't like being pinned under anyone or anything.

"I'm going to wake up your father," she said loudly to me. He worked the afternoon shift, he isn't going to be happy I thought.

Within a couple of minutes, which seemed like forever, a light come in bigger than the slivers from before. It was wide open and I had to adjust my eyes. I looked up and there was dad. He wasn't happy.

"Are you alright?"

"Yeah I think so" I responded. Yes I can breathe again, I thought.

"Get out from under there." he commanded.

I slid across the grass from under the ice shanty and got to my feet. He put it down right the way it was on the ground. He looked at us all and told us to go in for breakfast. We went right in and he followed. Breakfast was quiet. We all ate without saying a word.

"What happened out there? Were you guys hitting it?" asked dad.

"No, the wind took it" Anthony and I answered at the same time.

"Ok. When I have something out there leaning. Don't go near it." he said firmly.

"I want it laying flat." mom interjected.

Not another word was said on that subject. It was done and it will be laying on the ground. It was never leaned up against the tree again or any other project for that matter.

* * *

Sunday for us involved getting picked up by an old white school bus to take us to church. It would go through the town picking up the kids to take them to Sunday School. Eventually the bus was retired and then they would use their own personal cars to do it. Sunday School was fun as a kid. There was games and snacks and of course religious stories of Moses, Jonah, Jesus and Joseph. They were always the kid friendly versions. The 'you're going to burn in Hell' stuff is saved for when you're a teenager or an adult.

We spent many years going to the Derry Baptist Church. It started off small and grew over the years with two major expansions that I can recall. I never knew what really went on until I got older. The richer families called the shots and everyone went along with it. The church was funded by the richer families and it would be one of the reasons I left later on.

The Smith family owned most of the town. They owned the grocery store, the food processing plant, the fishing industry, the mill and even a restaurant. They were all part of the church and what they said goes. We went through several pastors over the years because I am assuming they wouldn't play ball with the Smith family the way they should. Cindy Smith and her husband adopted a two year old girl, Ashley. That kid had a sense of entitlement from day one. A spoiled, stuck up, little brat.

As she got older, she developed even more stuck up and snotty than you could imagine. She was allowed to run amuck and nobody would say anything to her because she was a Smith. If she didn't get her own way, she'd cross her arms and say "Do you know who I am? I'm Ashley Smith." in that stuck up, holier than though, snotty, condescending tone that I have grown to despise.

One day, I had enough. Ashley walked around like she owned the place and I was sick of her snotty, condescending tone and her sense of entitlement. Punching her in the face would have been nice but I had other plans. It would be too short lived and I would have gotten in too much Hell for punching a girl even though I am sure most would have thought it looked good on the little bitch. She'll wish I clocked her when I was done. I deliberately cut in front of her to get a candy from the bowl that was in front of the library before church service started. There was a half hour intermission between Sunday School and service.

"Uh," she squeaked in exasperation.

"Oh I'm sorry, were you next?" I asked in a snotty, condescending tone. It's about time this little bitch got a taste of her own medicine. I rolled my eyes at her.

"Do you know who I am?!" she shrieked in that holier-than-thou tone I absolutely hate. Those who have to ask that you're nothing. Just saying.

"Everyone does. You're *Ashley Smith.*" I scoffed in my best snotty, condescending tone. Mocking her.

"Uh," she squeaked again. Talk about stuck up.

"Uh," I mocked her again. "Yes and you really aren't a Smith. You're adopted! So I'd lose the attitude if I were you." I snapped back with my award winning snotty, condescending tone.

"Arrghhh!" she screamed and fell to her knees and bawled. "Wahhhhh!" she cried and whined until Cindy Smith came barreling over to us.

"What did you say to her?" she demanded.

"I got tired of her *'Do You know who I am'* crap and told her she was adopted." I responded still mocking her catch phrase.

"Why would you do something like that?! It wasn't your place to tell her!" she shrieked. Like mother like daughter. That's where she gets it, I thought.

"Oh, I'm sorry. I thought she knew." I answered using the condescending tone again.

" Besides. Everyone else does." I snapped staring her right in the face. I must have given her a dirty look as she scooped up the spoiled little bitch and took her to the restroom to clean her up.

That was awesome! The bigger they are the harder they fall. I kind of felt guilty about that for a few minutes. I honestly thought she knew. The whole damn church knew. How the hell she didn't is beyond me. It was the best kept secret in the whole place. Everyone knew but spoiled little *princess*. That one is for the books. She continued to use that catch phrase of hers throughout whenever she didn't get her own way. Snotty little bitch.

* * *

Years later she came into the pizza place I was working at for Halloween. It was shortly after I quit the church. That year we didn't bother giving out candy. She was about 12 or 13 then. She came in dressed like a witch and said "trick or treat" with the expectation in her voice as usual.

"Sorry , we aren't giving out candy this year?" answered my boss, Lynn. She's awesome. A really great person.

"*Do you know who I am? I'm Ashley Smith and my mom buys pizzas from you all the time.*" she said in her snotty, condescending tone I hate.

"I see all kinds of kids in here and you all look the same to me after a while," Lynn answered.

"Don't you think that '*Do you know who I am*' shit is getting old? Everyone knows who you are and you're nothing but a spoiled, little brat" I scoffed at her.

She stood there like a dear in the headlight for a second and then gave me a dirty look.

"*Happy Halloween*" I said dripping in sarcasm giving her a dirty look right back. I gave her another one and a look of contempt before I turned my back to her and went back to work.

That was pretty much the last I saw of her. I wonder if she ever became a courteous member of society from time to time but then it takes a second to realize I really don't care. If not, I'm sure she'll be put in her place by someone along the way. Good luck Ashley.

* * *

The town always had a summer festival called the Derry Fest. It always involved a parade and activities at the local arena. The activities ranged from a softball tournament to kids games and raffles. There was always a large beer tent where most of the locals went crazy. Binge drinking always brings out the best in people, doesn't it? You will find yourself doing crazy things you normally wouldn't do.

There was one year when it rained heavily and a mud wrestling pit was born. Watching people getting pulled in wearing white to join in the mayhem was funny although I would be pissed right off if I were the one wearing white. We'll just blame it on the binge drinking and pretend it never happened, right?

This year in particular, things got more out of hand when our first female fire fighter was pulled into the pit. A local guy known for abusing alcohol actually pulled her in while she was out of uniform to see how tough she was. She took it stride until he pulled her t-shirt over her head and while she was still in shock, he ripped her bra off. She was pissed and glared at him.

"I'll give you a $100 if you knock him out!"someone yelled.

She cocked back her fist and punched him right in the face sending him to the ground falling on his back and lading in the mud. He was out cold. Another guy took his shirt off so she could cover up. She got her $100 and the town drunk got arrested for drunken disorderly. What a wonderful night. It turns out he wasn't the only one thrown in the drunk tank that night for drunken disorderly. There were several charged with indecent exposure for mooning people who passed by and public urination.

At these events, there are always extra police officers brought in from other places for crowd control. I think there was even someone stupid or inebriated enough to relieve his bladder in the back of the police car. What a dolt.

* * *

Dad had a hobby of doing odd jobs and dabbled in pyrotechnics. We did a lot of small shows for private organizations. I can remember one day we were setting up as in us kids while they sat around and drank beer. It was 95 degrees in the shade and of course there was plenty of cold beer for them but when it came for soda or water for the kids, it was nonexistent. Thanks for thinking of us.

We let them drink and while we were dying of thirst, we were plotting on stealing some beer. Ten and twelve year olds plotting the beer heist. Don't judge. You would do the same. You are thirsty and a parental figure has no consideration for you on a hot day while you are doing their work for them so they can chug beer in the shade. Nothing but the finest parenting skills. Do the dirty work slave. If you think I was drinking piss or lapping up ditch water, you are out of your goddamned mind. Beer was available. Beer it will be.

I distracted them with directions on what else was to be done while Anthony pillaged the cooler. It worked perfectly. I listened to rambling on what was next while he made off with 3 beers. The fact is they didn't even know we took them. Another job well done by Piss Tank Productions which couldn't be made possible without child labor.

* * *

Dad's tactics weren't always pleasant. There was an incident where a printed sheet of paper contained "Fuck you" "Fuck" "Asshole" and a few other choice explicative words. Dad wasn't impressed.

"Here's how we are going to do this one: Each one of you is going to get hit once and you go back to the end of the line. The second time, it's twice. The third time, it's three times until one of you tell me who did it. And the guilty one will get whatever we end up with multiplied by your age," he explained.

One by one we got whacked and the line kept rolling. Whip! Whip! Whip! One each. Whip, Whip! Whip, Whip! Whip, Whip! Two each. It stung like a son of a bitch. The line seemed to go faster plus the blows in between intensified. We got up to twenty eight and it was bed time. So to give you the magnitude of this one pus two is three. Three plus three is six. Twenty eight times is four hundred and six total. Yes, you read it right 406 times. If you don't believe me, get out a calculator or spreadsheet and do it yourself.

Let me tell you, I never forgave him for it. The bruising and swelling that came with it was something else. I hope he feels like a bag of crap for it. Keep in mind two of us were innocent. Anthony did confess but never got the multiplier of 10. Could you imagine?

Dad tried to apologize but I never accepted it and my resentment for him was born. Apologies for something like that don't mean a damn thing. I have 406 reasons not to. Grab a plate and smash it on the floor and say "I'm sorry" Does it fix it?

I do like the analogy of bombed out bridge. Blow it to Hell. Say "I'm sorry" and then get in your car and drive on it. To repair it, it takes both sides to do it. If one side doesn't want to bother, your efforts are futile. I have C4. Keep building. It isn't happening.

Anthony never really apologized either 406 reasons for him. He did it and should have owned up it right away but instead we get a 3 hour torture. Had I known it was him, I would have sung like a canary.

* * *

Don't feel too bad, my evil side was being developed very well. I went with him to one of his friends' places and of course they were pounding the beer back. I let them go for a while one right after the other. The guy's wife came out and gave me a coke. She looked at them as I did. With disgust.

"Look at that," she said "Look at them guzzle beer and him ignore his own son."

"Well, I have you right now," I said.

"Yes, you're good company. It's sad he didn't care if you had anything to drink, did he?" she asked.

"No."

"They are so sloshed, I'll bet they can't even taste it anymore," she said.

"Let's find out," I replied as I picked up the empties from the deck by the pool. I dunked them in the above ground pool one by one and filled them to the fill mark and replaced the caps. I took them over to the beer fridge and put them at the back so they would get cold and ready for that next thirst quenching moment.

They kept drinking and drinking until I was sure they were into the pool water. They didn't stop or miss a beat. They kept drinking. I was dying on the inside. Too funny. It wasn't until the "beer" was gone that dad decided to take me home.

"Wow," he said in the truck. "He must have got some watered down pony piss or I had too many. I could swear that last one was water." He looked right over at me and it was time to put my innocent look on.

"Oh well, your mother will probably be mad we are late for dinner. We had to go," he continued. The rest of the ride was silent and I couldn't wait to tell Mom what I did and he didn't really notice. Mom just about died laughing.

* * *

Anthony and I wanted bunk beds. We got them but not the way we wanted. Dad made them out of 2x4s and plywood.. The unit was 3 feet wide and stretched the entire length of the bedroom wall. there was no bottom bunk. We were to sleep end to end along the wall. It wasn't just the fact the "beds" were cheaply made but the "mattress" consisted of a piece of foam you would use to put under your sleeping bag when you went camping. Broke the bank on this one.

I should mention there was no safety rail on the unit either. Every night one or both of us fell on the goddamned floor. Thump! I am actually surprised we never broke an arm or leg. If you want to add insult to injury, within a few months it was Kelly's turn for a new bedroom and he went out and bought her bunk beds with real mattresses which were off limits to us. It was a nice polished wood set and a glaring difference between the $100 welfare special. Ah life in the servant's quarters. I think that was pretty much confirmation where we stood.

I can refer to the bedroom as the servant's quarters for the simple reason that we had to cleanup his work shed on a regular basis because "we" always messed it up. Reality check. Those who drink and abuse alcohol always blame everyone else but themselves. He would drink and work in there and leave it an unsightly mess and forget where he put things and it was "our fault" and had to regularly clean it up.

Everyone had to drop whatever they were doing to help him find something he misplaced but it was always everyone else's fault. Never his. Not Mr. Perfect. Anthony got it the worse. Cinderella! Cut the Grass! Clean the shed! Cinderella!

CHAPTER 3

••••••••⬤•••••••

I have to apologize in advance, this book may jump around a bit. It's a bitch trying to remember everything in chorological order. It's been a while and mostly repressed memories which are never a good thing but we still do it. It's easier to try and forget than to deal with it. That's completely false. Deal with it. Take it from me, dealing with it head on is always better than trying to sweep it under the carpet. Eventually you will trip over it.

Back to my story, I'm no therapist. In grade 8, my world changed for the worse. About a week before school started, my dad took us behind the shed and said he was leaving our mother. He then opened his wallet to show us more than $1,000 and said, "This is the money for the bills, the groceries and the mortgage payment. If you want it, come with me. You don't have to answer now. Just think about it. Keep your mouths shut and don't tell her."

We of course didn't tell her and then when it came time for the split, Kelly and I stayed with mom. Anthony went to live with dad. Just before school and it's haircut time and my brother was down for a visit. We had a home barber kit in the house and my parents would cut our hair from time to time. Can you see where this is going? You guessed it, as soon as I was in the chair with the poncho around my neck. My brother got the trimmer and proceeded to cut my hair. He couldn't have done a worse job with a weed trimmer. A complete bald patch in the front and missing some longer ones beside it. It was a train wreck and of course it wasn't fixable without shaving my head completely. Hind sight that would have been preferred.

I haven't even gotten to bed yet and you can already hear the comments. Can't you? I think those do-it-at-home-barber-kits should be banned permanently without discussion. Everything should always be done by trained professionals especially when it comes to safety and your looks. What's next, do-it-yourself-dentistry? Yeah, get those wisdom teeth out in the comfort of your own kitchen.

Needless to say I was a walking punch line again. If I ever get asked why I let my brother cut my hair again, I'm going to flip. I didn't let him. He grabbed the trimmers and then I was committed after he cut from behind. Too little too late. To make matters worse, we had school pictures before I got it fixed. No retakes. Perfect, just perfect. That train wreck followed me to grade 9 where my lovely classmates made a point of telling their new friends at high school. Add to the effect I was that I was the shortest male in grade 9 and started to have a severe acne problem.

I always got a kick out of how they say high school is the best years of your life. I wanted to dig a hole, climb in and die. They were the worse years of my life. The story to that will be coming along to that soon enough. Hell is always brought on nice and slow. Before you know it, you are on the 7th layer and there is no escape. Burn baby burn.

We haven't finished off the grade 8 yet. We went through 8 supply teachers in the first month and finally got a full time teacher. He was a gym teacher and we pretty much had gym class most of the year. He did get the required curriculum done but the gym classes were extended. I am sure of it. We had a new French teacher and she liked me. She was really nice. Miss Bell.

It was shortly after the start of school, my mom met the biggest loser, waste of skin I have ever had the unfortunate privilege of meeting. Of course, when I met him he was trying to be nice and wore his mask well. I was cutting the grass for an elderly neighbor and was getting oil from the town hardware store and were on our way back to the car when this six foot guy with black hair came over from the other side of the street with a slightly out of date button down shirt and jeans. His name was Jerry McQueen. It turns out mom was seeing him after dad left and moved in with his new girlfriend right away.

Jerry lived with his mother, he was 37. This is a warning sign for anyone. Run like hell. She lived in a small one bedroom house. Jerry lived with her. Where's the privacy? I have so many questions after all these years. Most I probably don't want the answers to. She was nice, don't get me wrong. She was a hard working woman who let her sons take advantage of her. Jack, I met later.

Jerry started talking to me like I was a friend. We hashed over I was in grade 8 and cut grass for my elderly neighbors. I had 2 customers. He looked down in my hand and saw the green Quaker State bottle.

"That's good oil dude," he said and smiled at me as if he was winning points.

"Thanks," I said with a whatever attitude.

"I won't keep you, you have work to do," he said looking at me and smiling.

It took all I had not to roll my eyes. I smiled back at him. It was forced but I smiled anyway. I really was hoping it would have been just the three of us. Mom, my sister, and me. It's too soon. The fall back or rebound person is never a good thing. I know this now but when you're a kid, does anyone ever listen?

* * *

Jerry made a lot of promises about going away on vacations and some road trips. He had an older Chevrolet pickup truck , white. He was working at a food processing plant at the time and admitted to having a son named Timmy. Timmy was 6 at the time. He seemed pretty normal and decent. However, I never fully trust someone when I first meet them. It's always a game of feeling them out to see if they're legit or not. So far he was ok on that level even though I don't like it when people try to score points with me. I know it's an act. If mom liked him, give him a chance.

* * *

I went and visited my dad a few times and I got to meet Mary, his new girlfriend and I didn't much care for her. I found out she worked in the cafeteria at my dad's plant. The service must have extra special. She gives customer service a whole new meaning. He of course wanted me to give her a kiss. I'd rather kiss a rock. Her son was interesting. Jason who also conveniently was one of my brother's high school friends.

It was a weekend of boisterous nut smacking, cock grabbing, wedgies and pulling pants down. Inappropriate jokes and wicked wrestling matches took up most of the time when dad and Mary weren't around. Don't count dad out, he was in on the nut smacking, cock grabbing too. Three teenage boys were in the apartment and yes it was gang up on the younger one. I didn't mind. I nailed Jason several times in the sack. It was fun.

He knocked me down and I pulled myself up by his genitals. Oh the fun. He screamed like a little bitch. I got nailed in the balls good for that one but it was worth it. My visits came to an end when I heard her say derogatory things about my mother. Know your place bitch. Keep your opinions to yourself about people you know nothing of other than what you've been told. There's 3 sides to every story, yours, mine and the truth. I didn't bother speaking to her on it, she should know better than to trash mouth someone's parents in front of them.

I had it out with dad and he called me an asshole and then my visits with him came to a grinding halt after that. I never saw him again for about 17 years or any relatives on that side of the family either. It was like I didn't exist. The only ties he had to me was the child support he was paying. He kept trying to get it reduced and eventually succeeded from $75/ week to $40/ week.

* * *

Mom ended up giving Jerry a key to the house where he could go in and check on the place since they were going through a really bitter divorce. There were no holds barred and the gloves were off.

Nothing held back. There was always phone calls that ended up in shouting and screaming matches.

Jerry thought he'd be cool and tell us how he was in the army and how he was a corporal as his leaving rank. He then would impersonate a bugle player to wake us up in the morning. Yes, I am serious. The door would open without knocking of course and then he'd flip on the light and pretend to play the bugle with the military wake up call. What an idiot. What an annoying, blithering idiot! He thought it was funny. It's asinine. Luckily it was short lived.

There was one point where mom had enough and ripped the phone right out of the wall. This was before we had phone jacks. Jerry answered the phone and it was dad. He freaked and it was on. That fight was very heated. I can still see her putting her foot against the base board and balling up the cord in her left hand while holding the old rotary phone in her right and pulling on the cord from the wall.

"Don't do that! We need it for jobs to call us." pleaded Jerry although he never really applied for anything.

"I don't give a damn! You haven't even applied for anything yet!" yelled mom still tugging on the phone cord.

It didn't go the first time and she dropped the phone on the floor took both hands to the stubborn cord, wrapped it around her hands and pulled. It gave way and she nearly fell on her ass. The phone was dead!

"Goddamn son of a bitch," she said throwing the cord on the floor next to the phone.

We got a new phone with a jack within a couple of days and she would unplug the jack whenever their conversations would get ugly. It usually took less than 3 minutes for that to happen. I think he was just calling for his own amusement to see how far he could push her to going off on a tirade of language that would make Penn Jillette or Gordon Ramsay blush. Now I know where I get my filthy mouth and my don't give a shit attitude from, family fights and stuck up, condescending twats.

It wasn't more than 3 days after getting the key to keep an eye on the place, Jerry decided to move himself in without permission, of course and mom just gave it the doormat approach. Oh goody, here to stay. Just got out of mommy's house at 37 and it's time to free load somewhere else. I walked in from school to find him wiping his ass with a face cloth with faucet running and the bathroom door wide open. I hope you are as repulsed as I am just thinking about it. Needless to say I didn't use that facecloth again or any from that set either. Classy.

Within a month of living with dad, the relationship between Anthony and him was in trouble. There's nothing like getting a call at 10 PM full of screaming and yelling to go pick up your brother because they are fighting and can't live together any more.

When we got there, Anthony was outside the apartment building and dad was waiting for us. He even tried to get mom to sign a lined notepad regarding custody with spaces big enough to put whatever he wanted in it. She refused. good thing, he would have written in something about not paying child support at all and not being responsible unless we agreed to live with him and his new girlfriend who just so happen to work at the plant cafeteria where he worked. Anthony came home with us any way. He didn't know Jerry moved in at this point. They didn't like each other at all.

Around this time Jerry's uncle moved in with his mother . He came from Nova Scotia to stay here. He was a miserable, old man and it became apparent as to why. He was a second class citizen to the rest of the family. Jerry's brother Jack would slap him upside the back of the head whenever he did something he didn't agree with.

"Come up out of that," he say every time he slapped him upside the head.

Then his uncle would laugh. It must have been some sort of weird family bonding time or inside joke. I thought it was elder abuse and still do. Jack would come around when he wanted something which conveniently was around the same time as the pension checks came out. Jack was driving Jerry's mother's van. She didn't drive but apparently needed it for appointments.

Jerry's mother's name was Betty and her brother was Allen. They bought the van together. It was to go to the doctor's. Oddly the doctor was only a few doors down and around the corner. It was a two minute walk at the most. It really warrants a new van, doesn't it?

Allen eventually came around and he started talking to Anthony and I. He'd be nice one day and a grouch the next. Maybe he wasn't used to being treated like a real person. He'd get grouchy around pension check day. We never asked him for a dime. Jack did and she always gave it to him.

* * *

My brother came home one day and flipped out that he was moved in and the whole night erupted into chaos. My mother just started at a job that day and came home to everyone yelling and fighting. Dishes were broken and now there were holes in the walls from Jerry and Anthony. My brother Anthony redirected his aggression in my direction while Jerry stood by and watched and my sister hid in her room.

Anthony flipped out and advanced on me. I have never seen a look n someone's eyes like that before. I was hatred, anger and not human. He had me by the throat and squeezed really hard and while I was trying to understand the situation, he grabbed my head and slammed it into the drywall leaving a large dent. He smashed it there again while grabbing me by the throat with one hand and punching me in the side of the head with the other. This time a hole was in the wall. It sent a searing pain through both sides of my head.

He punched me right in the nose and I felt it snap. I struggled to remain standing while a stinging, aching pain right between my eyes as I felt a warming sensation drip from my nose. My eyes instantly started to tear up and I wiped my nose and it was bleeding. Another smash to the head off the wall, followed by a fist to the right side of my jaw while the other held my throat. I mustered up enough to knee him in the balls and made a run for it to my room. I didn't make it 6 feet.

He grabbed my from behind and hooked his finger in the right side of my mouth and pulled ripping it open. I elbowed him to get away. This was followed by several blows to my back, ribs and back of the head. I couldn't tell you how many or where. I know it was punches, kicks and any combination of the two in rapid fire progression.

He stopped and let go. I stood there leaning up against the wall for support. I was shaking and in a lot of pain. He went to the kitchen drawer and pulled out a wooden handled paring knife and stabbed the wall beside my head.

"This is your fucking head," he sneered leaving the knife in the wall.

I looked at and grabbed it before he could. I pulled the handle out and his hand went right over mine and started squeezing my hand trying to break my grip. I elbowed him in the face with the knife hand and ended up slicing his forearm on the recoil. Yes, Jerry stood there and did nothing like the spineless loser he is. I hauled off and drilled Anthony in the face with my left hand while he stood there in shock looking at his forearm. He staggered back and left the room. I threw the knife which stuck into one of the legs of the dining room chairs from my under handed toss.

I went to the cupboard and pulled out a medium sized cast iron frying pan and approached the living room which is in the front of the house. Luckily dad's riffles were gone, otherwise I probably wouldn't be around to tell the tale. He pointed one at me before and I am not sure it was loaded. It was the days before trigger locks and locked ammunition storage laws. I held up the pan and shook it at him.

"You want to go, mother fucker? Let's go!" I yelled shaking the frying pan.

"I'll smash your fucking head in!" I screamed and cried at the same time. I was still bleeding from the nose and the numbness from the right side of my mouth was setting in while it continued to bleed.

I have never been in a fight this violent in my life at this point and sure as hell didn't expect it to be with my own brother. I thought he was trying to kill me. No. HE WAS TRYING TO KILL ME!! I've had little skirmished with other kids, usually wrestling matches and the odd jab but this was as messed up as it gets.

He went to his room and slammed the door. I put the pan in the sink and was leaning up against the counter, shaking and crying. Jerry stood there and did nothing but smoke a cigarette. He didn't even offer a facial tissue or a paper towel to clean up the blood off of my face. He is a such a loser.

The bedroom door opened and Anthony was recharged and ready for more. He came right at me and without thinking I started the stupid chasing around the table thing. I should have grabbed the pan or any other blunt instrument. No, not me. I did the cliché horror movie bad decision of the soon to be dead victim. Running around the table, had there been stairs I probably would have run up them instead of out the nearest door. What the hell was I thinking?!

I made it to the view of the front door and at this time my mom came home. She took one look at my bleeding face and dropped her purse and keys and went right at Anthony who was coming around the table to get me. She clothes lined him and knocked him into the wall and grabbed him right by the shirt with both hands and pinned his ass up against the wall. She pushed him to his room and he went to make a swing at her. Mom picked him and body slammed him on the bed.

"Don't you ever take a swing at me you son of a bitch!!" she snarled and slapped him right across the face. He just glared at her.

She made me run to our neighbors who looked at me and immediately called the police. At least she had the decency to get my a warm cloth to wipe the blood from my face. She was a sweet older lady and had been friends with mom for years. The police came and mom called her on the phone to send me back.

When I walked in the door, the officer recognized me from a few months ago when he set up a speed trap on our boring street and for fun, he was clocking me on my bike. The speed limit on our street is 40 km/ hr and at 13 I got my bike to 27 km/ hr in a short distance.

He took my statement and it was decided to get him some help. Anthony went to the hospital psych ward in another city over an hour away for observation. The fact is he was a psycho and needed professional help. Jerry took me to his mother's place to settle me down. Truthfully I would have been better off at my friends place or anywhere else. I didn't go to the hospital but probably should have since I have permanent damage to the right side of my mouth. When I smile, it doesn't go as far as the left and the muscles aren't as defined either.

We sat and watched TV and didn't discuss anything. It was as if it were best to sweep it under the carpet. Ignore it and it goes away. That philosophy never works and never will. Pretending it doesn't exist or never happened is a passive way out of things. It did happen and maybe a trip to the hospital would have been a nice order of business and maybe seeing where your useless son's balls were wouldn't have hurt either. But let's watch hockey, everything gets better after watching hockey. The game seemed to take all night. When it was over, I got to go home and of course the house was still in shambles. We did a half ass job cleaning it up and my hatred for Jerry was growing. It will continue to grow I was sure of that.

* * *

The next day it was back to school and everyone was asking what happened to my face. I couldn't even lie to them. They knew my brother beat my ass on a regular basis. In fact, mostly every injury was inflicted by him over the years. I had some classmates who thought he was an ass for doing it. I still don't know why he was so cruel to me. It was as if his day wasn't complete without tormenting me in some way. They saw the bloody lip, the black eyes, the broken nose and all of the other bruises. I really don't think there was a lie I could have made up to cover for the mess I was. Falling from a tree? Flipping over my bike and being run over by an entire marching band, maybe.

It wasn't more than an hour or two before I was called to the principal's office. I went and my sister was waiting for me there too. There was a tall, younger woman with just over shoulder length black hair wearing a dark blue skirt and a blazer carrying a black briefcase smiling and waiting for us.

"Hello Justin," she said with a smile.

"Is there any place we can go and talk?" she asked turning to the principal.

"You can use my office," he said gesturing t o the door.

We went inside and she closed the door. She sat down on one of the chairs in the office. There was three opposite the desk with its executive style chair. She took the one closest to the wall and arranged it so we could all face each other. She placed the briefcase on her lap and pulled out a pad and pen before placing the briefcase on the floor beside her standing it up.

" My name is Stephanie and I am from the Children's Aid." she said. There was a pause

"I understand there was a violent fight last night and I am told there was a knife involved." she continued. I just looked at her and nodded. I couldn't lie. The right side of my mouth was already scabbing over. Kelly and I looked at each other and nodded in agreement. We would tell her everything.

We started at the beginning with the impending divorce, Jerry, last night's events, everything. We've been through a lot and the truth needed to be told. She sat in the chair and wrote it all down. She'd look up and smile and nod for us to continue whenever we struggled with what to say next. Her warm smile made it easier to tell her.

"Thank you." she said with her warm smile and gave me her card.

"I will be following up with your mother on this tonight, what time is she usually home?" she asked.

"By 5," I told her.

"Good, I will see you tonight. You did the right thing." she smiled at me, shook our hands and it was back to class.

* * *

For the record, out of every fight I have ever been in or any altercation I have ever had. This was the most violent. Not even an enemy has ever attacked me in the manner my own brother did. Nobody has ever left me with permanent damage to any body part before. I was bruised from head to toe. He beat the snot right of me for no reason other than I got in the way. Of what, I have no idea. It was unprovoked. Kelly would not have been as lucky as I was. Think about it, three years younger and a smaller girl. I have nerve damage to the right side of my mouth where he ripped it open and most of my school pictures from then on have a slight head turn to the right so you can't see it.

I have been told that brothers fight like that all of the time. Not to that level. That was nothing other than psychotic rage and to this day, I have no idea what I did to set him off and basically try to kill me. If that were the case of brothers fighting like that all of the time, why aren't more younger siblings hospitalized, dead or permanently disfigured? It is not normal.

I resent the comment and have little respect for those who could actually say something like that to begin with. If you had your ass kicked to that extreme by a sibling, that person needs some sort of therapy as well. That type of an attack goes much further than a case of sibling rivalry. It is psychotic. The look on his face and his eyes said it all. I really hope you never have to see it for yourself. It is terrifying when someone is out to kill you or harm you that severely.

CHAPTER 4

· · · · · · ● · · · · · ·

When I got home from school that day and put my stuff away. I went to mine and Anthony's room and tried to relax. It still felt uneasy in the house. I looked at all the holes in the walls. I couldn't believe it. The other shock was that it was from my body. Dad wasn't around to fix them and I doubt this lazy ass could pick up a hammer and nails let alone some dry wall putty to fix the walls.

Jerry came to my room and wanted to talk. I didn't want to talk to him. I was still pissed at him standing there like one of those Indian statues at the mall outside the smoke shop. Absolutely useless. There was a pause.

"So what happened today at school?' he asked.

"I had a visitor." I responded.

"What kind?" he asked.

"I'll tell mom when she gets home. You can wait until then." I said calmly.

"You'll tell me now." he said raising his voice slightly as if to try and assert himself. Where the hell was this last night?

"No I won't." I said.

"You'll tell me now." he said again.

"I don't have to tell you anything. You aren't in charge of me. I can do just fine without you." I said firmly.

He looked at me with contempt and walked away. That's right, walk away, loser, walk away I thought.

* * *

Mom got home shortly after and he immediately went to her like a younger sibling to go tattling. I don't even thing she was totally out of the car when he went racing towards in the driveway. How pathetic. I don't need him to go tattling to her about something he knows nothing of nor should he. I have a good relationship with her and don't keep secrets. I was going to tell her right away. I didn't need a pathetic loser like him to go over like a two-bit snitch. I can definitely tell what he was like as a child since people rarely grow out of it. If he didn't get his way, he'd be a stool pigeon and rat out whoever he could to make himself look good. My contempt for this douche bag was growing.

She came in the door and looked at Kelly and I and then casually put her jacket, purse and lunch bag on the counter in the kitchen. She sat at the dining room table and motioned us over. Jerry came over and sat down and looked at us grinning like a spoiled brat when the older sibling was going to get in shit because of his snitching. Did I mention I am really starting to hate this asshat?

"Ok, what happened today?" she asked.

"There was a worker from the Child Services that came..." I started.

"What did you tell her? You should know better than to talk to them. Are you really this stupid? They could take you away and make you wards of the court. Oh, you really screwed up now. Your mother and I will have to talk to this bitch and get her to change her mind. Do YOU have ANY IDEA how bad THIS IS?!" he was a ranting lunatic. He had only 10 words of what went on and he was ranting. Does he have something to hide? I am thinking so. Mom sat there in silence. It wasn't his place to say anything, he's a move in parasite and has nothing to do with anything. Maybe he's afraid he's going to be asked why he stood there like a statue. Forget about starting to hate you. I do. I absolutely despise you. I downright loathe you right now. No facts and you start ranting. A sign of a true dullard. Daft and oblivious.

"Do you think I can finish now or are you done ranting?" I scoffed. People wonder why teenagers have attitudes. Can't get a word in edgewise because you have some twat flying off the handle with no facts. It's called listening, dumb ass. Try it sometime. Get your facts first and then you can come to an informed decision. Amazing, isn't it?

"Don't take that tone with me!" he barked.

"If you would STOP INTERUPTING ME, maybe I will" I shot back. Those who constantly interrupt know they are wrong and try to discourage you from pointing it out hoping you will give up and give them the "victory".

"Ok go ahead," he said with a condescending tone. I gave him the look of death. Die! I had nothing but contempt for him.

I went on about how she knew about the knife and the mayhem from the night before. I told her everything. I did it because if this is how life was going to be, I'll pass. At this time I had no idea how things were going to go. I just knew things were going to get worse especially with this twat being around.

"When is she coming by?" mom asked.

"Tomorrow afternoon." I responded.

I never did find out what happened from that meeting nor did I see Stephanie again. I take it she thought things were going to be fine. Thanks for your help and for listening.

* * *

Life went back to normal if anyone can define that, please let me know. It was your typical grade 8 crap. It's your last year and it's time to raise Hell. My classmates were a bit unruly and then they started picking on Michelle and I for whatever reason.

At our school there was a low lying part down the hill to a creek. Michelle and I would walk and talk about things going on in each other's life. It turns out she didn't like Jerry very much either. When they first met, she said "fuck" and apparently she was a bad influence for me. It's laughable. Most kids know profanity by grade 3.

A group of the boys came charging down the hill at us and we were eating my mom's homemade bread. Michelle took a bite of hers and looked up at the group of 8 running down the hill at us. She chewed the bread and kept looking at them approaching and without warning she spit. That bread shot out like a shot gun and spread in perfect formation. I never saw 8 stupid jerks look so surprised in my life and take evasive maneuvers. Some dodged the soggy blast and others weren't so lucky. Direct Hit! Right in the face and on their shoulders. It was probably the funniest thing I remember from that year. They were completely grossed out and disgusted. Yes, a girl out grossed them. They left us alone after that. It was the most amazing spitting I have ever seen. Perfect timing and yardage.

* * *

It was a few days after the incident with the bread that Jerry's truck was repossessed for nonpayment of course. All of his repairs were paid for my mom. His mother bought a battery for it and he never did pay her back or mom either. I knew this guy as a loser and he was proving me right every day. He was a mooch and a free loader too. Why couldn't just get rid of this freeloader?

I also learned he was behind in support payments for Timmy and had to go to court. Surprise, surprise. Mom made him pay it and try to get out of arrears. Her payment schedule was good as long as he followed it. It was short lived. The only thing he cared about was trying to be a controlling twat and his cigarettes.

I feel bad for his kid but I know he's better off without him. I never got to meet him and he never visited him or even sent a birthday card or anything. This raised a lot of questions for me since his true colors were showing and he is a dickhead. An abusive waste of skin dickhead. I often asked when we're going to meet him and the subject was either changed or some lame excuse that he was shy or something. Being elusive means you have something to hide. A warning sign. Pay attention to it.

* * *

I think it was a few weeks later, some profanity was discovered in a school dictionary and our fill-in principal was out to prove something. He usually taught grade 5 and today he was in charge. He took Rudy's paper mate brand pen and scribbled on a piece of paper in front of the whole class. The ink matched and he proceeded to blame him for writing it and saying it was vandalism and vandalism is wrong. I wasn't going to stand for this.

"Excuse me sir, I have a paper mate pen too and so does half the class. Maybe we wrote it. You narrowed down the manufacturer of the ink. You are so clever. It was either that or Bic or Dixon. You had a 1 in 3 shot. Just because Rudy has a paper mate pen, it doesn't make him guilty." I said loudly for all to hear. I was walking up my pen to him and handed it to him. Rudy was part of the group of 8 from the bread incident.

This caused the room to get into an uproar. Soon everyone was going up with their paper mate pens. I think they even borrowed one to go up with. The whole class had blue paper mate pens. I was proud of myself. I've never seen such brazen bullshit in my life. trying to blame someone because they own the same pen as what was used to write some immature drivel in a dictionary. It was probably words like fuck, shit, dick, pussy or asshole. The usual. He knew a boy wrote it and since the dictionaries were a few years old, anyone could have written it. Blaming someone for that was wrong and I started a riot.

I didn't care for Rudy much but I wasn't going to let him go down for that especially since it was based on pure coincidental stupidity of matching ink. Could you imagine the justice system working like that? A bullet from a .22 caliber rifle killed someone and since you own it, you are guilty. Meanwhile anyone who lived in the rural areas were likely to have a .22 caliber rifle. It's a total abuse of power and should be squashed immediately.

Rudy never got in trouble for it and later even thanked me for standing up for him. He admitted he was shocked I did. He even apologized to me for being a dick. I accepted. He was just going with the flow and he thought it was harmless. It was. Had he hit me or something of that nature, I wouldn't be as easily forgiving. After this incident, they left Michelle and I alone. They even smiled and said "Hello'. Awesome. I didn't do it for that reason, however I am glad it turned out this way. I did it because he was being bullied by a teacher.

They say bullying is wrong and then do the same thing. That's a bunch of crap. Bullying is bullying and it's not cool no matter what pathetic excuse you think you have for doing it. Case Closed.

* * *

This was the first year we had Christmas without dad around and it was all about Jerry and his family. This was the first time meeting his brother Jack and his wife Lisa. We met his mother, Brenda. She was feisty. I liked her. Just to show you how much class Jack and Lisa had, they were sitting on the couch within a matter of a few minutes they were feeling each other up in front of everyone. I later learned Lisa was picked up in a sleazy bar by Jack. She had a nickname of "Loose Lisa" and for $5 she'd blow anyone so she can afford her cigarettes since she didn't work. I guess you can classify that as working.

Their table manners were a cry in shame. Rather than eating at the table, Jack and Lisa took their food to the sofa and slopped it all over the cushions and the floor. With this being the first time in someone's house, it was appalling.

"Justin, look at those two. They will eat everything in sight and wipe their ass with the table cloth. It's better they aren't here with us," said Brenda looking at Jack and Lisa with contempt. I nearly choked on my meal as I was laughing so hard. I had never heard anything put like that before.

"I raised them better than that. I guess when you hang around a filthy whore, you become a filthy, disgusting pig yourself. Make a note of that, Justin," she said looking at me with a mischievous grin.

I knew we were going to be good friends from that day on. She made me laugh. She was rude, blunt, vulgar and crass. I loved it. It was the shock and awe factor that made it funny. You wouldn't expect that from an old woman.

* * *

A LIVING HELL

It was towards the end of the year when we got the word, the house will have to be sold and we had to move. I think it was 30 days notice. It was short. It wasn't too long after that, the electricity was shut off and so was the gas even though we were still living in it. Just prior to that event, the shower had a leak and some holes were knocked into the walls to find the shut off. It wasn't there. More holes in the walls. The worse part they were never fixed and I know it greatly depreciated the value of the property. Between Anthony's rampage and Jerry's stupidity, yes it was greatly depreciated. The bitter divorce and the constant fighting I am sure ate up some of the proceeds in lawyer fees too. If you split and it's bitter, the only ones who win are the lawyers. It's a feeding frenzy.

It was time for the annual Grade 8 overnight class trip to Toronto and I couldn't go. I wasn't asking mom for the money. She had enough problems so I withdrew. The school offered to loan me the money and I declined. I wasn't speaking to dad at the time and I wasn't about to ask him. I sure as hell wasn't asking Jerry. Did Hell freeze over? I don't think so. We already had a house with no electricity and no heat which I kept quiet and so did Kelly. I wasn't adding to the burden.

It wasn't too long after that it was graduation. We went through a few classes on what to do and how to act at our big event. It was taught by Mrs. Winter. Yes, I still hated her. I can't forgive her for bullying me and humiliating me in front of the class. I sat through it and waited for our night to be over with.

That night finally came and I would be out of there. I don't remember much of the ceremony other than I invited dad and Mary to come to try and patch things up. He told me had to work. Fine, whatever.

It was at that time, another guy I went to school with, Ken, informed me his dad worked with mine and the shift was cancelled so they could all attend. Obviously mine had no intention of coming. Ouch. Every kid thinks their parents don't give a damn from time to time. I had it confirmed. Ken's dad told me the truth too.

I have been treated like crap before. I can handle being a second class citizen because you still count somewhat. I have never been

39

treated like nothing. I would have loved to be treated like shit at this point. It has a value and is useful. Ask a mushroom farmer.

"At least now you know here you stand," said Michelle. She wasn't being a bitch. She knew all too well what I was going through.

"Yup, I do," I said. I wasn't going to cry. I was pissed right off. I was more pissed off at being lied to than anything. Don't lie to me, spill it like it is. It hurt but I was expecting it. Mary's family was more important and since we had any electricity or gas at the time, it was pretty much confirmed then.

It was the ceremony where I got some good old fashioned revenge. Mrs. Winter was on stage with the rest of the teachers and principal I liked. It was my turn to go up. I shook all their hands but when it came to Mrs. Winter, I put my hand in her face and moved on t the next one. You want to berate me and humiliate me in front of the whole class bitch, I'll do it in front of the parents, the whole class and your coworkers.

You could hear the comments, "ooh" and "ouch" and "wow". Bitch take that, I thought. The principal was next and he was not impressed. He looked at me and smiled but I knew I was in trouble.

"You don't disrespect teachers like that, you get back over there and shake her hand." he scolded with a smile to keep his composure.

I smiled at the crowd and made my way over. I extended my hand and shook hers. I smiled. A mean one but I smiled and squeezed her hand a little harder.

"Now you know what it's like," I said to her with a smile before going back over to the principal and finishing my rounds. It was worth it. I hopefully taught that bitch a lesson about disrespecting others.

I won the French award that year. Miss Bell was awesome. To add more salt to the wound, Jerry came over when I was talking to her and tried to take credit for teaching me French since he was from Quebec. I stood there aghast. The gal and edacity! Who does that?! After boasting to the French teacher of how great he was and how he deserved the credit for helping me even though he never did, it was time to go. I started off back to the car with the lying douche bag and quickly ran back to Miss Bell. I knew her feelings were hurt and I had to fix it.

"I forgot something," I yelled back to Jerry and ran to Miss Bell.

"I am so sorry about that. He's an ass. You deserve all the credit and I can't thank you enough. You've made a very difficult time a lot better. Thank You," I told her.

"Thanks for coming back, I was just starting to regret my decision. Good luck with him," she said nodding her head in disgust in Jerry's direction.

"Thanks. I just couldn't leave like that. I am sorry you had to hear that." I told her. We gave each other a hug and I thanked her again before saying goodbye.

I still can't believe the nerve of that son of a bitch. That has got to be the most insulting thing someone could do to teacher. Insulting, condescending and just plain rude. Taking credit for someone else's hard work and insulting them with lies right to their face. The worst part is it looked poorly on me. It's just another reason I have pure contempt for him. Thankfully I was able to correct it. Somewhat, anyway.

* * *

I was still going to the Baptist church but he wouldn't have it. He was Catholic. We were going to be good Catholics. Hell no! I went to my youth group at the Baptist church. I liked them and they were my friends. It was bad enough we had to move away from my friends now and then pluck me out of everything to suit your needs wasn't happening loser.

I went to one Catholic youth group evening. It was at the priests house and I was the only boy. We watched a movie, "Lady hawk" and it was a boring evening. We watched the movie and it was small talk. The girls were nice but I really didn't want to get to know them. It was a forced meeting and I didn't appreciate it. I never went back.

I went to mom and told her I wanted to go back to the Baptist church. We had friends there and I hated the Catholic church. It wasn't anything like what I was used to. I didn't want to go. There was 3 of us and 1 of him. Majority rules. I didn't want to be without all of my friends at one time. It was decided we would go back to the Baptist church and he would stick to his Catholic church. Eventually he came over to ours. Perfect, just perfect.

* * *

The time came to move and mom and Jerry found one last minute that mom could afford. It was 2 bedrooms. We needed 3. It was the size of a 2 car garage if we were lucky. We probably could've gotten away with the 2 bedrooms without that useless douche. That meant major downsizing. We were moving from a 3 bedroom house to a 2 car garage. Maybe if the useless wonder could keep a job, we could possibly get a 2 bedroom house with a basement.

You should have seen this thing. It was ugly as sin and right behind the Salvation Army church. It had box tape covering the holes in the walls with paint on it. There was a gas space heater that heated the whole house. The cupboards were uneven, the bathroom was larger than the bedrooms. It had the hot water tank beside the bathtub. The largest room was the living room and it took up almost half the house. The windows were old wood and painted black around the frames. The floors were sagging and the kitchen sink looked as if it was picked up from the side of the road. The faucets were separate for hot and cold. If you wanted to wash your hands, you had a choice of freezing or burning them. It was a real hovel. The worst part is it was going to home for a while. It was in the next town, Palmer. Population 20,000.

Mom and the parasite got one bedroom, my sister got the other. I got the rollout bed in the living room that had to be folded up and rolled away every morning. My life officially sucks now. My clothes were in my sister's room so I had to put my outfit out the night before and get to the bathroom to change. To make room, I got rid of pretty much everything I owned except my clothes and a few personal effects. Sacrifices had to be made and I hated every minute of it. I had to give up the pets too. We had three cats and Michelle took them for us. They needed a good home and they got it. I got a hell hole.

Jerry and mom promised it would be temporary. It was just until we got on our feet and it was a last minute move. I had my doubts. He seemed to be all talk and no action. He couldn't even pay for a used truck. He couldn't seem to hold a job for more than a few months and mostly seasonal work. I'll bet he doesn't even have a high school diploma. He claims to have served in the military. He has a uniform but the stories don't add up.

He even tried to say he was in Vietnam. Vietnam was fought from November 1, 1955 to April 30, 1975. He was born in the mid 50s so the numbers just don't add up. US involvement ended on August 15, 1973. It may have put him at 20 at the time, however we were Canadians and didn't have involvement with that war. It just doesn't fit. He claims to have lied about his age but like any government division, proof of age is required. No exceptions.

I humored him and listened. It took all I had not to roll my eyes and call him a liar. There are libraries and now there are computers to use for fact checking. Just about every house has one. I did check and his numbers didn't add up. Plastic surgery doesn't cover bullet holes. He claimed to have been shot and no scar. LIAR!

If a real Vietnam veteran heard him, he'd be stoned to death. Most veterans don't go into graphic detail about the conflicts they've been in. They don't want to remember. Not like this. Glorifying a war and the killing of civilians and someone you are supposed to be fighting against who you can bet would rather be doing something else too. Like any other major conflict, the enemy probably didn't have a choice, fight or we execute you and your entire family. If you opposed or defied Hitler and his regime, you died. This was pure crap and a desperate cry for attention. Nothing more. It was probably done in a vain attempt to impress when all it did was disgust me.

The stories he told about being shot and conveniently had no scars to prove it. The torture methods he described could have been done by watching any of the numerous movies about the war. The bamboo cages, the helicopters, agent orange, walking through the jungle looking for snipers. All of which were pretty vague and sounded more like a scene from one of the movies. The stories he told could have been taken in graphic detail from the most popular of the genre like Hamburger Hill (1987), Platoon (1986), and Behind Enemy Lines (1986).

I can assure he you after he moved himself in, there were dozens of promises about building a better life, new house, new job and new opportunities. Promises of colleges and being able to peruse every career Kelly or I wanted. If it sounds too good to be true, it probably is. It made my bullshit detector go off.

CHAPTER 5

•••••••••●•••••••

Grade 9 was interesting. There were a lot of changes. I was really small and probably one of the smallest boys in the class. There were two lunch periods and luckily I met up with my older church friends in grade 11. We hung out on lunch while Michelle had her new friends. They were stuck up bitches.

I sat with them a couple of times and it was gang up on Justin time once again. Michelle sat there and I spit back some real zingers. I just got braces and my acne was getting severe. Add that to being the shortest boy in class and I may as well have painted a huge target on my back. The new name for me was Pizza Boy. A direct attack on my face, my self esteem was at an all-time low and I get some salt on the wound.

The medication I was taking at the time wasn't helping. The over the counter creams and washes weren't helping. The Pizza Boy comment pissed me off to no end. Fat jokes were my return fire. Several of them had fat asses. I used them all. When you have no consideration for my feelings or anything, game on. I insulted their hair, weight, some had severe acne too. Crater Face, connect the dots jokes were my specialty. It really pissed them off. Those who live in glass houses shouldn't throw stones.

One was really nice and I found out she lived by me and I started walking home with her. Her name was Joanna. I liked her. Her insults weren't insults. She joked to see how I would respond. Jokes about punishing me by tying me up and slapping me. That was pretty cool. I was turned on by it and wanted her to show me. She'd laugh and call me a freak. I probably would have loved getting my ass kicked by a girl in this case. I highly doubt she would hurt me that bad or even at all. She thought it was funny. So did I. She never insulted me for my acne, braces or the fact I was really short at the time. Not once.

The truth is, I walked 4 blocks out of my way to spend that time with her. I would have done 20. I enjoyed her company that much. We'd talk as we walked home, nothing really personal. She was just nice to be around. I let her do most of the talking. I liked listening to her. There was one day she didn't say much and I finally asked her why so quiet and she informed me she was moving away. This is in the days before Facebook or MySpace or even email. I really dated myself didn't I? Damn!

She said "Goodbye if I don't see her." That was on a Friday. "I'll see you on Monday" and she nodded. The following Monday she was gone. Damn. I really miss her. I really hope she is happy wherever she is. I was 14 at the time, looking back I think she really liked me too. I'm not sure if girls that amazing go with short, pimple faced, kids with braces. Let me enjoy it whether it was real or just a 14 year old kid's fantasy. There's a reason I didn't share feelings. I think you know why.

I went by her house on the way to school and the way home for the next couple of weeks and even pounded on the door to see if anyone would answer. I thought maybe they went to check out the house they were moving to or maybe a vacation first. I just kept going by, hoping for the chance to say goodbye properly and maybe exchange phone numbers and addresses. It didn't happen. I looked past the curtains one day and the house was empty. I never thought of doing it before, maybe it's because I didn't want to know then that she was really gone.

* * *

I pretty much stopped going to that table after Joanna was gone, there wasn't balancing factor between those mean bitches. She was doing it for fun and laughs. They were just plain bitches. Snotty, stuck up bitches. On the days I could hang with my friends in grade 11, I did. The lunches alternated every day. One day I had friends to hang with, the next day I was loser. The off days were depressing. I got through it by hanging in the library where the other geeks or losers were. I didn't fit in with them either.

* * *

Jerry heard I wasn't fitting in and was a loner at school from the store he shopped at. Their daughter was in grade 9 with me and she went and told him. Nice. Half truths. Had she seen me on the other days, I was with my friends in grade 11. They were concerned for my well being I guess. I can't fault someone for caring. He even started his own brand of baby talk at this time. How nauseating. I'll get to that in a bit.

I think this was the time Jerry was starting to sell HomeWare on his latest get rich quick schemes. It's multi-level marketing. For those who don't know how it works. It's simple, you pay for a kit and start selling their products and are in business for yourself. The other side of it is recruiting others to do the same. For example, you recruit 2 people and then they then in turn do the same and then before you know it as the chain expands you have everyone on Earth trying to sell each other the same products.

It is presented through dream sessions where you dream of living the life of luxury by selling their products with minimal effort. Because you recruited 2 people who have recruited 2 people who have also recruited 2 people each. You have an army of sales people under you all earning you money because they are all part of your team and divine leadership.

Mom of course paid for it and had to do most of the work. The douche even had delusions of grandeur of opening a store selling those products. As if that was going to happen. He couldn't hold a job for more than a few weeks. Let's look at the career path of this loser.

He had a job driving truck for the mushroom company and backed the truck into a barn on one of the runs for feces. That was over after that. He picked tomatoes, beans and corn. He worked for a food processing plant seasonal and never went back to that one.

47

His full time job was leaching off us like a grubby little parasite. L-O-S-E-R.

The baby talk. Ugh. I am getting nauseous just thinking about it. He thought it was cute. it was enough to make anyone sick. I mocked him every chance I got. Instead of properly it was "propery", love was "wuv", me was "meam", yes was "crest'" (yes, like the tooth paste, I wish he'd use it.) Is it making you nauseous? I would do some quotes but I'd rather not. Let's just say 2 1/2 years of that crap.

His sales ability was nonexistent because if Mr. Moneybags was nearly as good as he thought, we wouldn't be living in a 2 car garage and having to rely on the food banks for groceries. I am not proud of it but yes, that's what we had to do to survive. This parasite wasn't making things any easier. His HomeWare business was costing more than what he was making. His mother knew that too and rubbed his face in it when she came over.

"How much have you made?" she asked already knowing the answer. There was a pause.

"Let me tell you what you've made. Nothing. Let me tell you how much you're going to make. Nothing. That is nothing but a racket and a waste of goddamned time. Get off your ass and get a job." she scolded him. Wow, I really am starting to like her. Eat that Jerry.

"Back to your dirty, dirty ways," he said glaring at her.

"My dirty ways? You have no respect. You never have. I'm stunned you're still here and that they can put with you this long," she said looking at us. Now I really like her.

He glared at her and went back to the catalogue and started flipping through them. He never said a word. Just sat there sulking and flipping through the catalogue and angrily flipping the pages. This was too much fun. His own mother can't stand him either, this is perfect. We became good friends. I was quite fond of her in that case.

"I'll bet you can't wait until you're old enough to get out of here, can you?" she asked me.

48

"It would be better if he left. You can visit any time." I responded and smiled at her. She smiled back at me.

* * *

He would constantly talk about his "business" and it got to the point where I was snippy and snapping at him every time he opened his stupid mouth about it. I mocked him every chance I got. I had a part time job at a restaurant and I loved rubbing it in his face that I made more than he did at minimum wage 3 nights a week. His "business" was booming!

"I've had some sales and the business is doing good," he told me one day and I had enough.

"Oh the great 'business' that hasn't done anything for anyone. It's doing so well that we're still in this hovel. All the promises you've made are empty. We are stuck here and aren't getting out any time soon. If it was so great, why are we still here and why is mom still driving that same beat up old car? It's more beat up now because you've had 2 accidents with it and both of them were entirely your fault! Who paid for it? Mom did, that's who. I am sick and tired of hearing about that goddamned 'business'. All we do is hear it, hear it, hear it and it doesn't pay for a damn thing." I yelled at him. I gave him a look of disgust and contempt.

The accidents were from his stupidity. One was from backing into a parked car in the parking lot and cost about $600 in damages and the other was making a right turn and not watching from the left to check for oncoming vehicles. We all saw the red Volkswagen and told him to stop but the insufferable know-it-all just kept on going and hit the car in the right rear quarter panel and of course mom had to pay for both of them.

"Watch your tone when you talk to me," he said glaring at me.

"Let me know when you're done laying down the law, Money Bags," I scoffed and stormed off to the bedroom. The HomeWare gig didn't last long and what a surprise, he didn't make any money. It was all talk, lies and hokum. I am thankful it was short lived and it was over. Finally. Happy retirement on the islands since you made so much money. Those types of things are designed to fail. They always blame the person that does it for not following a proven and working system. Those are designed to fail, that's the beauty of the recruitment process. There's always another sucker out there that will sign up. If it sounds too good to be true, it is. They always say unlimited earning potential. There's always a kit to buy to get you started and running your own business. Everything has limits. Don't be a victim. Go to the website **www.pyramidschemealert.org** and save yourself or a loved one from being victimized.

* * *

It wasn't too long after the failed multi-level marketing fiasco that Jerry thought it was good to save money by buying in bulk. Peanut butter and jam in restaurant sized pails. You can guess who had to pay for it too. Not him. When it was brought home to our house, there was a big lecture that we had to save money (from a lazy waste of space who doesn't work) and if we were making a sandwich, you could only have one or the other. Sieg Heil! You Nazi tyrant I thought. Up yours you man, I'm having both.

"It's called a peanut butter and jam sandwich for a reason. You have both on it," I said.

"You will have ONE OR THE OTHER," he said firmly.

"I'll have both," I said defiantly. I rolled my eyes. Dumb ass strikes again.

"You Will have one or the other. I have spoken," he said trying to assert himself.

"Try and stop me," I said glaring at him.

"They can have both. I Have spoken", mom said looking directly at him.

"You kids are fucking spoiled. You're kept." he said starting to walk away to pout.

"You'd know wouldn't you?" I shot back. He stopped and gave me a dirty look.

"You don't pay for squat around here. You're a freeloader! You don't even work, do you?" I continued. The hell he was going to talk to me and dictate what I can have on a sandwich and have the nerve to say I am spoiled because I want as peanut butter AND jam sandwich. Kiss my ass. Oh yeah and one more thing- Fuck YOU!!!

* * *

Mom got a good job lead and enquired about it. It was with the Palmer Post Office. They were outsourcing the ad mail at that time. It paid really well. We delivered the junk mail everyone hates. Mom had 3 routes. I helped her whenever I could. Palmer was 20,000 people and there were 9 routes in total. Jerry had 2. He had to do it too. In theory.

We delivered Tuesday, Wednesday and Thursday. Thursday was the deadline. All of the ad mail had to be delivered by then since the sales started on Fridays. The task was simple, pick it up on Monday morning, take it home and put it all together and deliver it. The routes were clearly marked. We always did mom's first. She was more important, obviously.

We dropped Jerry off at his and we went and did hers. This unfortunately was short lived because Jerry was afraid of dogs. He was afraid of the big ones which is understandable but he was also afraid of the little ones, even the little Chihuahuas. What a pussy. I got stuck helping him with his. I have never seen such a piss poor work ethic in my life. What a lazy twat. Every time he heard a bark, a yip or even a squeak, he would refuse to do it. I did it. Send a 15 year old kid up to do it instead you spineless coward.

I got sick and tired of it. I lugged that stuff in the snow, wind and rain. On the cold nights, I nearly froze my ass off. He'd buy himself a coffee or hot chocolate but didn't get me one unless I asked for it. I usually had to threaten to leave him to do the work. It was his job, not mine. I did it as a favor, not for him, for mom because she made sure he paid for some stuff now. The freeloading days were over. It worked every time. Know your enemy and know them well. You can exploit their weaknesses and make them do things your way.

It was around this time we got into Tae Kwon Do , I enjoyed it, the working out was great and since I walked everywhere it didn't take long for me to start putting on the muscle. I looked good. Mom paid for it for everyone (the freeloader too) and took it herself. She looked good too. Things were looking up even though there was still the class division. I walked a little prouder. When you start to feel good about yourself, it shows. This is why I advocate doing whatever you want to make you feel better about yourself. It's worth every penny.

* * *

I was feeling good about myself and just finished grade 9 and was entering grade 10. Within the first few weeks of school, I had a girl ask me out. This was cool. I liked the feeling of someone taking notice of me. I still had the bad acne and the braces but I was getting lean and I liked the change.

She was a nice girl, blonde and came out of a group of friends that were huddled together, It was normal for girls to stand around in groups and gab. I didn't pay attention to it. She came over and asked me if I wanted to meet her for lunch. We had a McDonalds in town and that's where she wanted to go. She said her and her friends always went and they would meet me at the front of the school.

I as running behind and rushed to the front of the school, they weren't there. They got tired of waiting I thought and ran down the street to the McDonalds and looked for them. It was busy and I couldn't find them so I got my lunch and sat down. Another girl came over and said they were playing a prank on me. She had no interest and just wanted to see if I'd show. It turns out it was done on a dare. I was pissed right off. Goddamned bitch. To do something like that is just downright mean and callous. If you think playing with someone's emotions is funny, wait until it happens to you and then you'll see how funny it is.

* * *

52

It was shortly after that I got asked by some unpopular girls to go to a party. There was three of them and they were gothic looking and pretty much kept to themselves like I did. I thought, why not? It'll be interesting and eclectic for sure.

"What kind of party is it?" I asked

"Never mind, we need boys there. It's us girls and we need some boys there too. You obviously aren't interested." one said.

"I am interested. I just want to know what kind of party it is." I insisted.

"A Rainbow party. See if you can go." she said.

"Ok, when is it?" I replied.

"Friday night 8 o'clock" she said.

For the record I had no idea what a Rainbow Party was at the time and if I did, the following events never would have taken place. I should have asked anyone else at all. Anyone. I asked a few friends, they had no idea either. I was 15 and naive. I had no clue what I was being asked at the time. I went home and I had to know. I made the biggest mistake at the time. I asked my mom. I wasn't asking Jerry because I really didn't want his permission for anything. I didn't care what he thought. My dad wasn't interested in me so I had to ask her. I would have been better off standing up during the middle of a church service and screaming out a tirade of profanity and blasphemous remarks that her reaction. She freaked right out.

"Are you kidding me?! Do you even know what kind of party that is?!"

"No," I answered sheepishly.

"Ok, here's what you just asked me... You asked me if you can go over to a house with a bunch of girls where they each put on a different color of lipstick and then they each take turns sucking your dick. What the hell did you expect me to say?! You aren't going to a party with a bunch of little sluts and that's the end of it!" she explained and shouted.

See what I mean. Wow. I never made that mistake again. Any party invite or whatever in the future, I would ask anyone else, anyone else at all. A random stranger, a person I knew but didn't hang around, anyone else. That has got to be the most awkward conversations between a mother and her son ever. Research things yourself before finding out the hard way. I love Google too bad it wasn't available then.

CHAPTER 6

· · · · · · · ● · · · · · · · ·

The bathroom floor in the house was really soft at this time. When you sat on the toilet, it was a rocking ride since the floor was rotting away. Apparently there was a crack in the drainage pipe from the tub that was spewing water all over the floor. The floor had rotted to the point where it was soft to walk on and it was sagging under your weight.

The landlord got a look at it and hired a contractor to come and fix it. The contractor was shocked nobody fell through the floor. There was nothing left of the floor. The roll out tile probably had just enough to hold the floor together to prevent any of us from falling through. The house was a dive and I really couldn't wait to get the hell out there.

* * *

I was helping mom on one of her routes near the fast food area of town and she came back to the car carrying something in her hands. It was in January and it was cold. She was cradling whatever it was. I was waiting in the car with a hot chocolate since it was a small apartment complex. She opened the door and I could hear a kitten cry.

"Where did you find that?" I asked.

"In one of the garbage cans right on top in some trash." she said with disgust. She glared at the complex when she said it. It was if she knew which apartment had done it. The kitten was nearly frozen to death.

"Are we keeping it?" I asked since I had to give up my other three.

"I'll ask the landlord and if not, we're going to move. You kids have given up enough and I am tired of Jerry's crap. Without him. Keep that to yourself." she said. I was shocked and relieved at the same time. Kelly was home doing homework.

For the record I had that cat until I moved into my first apartment on my own. I was 23 and had her for almost 6 months after that. To the lowlife scum of the Earth that threw that kitten the trash: You are a cold hearted, waste of skin that isn't worth pissing on. I despise people like you who are inhumane to animals because you are just as rude, disrespectful and nasty to those around you. You make me sick. People like you often die alone and have empty funerals. You are never missed and we are better off without you. I hope you suffer when you die and I hope it hurts like Hell and die alone. Enjoy Karma.

When we got home with the kitten, mom took it to the bathroom to clean it up. It took three sinks full of water to get it clean. She was in her own filth and left to die and nearly starved to death. Luckily she survived. Jerry threw a fit.

"We're not allowed to have pets in this house," he said firmly.

"Or what, he'll throw us out? Let him. This place is a dump anyway." mom shot back.

"Where will we go?" he asked sarcastically.

"That's my problem. It's not like you pay the rent or anything." she shot back.

"I won't have a cat in the house. It's too small and they stink," Said Jerry trying to be assertive.

"So do you and we have to put up with you, don't we? Besides, if it's too crowded, you can leave. We prefer the cat to you. If you don't believe me, ask Justin and Kelly. So let me know when you're done laying down the law, Asshole" she snapped back.

"Don't you dare call me an asshole," he barked standing in the bathroom doorway.

"Well it's the truth, Asshole. What are you going to do about it, Asshole?" she said egging him on. She was still drying the kitten with a bath towel.

"Are you through?" he asked condescendingly.

"No! I'm Not! You say my ex-husband is abusive, but you're worse! At least he paid the bills and could hold down a job and had his own truck. You lost yours. He pays his child support. You expected me to pay yours. It's your kid. I have two of my own to pay for now but you expect me to pay for yours and neither of us has ever met him. Bullshit!" she said glaring at him. I know that look. It means you better back off . You're really going to get it if you don't.

"You leave my kid out of this," Jerry said pointing his finger at her.

"Ooh, big man. You've already left him out of everything. I'll bet he wants nothing to do with you. It wouldn't surprise me one bit. You'd rather spend your money on cigarettes, coffee, and lottery tickets and you haven't won squat, have you? All of your pretty little promises of a better life haven't amounted to anything and neither have you. We're still here in this dive and you don't even have the decency to lift a finger and pay for anything. Not even groceries and you pig out at every meal. Your fat gut you've gotten says it all piggy. So if it's between you and the cat, the cat stays!" barked mom going for the kill. She placed the kitten down on the counter and gestured with her hand in the air as if to say whatever and bring it on.

"We'll see," he said quietly and sarcastically.

"*We'll see* what?" mom spat back mocking him crossing her arms across her chest still glaring at him.

"Nothing, we'll just see." he said desperately trying to get the upper hand. He tuned to walk way.

"Nothing, your goddamned right, nothing. Don't you turn away from me. Look at me." she hissed. He knew what was good for him, he faced her. Instead he backed up a step towards the living room door .

"That's what you are, Nothing! That's all you're going to be too. Nothing!" mom barked and made her way towards him handing me the kitten in the kitchen as she backed him into the living room. She advanced him and backed him right into his chair. The kitchen was the first room at the main entrance with the living room to the right and the bathroom at the end of the kitchen.

He sat in the chair with his head slung low while mom stood over him glaring down at him. There was a pause. A long pause, she glared at him some more. She looked like a king cobra ready to strike. She stood over him menacingly for another second.

"What's the matter, nothing to say? Look at me when I am talking to you," she hissed.

"I am," he said in a child like voice.

"No you're not, you're looking at the goddamned floor. Look at me!" she barked grabbing him by the chin and raising his head with her left hand to look her in the eyes. She grabbed him by the shirt with the right and leaned over him face to face.

"There, that's better. Now you're looking at me," she hissed.

"You have not made due on one promise you made about anything. You said we would have a better place to live. You said we'd buy a house. You said you'd find a better job. You haven't done anything. You have made our lives worse. You have no problem getting me to spend money on you and your fat gut while my kids go without. They gave up their pets to move to this hell hole. Justin has to sleep on a goddamned rollaway bed in the living room. We are keeping the kitten and the kids are going to be happy. Nobody should have to live like this. If you have a problem with it, you can leave. Is that clear?" she sneered looking him in the eye just inches away daring him to oppose her.

"Ok. Alright, the cat stays" he whined.

"That's what I thought," she said menacingly and smirking while she let go of him. She shot me a smile. I smiled back. I was proud of her for putting that loser in his place. If he doesn't see what's coming, he's stupid.

Mom named the kitten Velvet because her ears were so soft and smooth to the touch. She was really affectionate and slept with me most of the time. She would sleep on my pillow and continued to do so until the day she died.

* * *

I was walking home from school my usual route when it turns out Anthony followed me home and wanted to talk. He was all apologies, I kept my distance enough not to be rude, but close enough where I could make a break for it if I needed to. I was very apprehensive. We were alone.

"Is Jerry still with you guys?' he asked.

"Ugh, yes," I answered rolling my eyes.

"Are you sick of him?' He asked.

"Totally."

"Do you think mom will talk to me?" he asked.

"I don't know but you can try." I answered. I wasn't sure. The last time I saw him, he brutally beat the snot out of me and threatened to kill me.

"Are we good? I am sorry about what happened," he said. He seemed sincere.

"I accept your apology but it's going to take a while to trust you again. I have permanent damage to the right side of my face because of you," I explained.

"Oh, I am so sorry. How did I do it?" he asked.

"When you ripped my mouth open," I answered not believing he didn't know how. I am not sure if he know I was apprehensive to be around him

"Sorry," he said quietly. I didn't answer.

"So where are you living now?" he asked.

"We're here." I said pointing to our lovely Hell hole.

"You're kidding." he said looking at it in disgust.

"Not much longer." I stated.

"Good, where from here?" he asked.

"I'm not sure." I said. I was lying. I wasn't saying anything at this point. I wasn't sure I could trust him again.

Mom pulled up and saw us talking. I'm not sure what she was thinking. She didn't take her eyes off of us either. I'm sure she was just as apprehensive as I was. She knew what he's capable of just as much as I do. Is he capable of murder? I would say 'yes' without hesitation. Having been on the receiving end of a brutal attack, I have no doubt in my mind.

I let mom and Anthony talk. I kept my distance. I'll let her make the decision. I'm not. Anthony is a psycho. She tried to get him help and dear old dad went and got him out because he thought it was his enemy Jerry that put him there. He had no facts whatsoever and pulled him out right away. Some parents are naive when it comes to their kids. They can do no wrong.

All he had to do was ask any of us to find out. He visited Kelly on a regular basis. Why didn't she tell him and better yet, why didn't he ask? He never bothered to know as far as I am concerned. He didn't care. That is evident. I never got so much as a birthday card, Christmas card from him or even a phone call. The only thing I got for years was disrespect and neglect. Had he made the attempt, he'd know. It was his own conclusion that counted. Forget the facts and go with your opinion because someone you hate is on the scene. It's easier that way, isn't it?

They talked for a while and then Jerry came home. He saw mom and Anthony talking and wasn't impressed. He had the "I won't have it" look on his face. He went in the house and grabbed a soda. I followed. I was expecting a fight between the two but remembered Jerry is spineless. He'll have lots to say after he's gone though. I guarantee it.

"Hello Anthony," said Jerry as he entered the living room. What a two-faced liar.

"Hello, " Anthony responded trying to be nice. You could tell he was being just as fake and trying to hide his contempt.

"So what brings you by?" asked Jerry being nosy.

"I came to talk and apologize" he stated.

"How did you find out where we were?" asked Jerry with a hint of malice.

"I followed Justin."

"Followed or did he bring you?" asked Jerry. Now he's pissing me off.

"Followed," replied Anthony slowly as to get him to make it register.

"Ok, carry on" said Jerry gesturing his hand.

"Thank you." replied Anthony. The sarcasm was thick as was the malice.

Anthony continued his visit without any further interruptions from Jerry. He seemed like he was sorry and he would come by and visit on the weekends when he was off for the next month or two. Jerry didn't like it at all. Every time he left, it would end in an argument as to how we could let him back in our lives after the attack on me and the carnage that took place at our old house. I don't have to tell you that when it comes to family, it's easier to forgive them than a stranger. The whole blood is thicker than water thing does have some weight to it. Without quoting the waste of space and taking up several pages of the same old rhetoric and avoiding repetition, let's just say the dumb ass never got it. We were tired of it and tired of him and his crap too.

* * *

We got yet another minister at our church and he had a teenage son, my age. His name was Josh McKay. I chatted him up after church the one day. He was pretty cool and it turned out he was in some of my classes. We were starting to be good friends. He got the pleasure of meeting Jerry after church and later asked me, "Does he ever shut up?" You already know my answer, "No."

* * *

To piss him off some more, Kelly had another kitten fallow her home from school and it instantly became affectionate to mom. She named her Precious. Mom missed the cats. We liked having pets. Unconditional love. It's nice to have someone snuggle up and give you attention after a hard day. It just makes the day worth it whether it's a dog or a cat. That unconditional child-like affection.

Mom would take off after work leaving Kelly and I with Jackass Jerry. She said she was visiting her friends. Particularly the one who lived next door to us when all Hell broke loose. What she was really doing is finding another place to live and Jerry wasn't coming with us. She had more than enough of his yelling, trying to bully everyone around, laziness, and the fact he was getting fat and disgusting where he wouldn't bathe as often as he should. What a swine.

Mom cam home early from work the one day and pulled us aside. She laid it all on the table.

"I found us a new place to live. You each will have your own rooms and Jerry isn't coming. I can't take any more of his crap and I know you can't either. I've hired movers and he's going to be told we are moving to Finch Bay (next town over to west) but we are moving back to Derry. We're letting him go to work and I am telling him we're moving so we can pack. We'll let him do the same. When he goes to work, I want the house empty and he'll come home to only his crap. Putting it out at the road is too much effort. Promise me you won't tell him," she explained.

"My own room, cool. No more sleeping in the living room on the roll out bed." I was excited and hugged her.

"We won't tell him. We hate him," Kelly said with a smile across her face looking at me and then back to mom.

"I'll play nice with him as much as it makes me sick like I usually do. I won't tell him. I can't stand him and I'll be glad to be rid of him." I stated.

"Ok. I'll tell him tonight I found a place in Finch Bay. Just go along with whatever he says and whatever you do, don't slip up or we'll never get rid of him," she said. She was concerned. He was getting to be a bigger twat every day. Like I even thought that was possible. I was wrong. It is.

By this time, we had to take the power bar to the entertainment unit in the trunk of the car because all he would do is sit on his ass and watch TV and fill his face. He was working and didn't pay for anything as usual. His money was all about cigarettes and lottery tickets. You guessed it, scratch tickets and he didn't win squat. The small winnings went right back into the next ticket and the one after that until he was out of cash. He had no problem eating us out of house and home and driving up the electric bill.

Of course if Kelly and I were doing homework he'd go on a rant as to why we should shut the lights out, it costs money. What a goddamned hypocrite. See it is possible to be a bigger dickhead. Now he is a twat. A useless twat. He graduated. Congratulations.

The weeks leading up to the move seemed to take forever. I loved working at the restaurant, it kept me away from him. I was a dishwasher and then a host. I really wanted waiter, I could have used the extra cash. For some reason, only management friends and ass kissers got it. I refuse to kiss ass to this day and have little respect for people who do. If you can't get anywhere on your own skills and talents, then ass kissing is for you. Don't forget to wipe your nose and mouth afterwards. Keep in mind, it'll only get you so far until a new boss like me comes along and then you are so screwed. Just keep your resume up to date, you'll need it.

Jerry was repulsive in every way, table manners and lack of hygiene. He was a swine. Watching him eat would make anyone sick, stuffing his face and talking with his mouthful. Burping and even farting at the table. If only I had a gun, I'd call it a mercy killing. Mercy on the rest of the world for not allowing him to continue. He actually thought it was funny. I guess it is when you don't pay for anything.

* * *

The day of the move was finally here. Everyone was up nice and early doing last minute packing and organizing boxes. The beds were stripped and put into garbage bags. We'd wash them at the new house. We needed to get the hell out of there. The movers were coming any minute. Jerry was up and making his coffee and smiling smugly.

"So, you and your sister will be going to new schools again," he said smugly.

"Yeah, I guess," I said dismissingly.

"Well we are going to Finch Bay. You won't be with your friends at Palmer. That includes that little bitch, Michelle," he said smirking.

"Don't talk about my friends like that you don't even know her," I snapped back.

"I don't have to know her, a friend of yours would be about the same as you. A smart mouth little punk," he said sarcastically.

"At least I have friends. Don't you have to work?" I shot back.

"Yes, I have time," said Jerry smirking at me with a holier than though look on his face. Oh buddy, if you only knew what was in store for you.

"I have packing to do," I said and walked away from him. Oh you wait buddy, you just wait until reality sinks in after work. I just wish I could see the stupid look on your face this afternoon. I would give anything to be a fly on the wall for that. It's going to be priceless. I fought back my smile. Ooh just to see it.

The moving truck came just before 8 AM and backed into the driveway. The car was parked at the church across the alley. There were two movers on the truck, a dark haired one with short hair and a guy with long, blonde hair. They got out of the truck and approached my mom.

"Hello, " said the blonde guy cordially.

"Hello," responded mom.

"Where are you moving this to? Derry, right?" he asked. Really?! You could read it all over our faces. 'Stupid ass shut the Hell up'.

"No, Finch Bay," responded mom.

"Oh, it must be the next one" he said looking at his sheets on the clip board.

"Ok here it is, Finch Bay," my mistake he said recovering.

"Are you on a time limit?" asked Jerry.

"Yes, we have yours and another right after. I got the two mixed up," he responded. Good recovery. You still let it slip. He probably saw through it with our luck.

"What's the address?" asked Jerry.

"143 Main Street E, apartment 2. I'll come here and get you at 4" mom responded without missing a beat. She rehearsed. Well played.

"Ok, if you don't need me anymore, I'm off to work," he said.

"We're good. Have a good day. I'll see you this afternoon," mom said with her award winning warm smile. She's good. She even kissed him goodbye.

Jerry was on his way to work on foot. We didn't say a word and moved stuff from the house to the truck. After a few trips from the house to the truck and we knew Jerry was out of sight, we breathed a sigh of relief. That was close. That was too close. I just hope he didn't figure that out.

"Sorry about that," said the blonde mover.

"Don't worry about it. Let's just get this done," said mom as she went back in the house for another trip to the truck.

"I'm sorry if I messed that up. I take it that he isn't coming with you," he asked me.

"No. He's not and he doesn't know it yet but he will tonight," I said with a smirk.

"I didn't think so. He didn't seem to know what the Hell he was talking about. I take it, you've had enough of him?" he pried.

"More than you'll ever know. He's a real piece of work. We'll be glad to be rid of him," I said brushing him off.

Not another word was said. Within a few hours we were loaded up and ready to go. The movers were in the truck. Mom, Kelly, the kitten and I were in the car and we were off. The stay in the house was long enough. I was getting my own room and moving closer to my friends and most importantly, no dickhead Jerry.

I was in charge of piling Jerry's stuff. I have never been the best at packing so I more or less piled it in the corner in the living room. His old, ratty bags and clothes, his paperback novels which will come in to play later in the story and the old folding loveseat he picked up at a used furniture store that turns into a bed by unfolding. The loveseat was shit brown. How fitting.

I had a bit of a conscience then for trash like him. I couldn't leave him with nothing to eat so I left him an aging banana (the oldest one we had) and a few cans of soup we didn't like. Split pea with ham is disgusting and looks like baby vomit. I left it for him with no can opener. I guess he'll have to put down the scratch ticket and get a can opener. I never left him any pots or pans either. It really showed how little he owned. Jerry is a pathetic loser.

CHAPTER 7

· · · · · · ●●●● ● ●●●●● · · · ·

The new house was a long and blue. It had two units, a front and a back. We were in the back. There was a long driveway leading up to it on a quiet long, dead end street. We had neighbors to the left and the right and a retirement home across the street. Awesome. To the rear was a large field and a woodlot that went down a ravine. You couldn't find the house from the main street because the woodlot and the ravine hide it. The large farmhouse on the corner and the Catholic church hide it as well. Mom is a genius. She should take a bow for this one. So what if he figures out we were back in Derry.

We moved most of the furniture through the back door and there were actually 2 1/2 bedrooms. There were two full bedrooms on the left side of the house and a smaller one to the front of the house. It could have doubled as a walk in closet. I liked the room. It was smaller but I like how I could look outside and face the porch to see who's knocking at the door. It was L-shaped from the way it was cut off from the front unit. It could work. I claimed it to some resistance from Kelly but I won.

I set up a TV and a small entertainment system in it and arranged the room where I could watch some movies in it and have friends over to do the same where it would be comfortable but not too weird that they were in my bedroom. The cats loved it too.

* * *

We just got settled in and it wasn't even a month in the new place when Anthony was waiting for me outside Palmer High School where I attended since Derry was so small. I came out the front door and there he was waiting for me. I paused for minute the second I saw him.

"Hello, what brings you here?" I asked.

"Hi. Do you think mom will let me stay with you guys for a while? I have to be out of my place by the end of the month. " he asked.

"I don't know, you'll have to ask her yourself." I told him. Secretly I was hoping for a 'no' answer. We all know how well it turned out the last time. However, we know you can't turn your back on family. This is going to be a tough call.

"When is she home?" he asked.

"Any time after 5. I hate to be rude but I have a bus to catch." I replied and made my way to the bus. I liked riding the one that dropped us off downtown Derry. I rode with my friends. There was one that went on my road but I didn't know anyone on there. If I did, I didn't really talk to them other than the odd 'Hello'.

I got on the bus and went and sat with Josh McKay and the others. Josh was adjusting very well to being in a new town and school. I wasn't too sure since he was a PK. Preacher's Kid. Most people who went to the high school weren't that religious.

The bus always let us off just north of the traffic light. It was a five block walk home from there. It wasn't far and I liked the walk. It was relaxing. I did that walk rain or shine, snow or sleet. I didn't care. They knew why I did the walk. The people on my bus I was supposed to take thought I was weird. I always pride myself on doing my own thing and not giving a flying care what people thought of me. It's my life and I'll live it my way. I don't need anyone else's seal of approval on it. If you were to try and live your life for everyone else, you're a servant and you will never satisfy everyone. There's always going to be someone who thinks they have the right to tell you how to live. Try it with me and we're going to butt heads. We'll be enemies in no time.

In my opinion there are three criteria on why you should interfere in someone else's life: they are going to or are hurting themselves, they are hurting others or intend to do so or if they are torturing animals as it is a sign they can do the same to another person. Otherwise, piss off and mind your own business. It's the secret to a long, healthy life. If someone wants you to know their business, they'll tell you.

I got home before mom and Kelly did. I made myself a snack and did my homework as usual. Kelly would get home within minutes of mom. She was still in elementary school and it ran later than high school. The buses were shared. We started and ended half an hour earlier than they did so they could use the buses after us.

Anthony couldn't wait, he was at our door before 5. He got a ride from one of his friends since he wasn't driving yet. Mom wasn't even home yet. He must have been really desperate for a place to live. He lived with friends and most of them I wouldn't trust as far as I could throw them. They had reputations for being thieves, pot heads and petty thugs. Never leave your cash or valuables out in sight.

Mom came home just after Anthony got there. She was surprised to see him. I also think she knew it was because he wanted something. Let's face it , our social schedule was wide open. If it weren't for my youth group and the restaurant I worked at, it would be completely open.

"Hi mom. How was your day?" he asked.

"Good. What brings you by?" she asked.

"To see you." he replied.

"Ok. What do you need?" she asked.

"I need a place to stay for a couple of months. I have to be out of my place by the end of the month."

"Ok. If I decide to let you live here for a while. It's two months maximum. You're going to pay me too. There's no more free rides. I am not a revolving door," she said in a matter of fact manner.

"Are Justin and Kelly paying you too?" he asked with a hint of condescension.

"No. We aren't talking about them. They are in school. You are not. You work and so does Justin. He buys his own clothes and supplies for school. He even helps around here and helps his sister with her homework too. You work and if you don't you will find a job. You can go ask at the grocery store. I go to church with him. You've also been on your own and have been paying for your own place for a while now. So don't you dare ever ask me if they are paying too. Are we clear?" mom asked with attitude.

"Ok. I wasn't giving you attitude..."

"Yes you were. You don't ask someone to help you and give you a place to stay and then give them attitude. So don't give me that shit that you weren't giving attitude because you were." she scolded.

"Sorry. I didn't think I was..."

"You're pathetic.. *Are Justin and Kelly paying too?*" she mocked.

"Oh. I "m sorry." he said half heartedly.

"That's fine. You're still paying. It's a lesson in growing up. You have to figure things out for yourself because you aren't always going to be able to run home. I won't be here forever. Then what are you going to do, run to the grave yard? *Mom, I need help.* It's a tough lesson but you've got to learn it."

"Ok."

"I shouldn't even let you back after what you did to your brother. You ripped his mouth open and he can't smile out half of his face. It's permanent. It may heal over time but will always have damage. If I get anything like that out of you this time, you are over 16 this time and you're going to be charged. You got off easy last time. We were getting you the help and your father had to come and mess it up. He got you out before anything could really be done and didn't even have the decency to ask why you were there in the first place. That should show you how much he really gives a rat's ass about any of you. Are we clear?"

"Yes."

"Good. You get the couch."

"That's fine. Thanks mom."

Anthony was moved in by the weekend. H didn't have that much to move thankfully. He took his spot on the sofa and packed up his sleeping gear every morning as I had to. He got the job at the town grocery store as a grocery carrier and stock person. It turned out he was working with our next door neighbor's middle son Ralph.

He was a tall, athletic guy with dark spiked hair. I didn't t know the other's names at that point.

* * *

We were driving home one night and made the mistake of driving down the main street that runs north and south. We passed Jerry's mother's street and her van was running light on. As soon as we passed it, the van began to follow. He was speeding and ran the stop sign at the corner of her street to try and catch up to us.

"Damn it," said mom loudly.

We sped up and went to the lake and turned around at the beach by the fish plant. He was still following. Mom went back into town and turned right. She pulled into the Catholic church parking lot and pointed the car to the exit.

"What are you doing?" I asked her.

'I'm going to confront the bastard," she said. Within seconds he pulled in right beside her and had the van pointed in the opposite direction so the driver's sides were facing each other side by side. He rolled down the window.

"What were you thinking leaving me like that?" he demanded.

"I got sick of your freeloading. You didn't pay for anything. All you do is use people and tell stories and make up promises you never follow through on. We had enough," she shot back.

"I knew the movers were covering for you when the one slipped and said Derry instead of Finch Bay." he said with pride and condescension.

"Well good for you. Congratulations, you solved the case, Sherlock." mom scoffed.

"What's the idea of not leaving me anything to eat?" he asked.

"I left you a banana and the pea soup you like so much." I said with a smirk.

"Shut up Justin, I wasn't talking to you! You little faggot!" shouted Jerry.

"Like anyone wants to talk to you. I see you're back at mommy's. There's a shock. Twat!" I shot back my voice dripping in sarcasm and malice.

"Easy Justin, " mom said quietly.

"Don't you call him a faggot, asshole!" she growled.

"And you wonder why we left," she said to him sarcastically rolling her eyes.

"You're one to talk, Living with mommy" Jerry said with sarcasm.

"Yeah I am, the only difference is I am 15 and you're going on 40. Nice van. Too bad it your mother's and not yours. Where's yours? Oh yeah, that's right, it got repossessed because you couldn't keep your payments up. Why? Because you're a pathetic loser that would rather mooch off of everyone else. How's those child support payments coming? Oh yeah, I forgot you don't even pay those either, do you?" I yelled back at him with my voice dripping in malice.

"Fuck you Justin!" he yelled.

"Fuck off and DIE!" I yelled back. I meant every word of it. I loathe his entire existence.

"That's Enough! Both of you!" mom shouted. I sat back in the passenger seat. Kelly was taking it all in and said nothing from the back seat.

"What the hell do you want, Jerry?" mom asked with impatience glaring at him.

"To talk," he said with desperation.

"We are. I told you why we left you and obviously we're through. What the fuck else do you want?" asked mom impatiently.

"To know where you're living and if there's a chance of getting back together." said Jerry.

"Where we're living is none of your business. If I wanted you to come with us, you would be there now. You moved yourself in without permission the first time. I gave you that key to keep an eye on the place. It wasn't for you to move in. When that time comes, you'll be asked. You just don't decide to move in someone else's house because you think you're allowed to. Ask first! If you want to work on our 'relationship', we'll start small. I'll meet you for coffee. You will never move in with us again. It didn't work and I am not going down that road again. If things go well in meeting, I'll see you again but you are not moving in with us ever again. The kids can't stand you as I am sure you figured out and to be quite frankly most of the time, neither can I. If you want to work on it, I'll entertain it so you get your answers. Are we clear?"

"Clear," he said quietly.

"Another thing, you don't ever tell my kids to 'fuck off' again," she said firmly.

"He started it..."

"What are you, a kid too? First of all, if anyone started anything, you did if you want to get right down to it. You thought you could come in and order everyone around like it was one of your military bases. This isn't the military and we will not be ordered around and screamed at. I am in charge, not you. I said you were in charge when I was gone. It was not meant for you to be bullying and shouting at them like a drill sergeant. Nobody wants to listen to that nonsense. Secondly, the 'one or the other thing with the peanut butter and jam' was plain stupid. I let them have both. They do go together you know and it wasn't as if you paid for any of it either. Thirdly, having Justin do your work delivering on your routes is nonsense. It's your job, not his. By rights you should have paid him half of it. He isn't your servant. Fourthly, did you not think that I was going to be told that you wanted to try and get me fired from the job? Are you seriously this stupid? Don't look so surprised, the boss told me. I had to talk him out of firing you for even suggesting it. Don't you EVER threaten me again! Then here we are now, you asking me for another chance. Answer me this, why the fuck should I?"

"Because I still wuv you.." he whined.

"That's another thing. I'm sick of your baby talk. It makes me sick. If you want another shot, talk right or forget it. Baby talk from a grown man is disgusting. Is that clear? Is it sinking in?" she asked with her voice dripping in sarcasm and contempt.

"I'll try.."

"You'll do more than try, mister. You'll do it and like it. I told you I got rid of one piece of trash and didn't want another. You're worse as far as I'm concerned. But you want another shot." said mom rolling her eyes.

"I do, I can change." he pleaded.

"Leopards don't change their spots. I don't want you to change. I want you to stop bullying, ordering people around and stop the damn baby talk. I want you to treat others with respect that you yell and order people to do for you. That's not the way to get respect. You get hatred that way. That's why we moved out on you. I will not live with a dictator now will I expose my kids to it. We tried it your way for 18 months and it didn't work, did it? Now maybe you'll try it my way." she said firmly.

"Oh, your way.." he said with sarcasm.

"We tried your way and it sucks. That's probably why you got divorced in the first place. They probably all hated your guts. How come you don't see your kid? Keep it up and I'm driving off."

"Don't do that..."

"Then lose the attitude. It's your fault and you know it." she affirmed.

"Is Anthony living with you?" he asked trying to dodge the truth.

"Once again, I'll say who lives with me and who doesn't. It really isn't any of your business." said mom growing impatient.

"So he is." he said smugly with contempt.

"It's none of your business. Are you done yet? Can we go home?" she shot back.

"Can I have your number?"

"Grab a pen. 555-3325, do you have it?" replied mom.

"Yup, It's on my cigarette package." he said holding up less than half a pack.

"Go home and write it out before you finish the pack. The way you smoke, it'll be before the end of the night." said mom. He smoked like a chimney. He was about a pack a day.

"I will. Good night. We'll talk soon." Said Jerry before he drove to turn around. We let him pull ahead as not to be followed. I couldn't believe mom was going to see this dickhead again. The definition of insanity is doing the same thing and expecting different results.

Here we go, round two. The thought of it made me sick. Completely nauseous. However, we can't tell our parents who they can date not even when we know how this will turn out.

We didn't discuss what just happened, she knew we were pissed off. She knew we hated his guts. I hated him more than anyone right now. It was nice to be free of the useless twat and now mom was going to see him. Ugh. Maybe she has her own answers to find out. I had my suspicions. He hated dad and dad hated him. I couldn't imagine why. Really?! I personally it was the cowards way to handle an enemy. When you don't have the guts to take on an enemy, they usually take it out on the person's car, pet, house or even their family. Hmmm. Could he really be that spineless and stoop to that level or is it just a coincidence?

Since fat ass's dad shot and killed our dog a few years before, it made sense. The people in this town are really that pathetic. Shooting a dog because you are too fat and slow to have a fist fight that you know you'll lose. It truly is a spineless and cowardly act.

Is Jerry that pathetic? I think so. He hates dad and got his ass kicked by him years ago when they were in high school. Jerry says dad hit him with a pipe across the head. Jerry has a small scar on his nose. That wouldn't be enough damage. A full force blunt force trauma like that would put him right in the hospital or possibly the morgue. Dad says he broke his nose by punching him in it. I have to believe dad on this one.

Jerry liked to tell tall tales. The Vietnam stories come to mind first. How you can be shot and not even have a scar. Yeah, right. Joining the army before 16 and getting involved in a another countries' conflict. Not likely. I'll go out on a limb and say highly unlikely. This makes him a pathetic, lying waste of skin. To answer the question of making dad's ex-wife and kids pay for having his nose broken and poor little ego bruised, I have to say yes. He is that pathetic and that much of a coward. I couldn't tell the others. I had to be sure. This requires skill. I'll let him believe all is forgiven and forgotten. Keep your friends close and enemies closer. Game on ass-hat, game on.

CHAPTER 8

•••••••••●•••••••••

Anthony did get the job at the grocery store. He worked as a grocery carrier and stock person. He was used to doing landscaping but now it was the grocery store. I was sure he was going to go back to landscaping. The owner of the grocery store was from our church. I'm sure that's how he got the job. Mom was likeable and still is. Everyone knows she's a strong woman with good values. Everyone knows she does the best she can and still does. It was a small town and everyone knew the bad hand we were dealt.

It wasn't more than a month after Anthony moved in that mom's cat Precious was missing. She was an affectionate cat that would suck up to anyone that would give her attention. She even sucked up to Anthony and he claimed to hate cats. He loved rubbing his hand her face and making the ears go back and make her growl. She always went back to him. She got into the habit of following whoever gave her attention last.

Anthony had a couple of hunting style knives. I kind of thought they were the type of knives hoodlums carried around. They had six inch blades and finger grips on the handles. The blades were similar in curve to that of a Bowie knife. Anthony loved his. He used them for everything from cutting up apples to steak. It was as if he were a biker/ outlaw wannabe. The type of vision you have of an anti-government militia Unabomber using a hunting knife to butter his bread. It was creepy.

These are the same knives he would pull out and torment Kelly and I with on a regular basis. This was done when mom wasn't home because we all know she would not tolerate that kind of crap in her house. She hated the knives but they were Anthony's. When he uses them on steak, she would roll her eyes and then get him a proper steak knife. She hid her disdain for the behavior well. She smiled when handing him the proper utensil t to use.

I knew where he kept them. I pulled them out a couple of days later after Precious never returned home. That cat was needy and clingy. The original thought was that she got out and needed to frolic in the field behind the house or in the gardens. The cat never missed a meal. It had been two days and she never came home. She liked to follow the last person to give her attention.

Anthony claimed to hate cats but she would go to him so he could rub his hands in her face and make her ears go back and growl. He'd stop and suck her up and then go back to rough housing her. This would carry on in the same manner every time he came she came to him. The cat loved attention. It apparently didn't matter if it was mixed with hostility or rough horse play. I thought it was too rough anyway.

When I pulled out the knives, I couldn't help but notice a brown stain along the base of the blade near the handle. I wasn't sure what it was. He did use the knife for everything. I also knew what he was capable of. I knew it every time I looked in the mirror. The cat that couldn't stand to be away from human attention was missing. It just wasn't sitting right.

Jerry came over and mom decided to show the knife to him. Great. A know liar is shown the knife. Maybe it was used to kill someone and maybe he brutally killed the cat and had stir fry like one of the Vietnam stories he liked to tell. This should be interesting. I thought it was blood but I needed answers. Anthony was working.

"What do you make of this?" mom asked Jerry.

"It looks like blood." he said like he was Sherlock Holmes.

"That's what I thought but we need to be sure," said mom.

"Why don't we take it to the officer in town. If anyone knows anything about blood and weapons, it's them. No offense Jerry but we need an expert opinion." I suggested. I was being nice. I hated the tool but I needed him to be an ally.

"That's a good idea, Justin," Jerry said. I was shocked. He was actually taking my side.

"Let's take it to him," said mom.

We piled in the car and drove to town, luckily the town's police officer was there at his hole-in-the-wall office. Officer Russell Turner was a man in his late 40s with a burly build. He was clean shaven with thinning dark hair and glasses. He was sitting in his office reading the newspaper. He saw us come to the door and looked over his newspaper at us and waved us in with his left hand while still holding the newspaper. He laid it down on the desk not to lose his place.

"Hello, what can I do for you?" he asked.

"I have a knife that has a stain on it and I want to know if it's blood," replied mom holding up the hunting style knife.

"Why would there be blood on it? Human or animal?" he asked.

"My cat went missing and I think my other son killed it. This is his knife and there's a stain on it." Mom explained hand him the knife.

Officer Russell took the knife and held it up to his face under his nose and sniffed it. He took in a few deep breaths to sniff it. I looked at him puzzled. He stopped in mid sniff and looked back at me.

"I suppose you wonder why I am sniffing it," he said looking directly at me.

"Yes. I am."

"I hunt and animal blood smells different than human blood. I will take it and run a AB test on it to see if it is for sure. That is if you don't mind?"

"Go ahead. How long do you need it for?" she asked.

"I'll give it back to you in a couple of days."

"That's fine. In the meantime, I am just going to come right out with it and ask him," said mom.

We left the office and went back home. I put the other knife away like nothing happened and was thinking up a good lie for Anthony if he asked where the other one went. I decided I was going to tell him to keep better track of his stuff and he's the only one who touches them. I have no interest in them. It's only a couple of days I thought.

Like clockwork Anthony came home that afternoon and went right for his knives. He pulled out the one from the shoebox he kept them in. Only one was there. He rummaged in the box and then looked at me as if to say "Ok asshole, where's my fucking knife and you better tell me. Now!" There was a pause while our eyes met.

"Where's my knife?" he asked accusingly.

"How would I know? You're the only one who goes in there. Maybe you left it out?" I said lying through my teeth.

"I know I put both of them in there and I want to know where it is god damn it," he snarled at me while trying to stare me down.

"That's enough!" mom said sternly raising her voice to him. She was still in the kitchen but was looking right at him pointing the knife she was using to prepare dinner.

"He took my knife and I want it back." he said in protest while pointing at me with his right hand.

"He didn't take the knife. I did. I want to know where my cat is and I want to know right now," she said staring him down.

"It doesn't matter you'll never see it again," he replied coldly.

"That's fine you'll never see your precious knife again either," mom replied just as coldly.

"Where is it?" he demanded.

"None of your business. You killed my cat didn't you?" she asked accusingly.

"Yeah I did. It followed me into town and I slit its throat and threw it in the dumpster behind the grocery store." he said without any emotion.

"I want you out tonight. You aren't to come back either. I will take you where ever you want to go. Then we're done. I don't want to see you around here again. Start packing and make your phone call. You are out of here. Is that clear?" Mom said without any emotion. She was beyond pissed off> I have never seen this side of her.

"I'm sorry. I didn't want to...." He started to make up an excuse. Really?! Like it was anyone else's fault.

"Save it. Start packing. You're out of here. If you don't pack right now, Justin and I will do it for you. Get a fucking move on.

You're out before the hour. I don't want to hear another goddamned word from you either. Get packing. Now."

"I don't have boxes..." he whined trying to get her to change her mind.

"Then use garbage bags!" mom shot back. She was trying hard to contain her fury.

He sat there like a deer in the headlights. Their eyes were locked in a stare down. Mom was looking at him as if she wanted to incinerate him on sight. He was looking at her in shock that this was even happening. "She couldn't be throwing me out in an hour." You could see him thinking it.

"What?! Am I turning colors? Do I need to get out the puppets and the crayons so you understand what I am saying? Start packing! Justin, get the garbage bags and help your brother!" Mom barked.

I grabbed the garbage bags and handed him one out of the box and grabbed another. I was placing his clothes in the bag and trying to be neat. He got up off the sofa and looked at her pleading with his eyes while I continued to pack his clothes in the bag. He looked at her for a minute in silence.

"Just so you know, her head came off when I slit her throat," he said a matter of a fact manner..

Mom glared at him and then ripped the garbage bag from his hands, pushed him aside and started throwing his clothes and whatever else of his she could in the bag. She threw it in like she was getting rid of a disgusting mess. She meant business. She was so hurt and angry, she couldn't pick him up fast enough. He was going to be gone in minutes.

"Make your goddamned phone call or I'll dump you off at the side of the road when I think you are far enough away. Dial!!" she barked throwing his savagely packed bag on the ground and handing him the phone like he was a filthy degenerate. The look of pure anger and contempt was very apparent on her face. She was hostile now. Her teeth were gnashed and she was showing them the side of her face in her sneer. The intense glare in her eyes could have melted steel. Her nostrils were flaring. If he didn't dial, she was going to lose it.

He took the phone from her and started dialing. He called a few people and then finally one said yes. He gave her the phone. The whole time she glared and sneered at him. She wanted to hurt him and was showing great restraint. I am not sure I would have been able to stop myself from doing severe bodily harm.

"Justin, load up the car with his crap and wait for me in the front seat." she said calmly. She was a volcano ready to blow. The calm before the massive, violent eruption. I grabbed what I could carry and managed to get it all in there in one trip. It was a struggle but I did it.

About two minutes later they emerged with Anthony leading the way. His head was swung low and he looked at the ground while he walked. Mom was in behind still trying to contain her rage and pain. He walked to the passenger side of the car and got in the back seat. He never did up his seatbelt. Usually she'd make him but this time if we were to be in a collision, I'm sure she hoped he would be mangled and severely injured. I was thinking it too. He actually decapitated mom's cat and told her like he was discussing the weather.

Mom looked straight ahead and drove to the town limits heading towards Palmer. She maintained her speed within an allowable higher rate of speed over the limit. She wanted to get violent on his ass. Anyone would. She kept driving and looking straight ahead. Not once did she look at him in the rearview mirror. Her anger and pain wasn't settling. He was going and that was that.

"Where to?" she asked coldly.

"Turn right on road 154 at the main road in Palmer. Then it's another 15 minutes." he said quietly. Mom picked up the speed. She wanted him out faster than that.

She turned on side roads and headed north to avoid the downtown core of Palmer. His ass was going to be gone as fast as possible. Anthony was smart he sat in the back seat without saying a word. It's good because on the side roads, nobody is close enough to hear you scream should something dreadful happen to you. There's deep ditches too. It would be a shame to fall in one of those. They're not going to find you for a long time down there.

"We're almost there. Turn right on the next side road and it's the fourth on the left."

We were in the middle of nowhere. The next side road had a gas station and convenience store called the Downtown Market right at the junction of 154 and whatever this one was called. Mom hardly slowed down enough to make the corner. She pulled directly in the long driveway that led up the large two-storey farmhouse. It was old and had painted white bricks. you could tell they did it themselves as there were runs of dried paint on the bricks in globs. It is a sin to paint over bricks as far as I'm concerned. Om jammed the brakes on the driveway. It was done in river rock style pebbles. The dust cloud caught up to us.

"Get your shit and get out." she said without even looking at him. She popped the trunk from the button under the dashboard.

He opened the door and looked at her to see if she'd look at him. He sat there a second or two.

"Go!" commanded mom.

"I'm sorry." he said quietly.

"Good for you! It's a lie. Now go!" commanded mom without even bothering to look at him. She looked straight ahead at the windshield. Her window was open about half way and the breeze blew her hair around on the left side of her face. She sat there emotionless and looked at the windshield.

He got out, closed the back door and opened the trunk and removed his stuff. He put it on the lawn and made his way to the driver's side of the car. He came up to her window, she still was looking at the windshield.

"Thanks for everything. I'll call you," he said calmly and quietly. She looked right at him as if he got up and yelled "fuck" in church. She was appalled.

"Don't bother. Don't ever come back or the cops will be involved." she warned. Mom instantly put the car in reverse and spun it around and the put it drive and drove off without looking back. Anthony stood there and was consumed in the dust from the tires. He stood there in disbelief. She was cold and he deserved it and he knew it too.

The whole car ride home, mom didn't show her anger any more. She was letting the hurt out as a few tears streamed down her face. They were for what she just did to Anthony but I think it was more for the cat. Rightfully so. It's another example of cowardly bullying.

CHAPTER 9

· · · · · · ● ● ● ● ● ● ● ● ● · · ·

We got the knife back from the police just as he said we would. Officer Turner was always good with his word. Mom drove up to meet him and I went along. Jerry was at home with his mother. We didn't bother getting him. It was waste of time. He would have talked Officer Turners ear off with his fabricated army stories. I knew they were desperate and pathetic lies. There's no way they weren't. I still have the knife Anthony used to kill mom's cat and I will never give it back to him.

* * *

Josh and I were becoming good friends or so I thought. It was my grade 10 year. It wasn't long before he made new friends and then I saw less of him and then it was like I hardly existed. His new friends' parents had money. We didn't have enough so I got brushed aside. I went from hanging out and goofing off to the casual "Hello" in the hallway or when we were in the same class or at church. It burns my ass to get tossed aside like I don't matter. There seems to be a pattern here, doesn't there? Family and now "friends". Then before you knew it he was Joe Popular and had a girlfriend too.

I started hanging out with Michelle again. I was over the fact I got tossed aside tossed aside for those conniving, two-faced bitches. We were rebuilding our friendship. It wasn't long before we were back where we started. I decided at the same time to get more active in the church. I needed some more friends and I didn't want people to think I was a total loner like I got labeled in grade 9. I wasn't going through that again.

Josh invited me to come out to Friday Night Youth Group. It was for teenagers and something to do so I decided to go. We'd play floor hockey, watch movies and snack on chips, candy and drink soda. There was always bible lessons sneaked in there too along with prayer time. It was ok and fun to be out with some other teenagers.

Pastor Tim and his wife Deb ran the show. They had 3 kids with their daughter Maria being the oldest followed by Daniel and Jacob. Maria was tall and lanky with shoulder length brown hair and wore glasses. She was almost as tall as me but then again I was kind of short for my age. Her brothers wore glasses and were lanky as well. In fact, so did Pastor Tim and Deb.

In the beginning things were ok and then I felt they were starting to interfere in my life. Deb thought I should quit my job at the restaurant so I can come to church more since I would miss a lot of Sunday services. I was a host at this time and Sunday Brunches were and still are very popular. We had a buffet service every Sunday. I got one off a month and Deb didn't think that was right. I go to church and everything else was going to have to work around that. She actually pulled me aside and wanted to talk about it on several occasions.

"I didn't see you in church again on Sunday. That job of yours is interfering with your spiritual life. You should quit it and find something else." stated Deb.

"No, I need the cash and I attend on Fridays as well as Sunday Evenings when I can. My spiritual life will be just fine." I assured her. I was shocked she would even suggest this.

"Well if you were under our house, you wouldn't be doing it. Church comes first and always will." she affirmed. This was very true. Maria was the same age and wouldn't think of having a part time job. It was apparently forbidden. I looked at her and couldn't believe what I was hearing.

"Well your family's situation is different from ours. Your husband has a good job and you live in the church's house. You don't pay mortgage, insurance or utilities and most of your income is disposable so it's easy for you to say. My mom scrapes by and has a dead beat loser of a boyfriend so I work part time and get whatever I need or want myself. I won't ask her for anything. I don't want to add more stress and problems."

"Maybe she should find a better job than." she said smugly. I could sense the judgment and superiority she felt saying it. It sickened me. Condescending bitch. I shot her a dirty look.

"Well since you have all the answers, why don't you tell me where or are you just going to pray about it?' I shot back, my voice dripping in malice and contempt.

She stood there with her jaw dropping and in total shock.

"Ugh," she squeaked with a pretentious dirty look mixed with shock on her face.

"Oh, you don't have all the answers? Then don't judge!" I attacked. I glared at her and then went to join the others. I was pissed off now. How the hell can someone make snap judgments like that without really knowing what's going on? Cheap advice from the ivory tower. She can't even relate to me and she has all the answers? Yeah, right. I don't think she has struggled with anything. I didn't care if I was out of line. She was first. I was defending myself as far as I am concerned.

I stewed on it for another week since I missed church service on Sunday. I was working. I usually ran the brunch buffet. I couldn't say "no". I needed the money. It wasn't as if I had anyone else to turn to. I still wasn't talking to dad and had no intention in doing so. I don't go crawling back, never have, never will. I thought if things don't work out with someone, why go back for seconds. The definition of insanity is doing the same thing over again expecting different results. Much like Mom and Jerry. Pass the Prozac. We clearly need meds.

* * *

I don't know what I was thinking but I went back and Pastor Tim saw me and motioned me to come in his office. I looked at him and thought, "Oh no, I probably should have held back last week. I need to work on that." I entered his office and he smiled at me sheepishly.

"Please close the door and have a seat." he said kindly and motioned to the set of chairs in front of his desk. He was standing behind one and they were angled just right to carry on a conversation while still facing the desk. I sat down in the one to the right facing the desk. He sat in the other. I was surprised he didn't sit across the desk. This is new, I thought.

"I understand you were upset with my wife last week" he began. His voice was void of anger, more concerned than anything. he looked right at me while he spoke and leaned into his lap with his hands netted together with his forearms resting on his knees.

"Yeah, sorry about that," I half heartedly apologized. I wasn't sorry for standing up for myself or what I said. Perhaps the way I said it was over the top.

"It's ok. We talked about it. I know you are having a hard time and it's a lot for someone to go through especially your age. You don't like it where you are now and want things to be better but want to be a kid too. However, when you disagree try to be more diplomatic. If you feel yourself getting hot under the collar, just excuse yourself. It's always better for you to collect your thoughts and then reproach what's bothering you so you can do it rationally," he explained. It was like a friend talking to me. Wow I had a new respect for Pastor Tim. The guy gets me. If he doesn't, he certainly has the education to relate.

"Ok, I will apologize to her," I reluctantly agreed to do it. It's sometimes better to do it than let the bad feelings brew. Nobody said I had to mean it. The reality is, I was sorry but for other reasons. This is how I apologize to this day. I am so glad people can't read minds, we'd all be in deep shit. I am sorry she feels it necessary to interfere in people's lives. I am sorry she feels she has the right to dictate what I do in my own life and be condescending about it. I am truly sorry she feels I should give up everything and pray my life away. Yeah, ok. What I as the most sorry about was the fact I didn't have a lot of friends and there really wasn't much else to do but subject myself to this crap so I can have a night out or I could always stay home and listen to the other anything else that measured up to a steaming pile of excrement.

"I am sure she will appreciate that," he said with a smile. Either he was genuine or he kind of knew what I was thinking. It really didn't matter if he did. I really don't think he'd tell her.

I excused myself and went to "apologize" and get that out of the way. Luckily she was receptive. I am sure she meant well and had the best intentions of what the real world isn't familiar with but whatever. In fact she seemed to take it too well.

* * *

When I got home, Jerry was there with mom. It was odd as he was always working the afternoon shift and was normally done at 12 AM. It was just shortly after 11 PM. I looked at him and realized something was wrong.

"How come you are done early?' I asked.

"I left. Someone threw a an entire spaghetti squash at me and hit me in the arm. The supervisor didn't do anything about it, so I left," he explained.

"You walked of the line and abandoned your job?" I asked.

"Yeah, I did," he stated.

"Are you nuts? You pretty much fired yourself. You'd be lucky if they took you back. There are channels to follow for this type of thing," I replied as a matter of fact. Yes I paid attention in the orientation at the restaurant I worked at.

"There are laws against that type of behavior and there is a chain of command to follow including supervisor, union representative and human resources up to and including plant manager, " I continued.

"Well aren't you the fucking book of knowledge," Jerry sneered with sarcasm and condescendingly. It's on now.

"Do you forget I worked there for the last 2 summers?" I asked condescendingly with the same level of sarcasm as he gave me.

"Oh, now you are the big shot bread winner of the house," he scoffed.

"Really? At least I can say I never walked off the job. It's probably like the last one you had where you walked off and threw your hard hat and work boots in someone's lawn like a spoiled brat kid when things didn't go your way," I shot back glaring at him. He worked at another plant and walked off the job after a brief confrontation with another employee about job rotation. Needless to say they never took him back. You would think the dumb ass would learn from that experience and not repeat it.

"I had a spaghetti squash thrown at me and it hit me in the arm," he pouted.

"Oh yeah, where's the mark and where's the bruise?" I charged.

"Right here," he said rolling up his sleeve only to reveal his bare arm with absolutely no trace of impact. There wasn't even a pimple to blame it on.

"There's nothing there. It would leave a mark so it didn't hit you very hard or at all, did it?" I scoffed.

"We'll see. A bruise takes a couple of days to show up. Then you'll be eating those words Justin," he sneered.

"Good, we'll check in the morning and every day for the next couple of days and I will even put money on it there won't be a mark, will there? It'll be just like the day we'll meet your son. Never! He probably won't have anything to do with you and it's really hard to imagine why, isn't it?" I shot back dripping in malice and sarcasm.

"If you ever talk to me like that again, you little bastard...."

"Go ahead and hit me and I will make sure your night gets a lot worse when the cops come. I may have to tell them about your alleged weapons you hid too," I said with superiority as I interrupted him. I glared at him and smirked. Try it. Just try it. I have your number. He looked at me with the deer-in-the-headlights look and then walked towards the door.

"I'm going home," he announced and walked out the door. He got in his mothers' van and drove away. Jack recently lost his driver's license because of repeated speeding violations. There's another one who you think would get a clue after the second or third time. But then again, I guess not.

Home by the way was a one bedroom house, his mother owned and now shared with Jerry and her brother. So many questions are raised over that arrangement I can't even begin to tell you how buggered up that is.

"You really don't need to be so rough on him, maybe he's telling the truth," mom said to me calmly.

"You really don't believe that line of shit, do you? There's no mark on him anywhere and a spaghetti squash is huge. It's going to leave a mark."

"I know. He can't hold a job and makes a lot of false promises," mom stated.

"All the more reason not to believe a word he says. Everything he said has been completely made up. Things will be better. Yeah , right. They are worse. We've been through hell with that piece of trash and he can't deliver on anything. He has a pitiful excuse for everything. That's why we left his sorry ass in Palmer and he follows us wherever we go. He is a fat, lazy, lying piece waste of skin and we are better off without him. The only thing he's done for us is bleed us dry and mooch off of us like a parasite."

"I know but he won't go."

"I am doing everything I can to make him feel unappreciated and unwanted. It works. He's gone to home to mommy's couch or floor for the night. He can sleep on the roll away bed. Try it, it feels great to dish it right back at him. I love throwing it right back in his face," I scoffed.

"I can tell. You have every right to be angry but it isn't all his fault, " she replied.

"Most of it is. He is a liar and a waste of skin and you can do a hell of a lot better," I shot back. Mom stood there silent, she knew I was right.

"Ok, it's getting late. I am going to bed. Don't stay up too late. Goodnight," she said and we gave each other a kiss on the cheek and she was off to bed.

* * *

I went and visited Michelle that Saturday at her parent's house. We have the relationship where we share everything. All of life's steaming piles of excrement are discussed and mocked with their well deserved ridicule. We didn't see eye to eye on everything but we understood it. I proceeded to tell her about Jerry and the spaghetti squash incident when her mother started snorting and howling with laughter. I stopped talking and looked at her.

"Oh that's rich. Is that what he told you?' she asked in between snickers.

"Yes," I said as I started to snicker. This was going to get good. Michelle was covering her mouth trying hard not o burst out into a side-splitting laughing fit. I looked at her.

'Ha," was all she could muster in between the snickering and giggling she was doing. She had tears rolling down her face from trying to suppress it.

"Well let me tell you what really happened. I was on the same line. You don't seriously believe that line of shit that loser told you, do you?" she asked still trying hard not to join Michelle in a snickering and giggling tear streaming mess.

"You're going to love it, Justin," Michelle squeaked holding back her laughter.

"I was working down the line from him and we were scooping out the guts and seeds on the spaghetti squash like I am sure you remember from last season. You remember little Kim with the high pitched voice?" she asked me.

I nodded I did while I was taking a drink of my coke.

"Well he wasn't getting all the seeds out and Kim shouted across the line 'No! No! No! Jerry Dig it all out!' "You have to get all the seeds out not just a few!" She did this with a perfect high pitched voice with an Italian accent that sounded like Mickey Mouse on helium in Rome. I snorted the mouthful of cola out my nose all over my shirt, her armchair and the floor and burst out laughing as I could see Kim doing this. Michelle's mother had her arms flailing like Kim would and with the voice it was too much. I was laughing so hard I thought I was going to piss my pants "This happened like three times in a row in a couple of minutes and he finally picked up his squash and threw it down the waste auger at the bottom of the line with the spoon and walked off the line like a spoiled brat kid." She had her arms raised and imitated throwing the squash down the waste auger.

"There it is! The proverbial flying squash!" Michelle squeaked howling with laughter.

I looked at her and joined her howling with laughter. This is too much I thought, big bad ass. Big baby!

"She threw a squash at me and hit me in the arm!" "No! No! No! Jerry. You're a loser," I squeaked out like Mickey Mouse on helium in Rome. We were laughing so hard and couldn't stop. I never thought the truth could be so funny. I had to wait for the right opportunity to tell this one. I had it. We were having a dinner party next weekend. Oh yes!!! Jackpot!!

CHAPTER 10

•••••••••●•••••••

At the dinner party, he had his friends over and his family. Most of all, Brenda was there and this was going to be awesome. Epic! This will knock him down to size and humiliate him. It is so on dickhead. I let him talk smack while he drank beer and eat the hors d'oeuvres to his friends about how great he is and then he started the story about how he no longer worked at the vegetable plant. I let him finish and wallow in the supporting comments from his friends. Now it's Showtime.

"Wow Jerry, that story gets better every time you tell it. Who here wants to know what really happened?" I said loudly so everyone could hear me.

"Ok, go ahead you little know-it-all," Jerry scoffed trying to still look good in front of his friends as little as there was.

"Well you know Michelle's mother was working on the line with you right?" I asked.

"She was across the plant on another line, but please continue" he said in a snarky tone.

"She was on your line and I believe her." I reiterated right to him. "Anyway, they were doing spaghetti squash and he wasn't getting all the seeds out and Kim called you out" "No! No1 No! Jerry! Get all the seeds out!" I called out in the Italian Mickey Mouse on helium voice. "Oh and what did you do, threw your squash and spoon down the auger and walked off the line and out of the plant like 2 year old on a temper tantrum," I said smirking from ear to ear. The shocked look on everyone's face was priceless. You could have heard a pin drop.

"She's a liar!" he screamed.

"No she isn't! That's the way I heard it too! You're the liar!" Brenda shouted at him. He just stood there with the deer-in-the-headlights look again.

"Good work Justin, I was waiting for that." Brenda continued and smiled at me.

"What the hell is the matter with you?! I worked there for 27 years and you didn't think I would find out?! You are an embarrassment and a lazy son of a bitch! Do you have any idea what it's like to have an embarrassment like you around?! With all your big talk, you are nothing but a pathetic liar! The way you mistreat these kids and lie to everyone, you make me sick! Good for Justin. He call your ass out in front of everyone! It looks good on you! Let's see how your friends look at you now, you son of a bitch!" she scolded and looked to everyone around. They were speechless and frozen in shock. It was beautiful. All eyes on the fraud. Revenge is real fraud. t was beautiful. see how your friends look at you now, you son of a bitch!" she scolded and looked to ly sweet and best served cold. Ice cold. Know your enemy and their weaknesses. Most of all, have fun.

The room was speechless and then they started laughing. Jerry glared at me. How dare I tell the truth and how dare I call him out in front of everyone. Serves you right. All the yelling, swearing, baby talk, free loading, lies and the way you treated us over the past few years, you damn well deserve it. "Put the lights out!" " You will have one or the other." Enjoy your helping of karma because there is plenty more where that came from. I walked right over to him grinning from ear to ear.

"They're laughing with you," I said with my voice dripping in sarcasm. "No, they're laughing at you. You should know better to tell lies. The truth will comes out when you least expect it, doesn't it?" I hissed. I smiled at him the most evil smile I could and dared him to do something else with my eyes.

"You are an evil boy, Justin. Pure evil." he sneered.

"You catch on quick. Would you like to know what else is in store?" I hissed. He looked at me in disbelief. I smiled back at him at went back to sit beside his mother where I looked at him and smiled. He glared at me and then left the room.

* * *

I was still the odd man out at school. Church friends didn't want to hang with me since I didn't have money and I didn't want to be with the nerds or the geeks (I hate labels) since I didn't share that much interest with them. I just wanted to fit in with the kids that liked what I like but they were far and few in between.

* * *

That Friday night , I went to the church youth group activities and there was an new agenda. Etiquette courses. We were apparently a group of no class, white trash , Neanderthals. Deb apparently viewed us as members of the knuckle dragging club that communicated through a series of grunts and animalistic behavior. She wanted to get us on her playing level so she wouldn't be embarrassed being seen with us in public. She never said it but over the course of the next few weeks, it was obvious. I found it insulting and condescending on every level. Some of my friends were so insulted they weren't going to do the program. I had another idea.

This first week we had a special guest, one of Deb's friends that sold Mary Jane Cosmetics and we were going to learn how to wash our faces with the highly expensive line of Mary Jane products. Yes, Mary Jane Cosmetics and a sales pitch in church. In the largest study room, there was a partition that separated the room into two smaller rooms.

There were large banquet tables set up in a horseshoe formation so everyone could see her at her little table in the front. They set up the table for a makeover at every spot. Each seating had a small bar of soap, paper towels, a paper plate, a sample perfume vile, a plastic cup of water, make up remover pads and of course Mary Jane catalogues and brochures.

"Everyone please take as eat so we can begin," beamed Deb. She looked right at me and smiled. She was going to enjoy this. "Every other seat for boys and girls."

Bugger me, I thought to myself as I took a seat next to my friend Marilyn. I just finished talking her out of skipping the courses. I was going to have fun with them no matter what. This was my night out and I needed fun in my life.

"This is Mary Herman. I want you to pay attention to her and save your questions to the end," instructed Deb as she extender her towards Mary.

'Thank you Deb for having me." she said moving to the centre of the room to her little table full of her products. "First how many of you make a habit of washing your face every morning when you wake up and evening before bed?" A few hands went up. Mine included.

"Oh. I thought the number would be much higher. Then again, some of your complexions tell me otherwise." She said with a judgmental, condescending tone. I glared at her and she caught it.

"Perhaps I should clarify that statement," she said looking right at me. "How many of you are using bar soap to wash your face?" Less hands went up this time. She looked at me for a minute.

"Your hand went up the first time but not the second time. What are you sung to wash your face?" she asked me with a false sense of sincerity. It was a sales pitch, a well rehearsed sales pitch.

"Oxy face wash," I replied.

"How is it working for you? I would assume, not the greatest since you still have acne. My son uses something else and he doesn't have acne at all. I will show you and you will want to get rid of the Oxy."

"My problem goes beyond a facial wash, I am on medication too. I am assuming this magical bar is the solution to all of my problems, isn't it?" I asked with my voice dripping in sarcasm. I was offended.

She is not even a certified beautician or dermatologist and she knows better than the pharmacist and my doctor? She is a sales consultant and a commission based one at that. We all know the type, she has to sell the product to get paid. Clearly there isn't any level she won't stoop to do it including selling to teenagers in church. I was very sensitive about my acne problem and tried just about everything I could over the counter and even had several prescribed medications and creams to try and elevate the problem.

In three years time, I will be put on Accutane (isotretinoin) by a dermatologist to get rid of it. We will get to that later. This bitch is going to talk down to me like I am a complete idiot to pitch her product because she knows better than medical experts? And I am the next president.

"Well, we have a skeptic in our midst. I will prove it to you," she said with a smile looking directly at me. Her face was smiling but I know it meant shut the Hell up. You are costing me sales.

"Please continue," I said motioning my hand towards her smiling at her. Yes, please continue. Then get on with your sales pitch to teenagers in a church. You are pathetic in every way.

"Ok, let's begin. Please pick up your make up remover pad and wet it in the cup and now I want you wipe your face with it and remove any excess oil and dirt.." Everyone followed her instructions and put the dirty pad down on the paper plate.

"Now I want you to open your bar of facial cleaner out of the packet and wash your hands with it before you touch your face with it. When you have done that, I want you rinse your hands well and then lather it up in your hands again and wash your face. Make sure you get a good lather and cover your entire face. Don't rinse it off right away, I want you to let it sit for a minute and soak up all your oil and dirt. After a minute , wet your paper towel and wipe off the excess soapy lather then pat dry with the other towel."

"The soap is formulated for men and women as your chemistry is different by your gender. This is why you were asked to alternate when you sat down. Does everyone feel cleaner now?' Silence.

"That's good, I will be glad to answer any of your questions you may have about our facial cleansing system. There is a brochure and catalogue at every one your seats for you to look at your convenience. My name and number is on the back and I will be glad to help you should you need me," she said smiling at us like a used car salesperson.

"Now let's thank Mary for coming out and sharing that with us tonight and then we can all head to the gym and have some fun with Pastor Tim," said Deb smiling at us like she was an elementary school teacher in the primary level. We gave her a half hearted round of applause. I looked around the room to see the unimpressed look in everyone's eyes and the forced smiles.

I picked up my pile of useless crap and made sure it went straight into the waste bin on my way to the gym. Mary and Deb caught me doing it and shot me a dirty look as I tossed the refuse. I could see them in my peripheral vision, I turned and flashed them a malicious smile on my way through the to the gym.

When we got to the gym, it was set up for volleyball. The night isn't a total loss now. I liked volleyball. It wasn't worth going through the torment to get to it though. How condescending and demeaning.

"Hey Marilyn, I heard next week's lesson is how to wash your ass," I joked.

"Oh my God, you're bad. That's hilarious,' she squealed.

"What did you say?" shrieked Lynn, a mutual friend.

"Next week is how to wash your ass," I joked.

"Are you serious?! I won't be here for that! Oh my God, tell me you're joking!" shrieked Lynn.

"Relax. He's joking," reaffirmed Marilyn.

"At least I hope I am. We just learned how to wash our face. That was condescending enough and you can bet your ass the rest will be too. I promise to treat them with the right amount of respect they deserve. I can guarantee, the old 'No sex before marriage' thing will be on the list for sure. I wouldn't be surprised they discuss table manners as well and how to hold a fork," I scoffed.

"Justin, keep it down. Here comes Maria and her brothers," warned Marilyn.

"Hi Justin. Do you have a minute?" asked Maria.

"Sure"

"My mom saw you throw out the soap in front of Mary. That wasn't cool. Why did you do it?" asked Maria. I knew she wasn't impressed and was set up by her mother to ask me.

"Like I said down there, *this* isn't going to go away from a catalogue ordered bar soap." I said with malice motioning my hand over my acne laced face. "I am on a medicated face wash and was prescribed medication for it. For her to say to use that soap instead of the products I got from the pharmacy is reckless, irresponsible and condescending. She is NOT a doctor, a pharmacists, or even a beautician. She IS a commission based sales person that sells out of a catalogue. You might as well have had an Avon representative here too. I found the way she spoke to me about my problem highly insulting so I put that crap right where it belongs. In the trash! You can tell your mother I said it too! I am offended! It suggests I don't shower or wash my face like I am some filthy, little vagrant!" I charged. I was on the offensive. I glared at her with my eyes narrowed on hers. Mine were like razor blades savagely slicing her to shreds along with my sharp words.

I was pissed and if she didn't know it before, she knew it now. I was offended by the nature of the entire evening. Not only is it something you teach small children but the fact you have to demean us as a group. Who the hell do you think you are to even suggest not to follow medical advice? All for a sale you haven't got a hope in Hell in getting from a teenage boy let alone a group of teenagers as a whole.

"Oh. Ok. Thanks Justin," she said retreating. She was speechless and there was no way she was going to change my mind. She kept away from me for the rest of the evening. For some reason the subject of my behavior on the soap was never brought up again. I am sure it was discussed extensively behind my back.

* * *

Josh wanted to prove his love for his girl friend and carved her name into his arm with a knife. I thought it was dumb. If he was old enough he probably would have gotten it tattooed there instead and we all know how well that works. Cover ups are a bitch or else you have to keep dating girls by that name. He wore a bandana on his arm and peeled it back to reveal her name in written in scabs. "JAMIE"

"That's a guy's name too. So if you jump ship and go with the other team, you can have a boyfriend name Jamie too." I joked. Whack! Josh punched me right in the shoulder and it hurt.

"That's not even funny, Asshole," Josh said his eyes narrowing at me. Yes, he swore. The pastor's son swears. If only his dad knew along with the fact he had "Jamie" carved in his arm. I could picture it now. The fireworks.

"It was joke. You can't take it. Can you?" I said to him my eyes narrowing.

"I can take a joke. That wasn't funny. I'm not into dudes." he stated coldly. Homosexuality is a hot button subject among Christians especially the Baptist. Apparently you can't even joke about it.

"Wow, you are touchy. It was joke. You have 'Jamie' carved into your arm. I realize it is a girl's name but also a boy's name too."

"Yes, it is. This one is a girl. Now leave it alone," he warned.

"Got it. And don't ever hit me again."

"Don't joke about me being gay again."

"Got it," I said in agreement. We weren't very close after that. We only saw each other on the bus or in passing in the hall. He had his new friends and I wasn't invited to be around them except for if we were going to McDonalds for lunch once in a while.

* * *

It wasn't long before he broke up with Jamie and I he knew I thought she was very attractive. I knew it broke the friend rule of going out with an ex. I didn't think I had a shot and was quite timid about it. In fact, I was pretty sure I didn't have prayer. I had just gotten braces and the acne was bad. Centerfold material for Not A Hope In Hell magazine.

"You like Jamie, don't you?" asked Josh.

"Yes, but girls like that don't go out with guys like me. Look at my face. Look at my teeth," I said showing my teeth.

"If they like you, it doesn't matter. It isn't forever. Besides she said you were really nice when I went out with her," he said.

"Really?" I asked. I thought he was full of it.

"Yeah, really." he said.

"What do I say to her? What do I do?" I asked.

"Well, you don't have any classes together. Write her and ask her to lunch and give it to her before class. I will give you her schedule. If it's too soon, be her friend and then take it from there." Josh suggested.

I am going to make a long story short. I was lied to, she wasn't interested. After several notes back and forth she agreed to go to lunch with me where I ended waiting at the restaurant like an idiot the entire lunch period when she didn't even show up. I felt stupid, betrayed and like a full blown blithering idiot. I was pissed at her and Josh.

Josh should never have suggested it or encouraged me to do so. It think he did it for a laugh at my expense. As for Jamie, here's my advice to girls like you: If you aren't interested, come out and say so. Save the other person the embarrassment.

Being honest is a tough pill to make someone swallow but do it with tact and dignity. An example," I am really flattered but I am not interested in you. I am not the right person for you but you'll find someone that is."

To lead someone on not to hurt their feelings or to stand them up makes you a twat. Be honest. it is never okay to toy with someone's feeling or emotions. In these cases, always tell the truth. Needless to say I didn't trust Josh much after that.

CHAPTER 11

Anthony was back in my life again shortly after since he was still working at the grocery store. He met someone new. He had a girlfriend now. They met at the grocery store when he was stocking shelves. Her name was Tina. She was tall, slim build with curly brown hair and glasses. I thought she was nice and deep down I thought she deserved better. It wasn't a very nice thought. However, some things take time to get over them if you ever can at all. With family it's even harder but sometimes people need to be cut out of your life. Look at dear old dad. I don't miss the yelling, swearing, drinking and belittling comments.

It wasn't long before they got their own little one bedroom apartment in Palmer. It was a nice little place considering the size but who am I to judge after the dump we lived in? It had one bedroom, a kitchen and a living room. The bathroom had an old fashioned partition that folded up like an accordion and retracted into the wall. Not much privacy when you can hear what the other person is doing in there. When you hear someone taking a piss you might as well be in the same room as them watching.

He was being civil to us again and all apologies over killing mom's cat. We agreed to see him again and since he was dating Tina, maybe he changed. With family, it's very hard to write them off totally. We keep trying to make it work, blood is thicker than water.

We met up with him for coffee and started to like Tina. Maybe she was what he needed. She worked at the coffee shop so he spent a lot of time there. We all did. She encouraged us to talk and get things patched up. Family was important to her as she was close with hers. I started to hang out with them on my own after school. I wanted to make it work and if he was willing to do that, we could try again. Jerry, of course was against the whole idea.

"I just don't believe you people," he sneered at mom and I.

"What?" mom asked with contempt in her voice.

"You people make me sick. Anthony can attack Justin, kill your cat, steal from you and you keep taking him back. I don't get it," said Jerry with disgust.

"We got rid of you and you keep coming around, don't you? You aren't family, he is. Would you like me talk about what you've done? You're still coming here in this house," responded mom.

"What did I do?" whined Jerry.

"Let's see here,. You lied about making a better life when all you did is sponge off of us. You can't hold a job to save your soul. You are over 40 years old and live at home with your mother in a one bedroom house with her brother. You are an abusive, controlling twat. You eat like a pig and you're getting fat. You don't even have a car of your own and live off of everyone else. You don't have the right to say anything to anyone," sneered mom. She knows how to hit them and make it count.

"That was low," sneered jerry.

"And true. All of it," smirked mom.

"When he slips up and hurts you again, don't come crying to me," said Jerry with a holier than thou tone in his voice.

"I don't think that will be an issue. I never crawled back to you, you came looking for us because you can't accept the fact it's over. You will never live with us again. You are a visitor and that is how you will remain. In fact, it's rude to come over unannounced. I want you to call first from now on. Is that clear?" replied mom.

"What the hell brought this on?" whined Jerry.

"You are always here. How am I supposed to do anything when you are always here? You need a job, then maybe that will occupy your time enough where you don't have to concern yourself with my business all the time," suggested mom.

"If you want me out, then just say so," shot back Jerry.

"Fine, it's time you left for the day," replied mom.

"If that's how you want it...." started Jerry.

"Don't even start. I don't have time for your bullshit," shot back mom.

"Fine. Goodbye," said Jerry pouting as he went out the door with his hand waving to his back at us.

"What a baby," said mom as she looked at the door with disgust.

"He'll never get it, will he? We hate him but he still thinks he's in the right," I said shaking my head.

* * *

Anthony and Tina were going to have baby and moved into the front apartment. I was working at the restaurant and got a call late at night when I was working on the float for the town's summer festival parade. I was an uncle at 16. Cool.

Little did I realize it would be short lived. So I will make this brief. I saw my niece up until she was 2 years old and it was far and few and in between. I think I saw her first birthday and that was it. I remember Anthony getting abusive to her and punching Tina in the face while she carried the baby outside. The relationship was rocky from the start and it wasn't long before they moved out but not before he sprayed the house for spiders outside and my cat too. The cat died the next day from direct contact to insecticide. I should have seen that coming.

I never saw my niece again until later on in life when she was 16. They had another girl that I never met.. Their names will not be mentioned as I was never a part of their lives in any way. They are strangers to me and will remain that way. They have been poisoned against the Williamson family in its entirety and I really don't want to know what they have been told over the years. Before Tina left after ending the relationship with Anthony, the following conversation took place.

"I left your brother and you and your mom will never see your niece again," reported Tina like she was reporting the weather.

"Ok, I get why you left him but how come we can't see her?" I asked.

"It's because your mom's a bitch. It's her fault Anthony is the way he is. He told me everything," she said in a matter of a fact tone.

"You can partially blame our dad. He was a drunk and abusive too. Like father like son. If you want to take her out of our lives, go ahead. You had the intention of doing so anyway. You will not stand there and blame mom for his actions and mistakes. He is old enough to know better. Besides I have heard enough about your mother to say that is what makes you the shit disturbing, manipulative, control freak bitch you are but I also know we make our own decisions," I responded in the same reporting the weather tone.

"Are you saying I deserved everything I got?" she asked in shock.

"No. Nobody does. However you knew him long enough not to push the buttons but you did and I have seen you smirk when he got angry and threw things. You enjoyed it. You are a shit disturber. If you think I am going to beg your highness for visitations, you have another thought coming because that's what you want otherwise we wouldn't be having this conversation," I told her flat out. I was calling her on her crap and got a dirty look to confirm it.

"You're just like your mother," she shot back with the dirty look still on her face.

"You're a shit disturber. No one will see the kid except your family. That's what you want. Then that is what you will have. Goodbye Tina. Have a nice life." I flatly said as I turned and went into the house.

I told mom about our conversation and she wasn't the slightest bit surprised and had the same attitude I had. We did see her and the two kids at a coffee shop with Anthony on a few separate occasions. We pretended we were strangers and let the bitch have it her way. We already knew we were poisoned to the kids. They were perfect and we were scum. By the way Tina I know about the contest you had with your 15 year old cousin to see who could get pregnant first. You were 20 years old. Enjoy the delusion of being perfect.

I saw her again years later and the kids were grown. The oldest being 16 and the other 14. Tina tried to be civil and I did the same. She offered to let me see them again. I took her information and thought about it. I decided we will remain strangers as there is far too much damage done over the years and after being introduced as "A Williamson." I took offence to it and it was a major part of the decision process. The other was the fact I was a stranger and after all these years I wasn't introduced in the proper way as their uncle. They had no clue and it will remain that way.

For closure, Tina works in fast food. She is not even a crew trainer. She is a cashier/ order taker. She did get Anthony back in style by showing up where he was working with the new van her new husband bought her to show him the ring as well. I may not like her but he had that coming. As for what I do now, you will have to wait. No peeking to the end to find out. Like any good story, the best is yet to come.

* * *

I went over to Josh's place a few times and another friend joined us. His name was Wade. He was a couple of years older. With Josh's parents away or the night at a church function, we decided to spend the night in at Josh's place watching a movie. We went to the locally owned convenience store and a guy from our high school, Jim was working in the store. It was his parent's store and they weren't around.

After mulling over who saw what in the movies, we couldn't agree on anything.

"Why not a porno?" Josh asked jokingly.

"Why not?" I added.

"Ok Let's get one. Sorry Justin, no gay ones," joked Wade.

"Piss off! Are you sure you want to get one of these? I wouldn't want you to get penis envy when you see the guys in these films. You are going to realize that 3 inches just doesn't cut it" I shot back.

"There's going to be no jerking off. I wouldn't want Justin to think it's a dick buffet although it would be all you can eat and then some," fired back Wade.

"You don't have to worry, Wade. I already flossed. I wouldn't want that little thing to get stuck between my teeth. Here does this make you jealous?" I fired back while holding up my pinky finger in a baby talk tone.

"At least girls will go out with me. How did that work out you and Jamie? Oh, I know what happened, you were shocked she was a girl!" shot back Wade. That went too far. This means war!

"You're a fucking cock! A cock sucker! Fuck off and die!!" I shouted at Wade. "And you, Josh. You set me up for that and lied to me knowing I'd be made a fool of. That was an asshole of a thing to do. I hope one day you get the same and then we'll see how funny it is." I said to him with my finger in his face my voice dripping in malice. I was so pissed off I was shaking. Way to rub salt on the wound asshat.

"I didn't know it would go down like that," insisted Josh.

"Don't lie to me! You knew damn well I didn't have a shot with her but you kept pushing me, didn't you?! I hope you're happy with the results," I said coldly glaring at him.

"Ok, I'm sorry," said Josh surrendering.

"Thank you. That's what I wanted to hear. Now lets' get the video to your place and get the pizza," I said brushing the Jamie incident aside.

We got the video sleeve to the check out and Jim looked at it and then looked at us and chuckled. He took the sleeve and looked at all three of us for a minute and then back to the sleeve of the porno flick.

"You have to be 18 to rent this you know," said Jim chuckling.

"Come on Jim," pleaded Wade.

"ID please," insisted Jim smirking.

"Are you kidding me?" asked Wade.

"Yes, I am. I see your parents are out for the night," snickered Jim.

"You're not going to tell them, are you?" asked Josh with concern. He should be concerned. His dad is a pastor at the Baptist church. I could almost hear him freaking out now.

"No. I don't care what you do. This is funny to me, to see the Pastor's son renting a porno. Should I put your dad's name on the rental slip, Josh?" joked Jim. Josh was horrified. It was hilarious. Wade and I were howling with laughter.

"What do we put it under?" asked Jim.

"Mike Hunt. And we'll use the other half of the duplex I live in as the address. It's vacant," I suggested. I saw Porky's again the other night. Mike Hunt was fitting to this situation.

"Ok Mike, sign here, Just make sure you drop it in the night box" snickered Jim. I happily obliged and signed it M. Hunt.

"I will. Thanks Jim," I replied. Josh and Wade were both looking at me.

"What? You don't think I know how to have a good time?" I asked them as we left the store porno in hand.

"I'm shocked," said Josh still trying to absorb what just happened.

"Then maybe we should hang out more often and see what else I can get, " I suggested.

"I'm scared to ask but curious at the same time," replied Josh.

"You'll have to wait and see," I said with a smile.

Luckily the pizza parlor was just around the corner and our pizza was ready. Josh, of course had to try and flirt with the girls behind the counter. They were sisters and both attractive with their long flowing black hair and almost perfect complexions. I kicked him in the side of the shin. It was time to go. We were on a time limit and even though it would have been funny as hell and type of stuff you bring up many years later, we didn't want his parents coming home to find us watching the movie at his house.

We got our pizza and split the bill three ways and were on our way to Josh's house. He only lived 2 blocks away. We of course did a double checked of the house before taking the movie down stairs to watch on the big screen TV. Pastor McKay and his wife were out. Josh was a good boy and could have friends over pretty much as long they went to church. Tonight isn't church service however we were going to watch people service each other.

We got some plates for the pizza, grabbed some soda since there wasn't any devil juice in the house but the show must go on. Tonight's feature was about 3 aspiring young ladies who wanted a shot at fame and fortune and a talent scout was only able to choose one. Let the show begin. The opening scene was just starting and the clothes were off.

"Hey Justin, no beating off. I don't need to see your little dick," said Wade while he stared at the screen.

"Really Wade? We're going to go down t this road again? Why don't you get yours out then we can all have a laugh especially when your premature ejaculation kicks in. I'll bet it isn't out of your pants for more than 5 seconds if you can even get it before it goes off." I joked.

"Justin are you looking at the dicks or the pussies?" asked Wade.

"Both, and so are you, bitch. It's a sex scene. Don't hand me that crap you aren't looking at his dick because you are. If you didn't want to see dick you would've pushed for lesbian porn and you didn't did you? You want to see big, hard, juicy cocks, don't you?" I responded. I grabbed my crotch over my jeans and give it a shake when he was looking at me. Wade shot me a dirty look. I was right. Just like any other homophobic prick out there. If you didn't want to see dick, you would watch lesbians. The fact is heterosexual porn has dicks. They are big and hard and usually above average in size as well as girth. People watch it, fantasize and pleasure themselves to it. I am comfortable with myself and I can admit it, can you?

"I don't go your way Justin. You never had a girlfriend so maybe you try a boyfriend," brushed off Wade.

"Well your girlfriends don't stay with you a month. Maybe you need a boyfriend yourself. Hanging with your buddy. You can share everything together," I shot back. This only earned me another punch in the shoulder and a few minutes of awkward silence. Josh was smart, he wasn't saying a damn thing.

"Why are you so quiet?" I asked Josh. He was in awe staring at the screen.

"I'm jealous of the size of this guy's cock," he responded still staring at the screen.

"Well it is a big screen and it's a close up. It's taking up the whole screen. Wow, I guess it is true the camera adds 10 pounds." I said laughing my ass off.

"Wow Justin, can you go a whole sentence without swearing?" asked Wade in a condescending tone.

"Why yes I can, Wade. I can go for great lengths of time without swearing. I do have a part time job and I can go an entire 8 hour shift without using any bad language altogether. I am sure this amazes you. In fact, I can even go through all of my classes without even using a single profanity of any kind. Before you pass judgment over my potty mouth I would like to see you go an entire day without being a snotty, judgmental, holier than thou ass-hat. Now there's a challenge. I swear at you because you look down on me and treat me like a second class citizen. You don't deserve my respect," I replied in the same fake upper class act he was pulling. I even made sure it had just the right amount of sarcasm for this pompous ass.

"I treat you like a no class citizen because you swear too much," Wade responded in a cocky tone.

" You treat me like crap because you are like everyone else. My parents got divorced and now we are scraping by and have had to use assistance. I live in a duplex and my mom doesn't make the money your parents do so it gives you a superiority complex like everyone else. You think you are better than me because your parents have good jobs and make more money. Here's the reality check, when we are older you may not be as fortunate. Then we'll see how high and mighty you are, won't we?" I was getting pissed. It was the same reason Jamie wouldn't have anything to do with me. I was an embarrassment to be around. Mom couldn't afford to give me the nice clothes and things they took for granted. The judgmental looks of disapproval were plentiful. I was poor white trash to them. I was a joke. Great friends.

"It doesn't matter. I am sure I will be doing better than you," said Wade in his pompous ass tone. The look of disapproval and judgment confirmed exactly what I said. Wade is a twat!

"That's enough. I am friends with both of you and if you can't get along, we can't hang out. Not together anyway," scolded Josh.

"I ain't the one with the problem. It's him. Every time he opens his mouth, it's an insult in my direction and it's pissing me off," I sneered and glared at Wade. I absolutely hate him. I will not be silent while I am being disrespected by a condescending prick like him who never worked a day in his life and has everything handed to him. Then he thinks he can look down on others. I will treat him with the same disrespect and then some. What an prick! 'Do unto others', twat.

"That's your opinion," said wade giving me a sideways glance. He clearly can't be bothered engaging. Contemptuous, pompous ass son-of-a-bitch.

"Anyway..." I glared at Wade. "Wouldn't it be funny if your parents came home right now?" I asked Josh trying to kill the tension in the room.

"Oh my God! They'd kick you both out and then kill me! I'd never be able to see either of you again," Josh exclaimed in horror.

"Well if they do, I say we get our dicks out and go for it. Watch the fireworks," I joked.

"They would have me committed! I'd be disowned! Having my dick out with two other guys! Oh my God!"Josh was freaking out. It was entertaining but I could totally understand the fear. They were hardcore. I'd be scared too.

"I'd jerk off and finish in front of them. What would they say don't cum here again? Thanks for cumming by, now get out!" I joked trying to lighten the mood. "Oh wait, we're in an etiquette program so as long as your pinky fingers are up, whatever you are doing is in good taste. So, when you're beating off... Pinkies up!" I was on a roll. Even Wade was laughing. I was surprised, but I'll take it as a compliment.

Luckily we finished the movie and the pizza before they came home. We even left before that happened. I made sure I had the movie in the plastic bag from the convenience store. I lived five blocks away from the store. Wade and I left at the same time and walked together in silence. Once we got to the main street, Wade couldn't wait to ditch me. At least he said "Goodnight Justin, see you later," We all know how much he meant that but etiquette is about lying. Pretending to care when you don't and saying things you don't mean. I replied with a simple "goodnight" I am not a fraud. I dropped it in the night drop box even though Jim was still working. He looked over when he heard it fall in to the bin. He smiled and waved. I always keep my word.

CHAPTER 12

······●●●●●●●······

I learned my friends Kara, Rachel and Marisa were having an issue with someone we grew up with. Jane, it seems had been a bit promiscuous and become quite annoying. She was bragging about her new boyfriend and having multiple orgasms with him every weekend. She apparently even tried to give her neighbor's (Kara) boyfriend a hand job one night at one of their latest parties too. Rural communities don't have much to do so high school kids drink underage, smoke pot and have sex with whoever they can. With only a cop or two in town, it's virtually undetected.

They wanted to get her and have some fun doing it. They were really going to prank her ass good. It started out harmless enough with a cucumber covered in a condom and an envelope with newspaper letters saying "Keep it fresh." Inside the envelope was a note made out of newspaper letters.

A cucumber is good to eat
It makes a healthy treat
When it's lust you seek
It stays hard for a week

Jane was freaked out. She found it mildly amusing and offensive all at the same time. The fact that she was violated by someone entering her locker without her knowledge was a bit much for her to handle. Little did she realize, it was her best friend and neighbor Kara that gave me the cucumber and the locker combination as well as the location of it. I provided the condom, a free treat from Health class. It was very funny. I provided the poetry, a talent I was sure to develop.

I wasn't sexually active at this point and really didn't have a need for it. Ok, I am a liar. I wanted to but I didn't get a second look from anyone. The closest thing I came to a sexual relationship was the Rainbow Party invitation from last year and we know how well that worked out. Plain Jane was getting action and I was bit jealous. In fact a lot of my friends claimed they were getting action, even the devout Christians. My life sucked. I would welcome an advance from anyone at this point.

* * *

I went back to youth group night at the church again. I liked hanging out with Josh even though I was a bad influence as his father pointed out. I wore gothic and horrific shirts with skulls and rock shirts like every other teenager. To them, I was Satan.

It was time for another etiquette course. This one was on table manners. We all sat around a banquette table with an informal setting missing the teaspoon and of course no wine glass. Drinking wine is wrong. Deb actually tried to convince us that the Biblical term for "wine" was grape juice. Jesus turned the water to grape juice at wedding. Really?! Not a wedding I would like to attend. Let's toast the bride and groom with 7Up. Please.

"Tonight is about table manners," Deb began. "Can anyone tell me some bad examples of table manners? " she asked only to get silence.

"Ok. Justin, you work in a restaurant. Please give us examples."

"Alright. First of all manners don't seem to apply in restaurants. There are lots who use them but not everyone. You will get someone snapping their fingers at you like you are a mutt or a servant. They talk with their mouthful, whistle, grunt, slop food on the floor, pick their noses, wipe their mouths with their hands and I am told there is a high percentage that don't wash their hands when they use the restroom. We have a buffet and there you are going to see the worst behaviors ever. You might as well fill a trough with pig slop and let the hogs at it. There are only a few but they stand out and they are the ones you remember. "

"Justin!" said Deb raising her voice. I apparently gave too much information. Oops.

"I'm sorry, was that too much?"I asked trying to be sincere.

"The trough comment was too much," she replied.

"You're right. Hogs have more class," I said in a matter of a fact tone.

"Justin, you made your point. Exactly what I wanted and then some. Obviously you are to wash your hands when using the restroom. Don't talk with your mouthful, pick your nose, grunt, whistle, or slop food on the floor. What else?"

"Let your kids run amuck, yell and swear at the staff..." I started to add.

"Keep your hands on the table?" suggested Deb with a hint of condescension in her voice. She sat down at the head of the table and moved her hands from the wrist resting on the edge of the table. "Always," she said with authority. She then moved her hands up until the mid part of her forearms were resting on the edge of the table. "Sometimes," and then put her elbows on the table. "Never" she said again emphasizing the never.

"May I ask where we are going when all this is done? I mean obviously there is a point to all of this," I pried.

"Yes there is. We are having a night out that you will never forget around graduation. We are calling it Summer Celebration. But first we are doing these etiquette courses. I want you to look high class," replied Deb again with a hint of condescension and a trace of judgment in her voice. This time it was masked with a smile.

"Salt and Pepper are a pair and go around the table together," said Deb in her authoritarian tone while holding them up together in her cupped right hand.

"What if you only want the salt?" asked Josh.

"They always go in a pair. Never separate," repeated Deb.

"Your napkin is to be folded corner to corner and placed in your lap with the widest part towards your waist," she continued and held up her napkin folding it corner to corner.

"Why is that?" asked Wade. He was obviously determined to drag this out as long as he could. What a douche bag.

"It covers most of your lap in case you drop something, it lands on the napkin and not on your pants or dress. Let's face it, you don't want that," replied Deb.

"So to wipe your face..." Josh started to ask.

"You take the right of left side in the corner and do a quick wipe and then return it your lap," interrupted Deb. Apparently that is completely acceptable. I thought interrupting someone was rude but I guess if you are the guru of manners, you are an exception to the rule.

"Where is it customary to belch at the end of the meal to compliment the chef? I am asking in case we are eating in that type of ethnic restaurant." I asked only to get a look of disdain from Deb and a few chuckles around the room.

"If you do that, I will leave you there. I believe it is the Middle East where that happens, however, I am more apt to believe that is an urban myth. Burping loudly is rude and disgusting. I fail to see how that can be a compliment to anyone," replied Deb with her eyes narrowing in on me. She obviously wasn't impressed. Wade can ask a stupid question, so can I but at least mine gets a bit of a laugh rather than people rolling their eyes.

"I have no intention. I am making light of the situation because everyone in here has laughed at burp, fart, sex, and bodily function jokes. As far as I am concerned etiquette is an act. Trying to make people believe you are something you aren't. I see it all the time at the restaurant. We get people who come in dressed like they won the lottery only to order the cheapest meal we have, be rude to the server and not tip. You would be lucky if they ordered anything to drink," I stated.

"You're right, it is an act. To act properly in public and not to embarrass yourselves," reaffirmed Deb. Personally I think it was so we wouldn't embarrass her.

"Okay, fine. Even as rude as people get, I have never seen someone burp in someone's face or fart and say 'here's one for you' or something like that. Most people have more class than that. They don't cough in your face, pick their nose and wipe it on your sleeve or dig in their ears or blow their nose when they are at the table. I have never seen a food fight either. There are boundaries. I highly doubt anyone is that much of a pig in here either. Everyone in here has eaten in a restaurant that wasn't fast food. Nobody cares if you use your dinner fork for your salad. The only concern is you don't use your hands. Nobody cares if you use a tea spoon for your soup, they only care you don't drink from the bowl. In fact, I highly doubt we are going fine dining. I will say a family restaurant or a buffet. As long as we say 'please' and 'thank you' and do the obvious like use the serving spoon provided in the buffet we will be fine. Mom may not make a lot of money but she didn't raise pigs. I find this lesson highly insulting and patronizing. I wasn't raised in a barn or a cave and neither was anyone else in here," I ranted only to have everyone looking at me and slightly nodding their heads in agreement. Of course nobody spoke up. I was being stared at in total disbelief and shock by Deb. Her eyes narrowed more with every word I spoke. I could have swore I saw a vein bulge in the side of her temple. I didn't give a rat's ass.

"Thank you, Justin. We are going to a buffet. We are on a budget. However, please try to control your rants and ramblings. What you said has merit but I think it was best saved for afterwards on a one on one basis. It is rude to speak out of turn like that especially when I am trying to instruct the group," She scolded. I was rolling my eyes. Yes, that is how I handle stupidity and those who annoy me. Who the Hell died and put you in charge of the town's kids and deputized you the goddamn manner police?

"And don't roll your eyes at me," she snapped. I instantly did it again."There, you are doing it again!" I couldn't help myself. I was annoyed and bored with her tactics. It is an automatic reaction. It's more involuntary. We all do it or something similar it fits the situation. Here, let me do it again. I rolled them again. Deb glared at me and continued her manner patrol instructor mode. I tuned the rest out.

* * *

It wasn't too much time after they moved in where I was approached by Kara to do another prank on Jane. It had more to do with her alleged whoring around. Everyone heard Andrew Dice Clay's version but I figured we could step it up a bit. None would be possible without the girls input. They all had their hands in it. Whether through ideas or any drawing that were attached to the package.

Hickory Dickory Dock

Your mouth around a cock

A stroke and a slurp

You made it spurt

And swallowed every last drop

We all decided to walk by Jane's locker the next day. She arrived right on time and found the envelope and ripped it open right as we conveniently were walking by. Michelle, Marissa, Kara, Betty and myself all appeared shocked when she started shouting and pouting.

"What the hell?! Why does everyone think I'm a slut?! Who's writing this stuff and putting it in my locker?!" pouted Jane.

"What's wrong Jane?" asked Marissa in her best acting voice trying to show concern. She was good. She almost had me fooled. The rest of us moved in towards Jane and pretended we cared. We had Academy Award worthy performances of concern and sincerity. She showed us the poem. We laughed. It was good quality smut and deserved a laugh.

"It's not funny!" she pleaded.

"It is funny. But not that you got it in your locker. It shows some talent that's for sure. It's funnier than Andrew Dice Clay's version," I interjected. Of course it was, I wrote it. I deserved some credit. It's hilarious.

"It is funny, but not against you," agreed Kara. Good, give me more credit. It was your idea but my creativity I thought to myself. I tried not to smile. Kara was covering for herself more than anything but as long as it deflects the blame off of me, I am good with it.

"How many people know about your escapade at the party?" asked Rachel with fake concern and a hint of judgment.

"I don't know," whined Jane.

"You're starting to get a reputation. I would keep my mouth shut when it comes to whoring around," suggested Marissa with tones of judgment. Marissa was a large girl with shoulder length blonde hair. Her face looked like a bag of smashed assholes and had a fat ass too. She was clearly jealous since nobody would want to have sex with her. I couldn't talk much either. I was short, scrawny and covered in pimples. I was jealous too. I admit it. Jane wasn't much to look at but she was getting laid. She was cheap and easy but getting laid none the less. God, our lives sucked. Everyone of us was flawed and wouldn't get a second look. The girls were fat and I was scrawny. Jane was getting sex. Jane?!

"Don't judge, Marissa! You're just jealous nobody wants you! You probably wrote the notes and put them in my locker! You're a pathetic bitch!" shouted Jane. Marissa was fuming. She was showing restrain and wanted to plow her in the face. 'Don't you dare give it away, Marissa' I thought. We all looked at each other thinking the same thing.

"Why would I be jealous of a slut like you? Enjoy your reputation. Your parents must be proud. Don't blame me for your problems. Try keeping your legs shut!" fired back Marissa as she turned and walked away. She held up her right hand over her shoulder with her middle finger extended as she walked away down the hallway and kept it there as she turned the corner.

"Nice going Jane," chimed in Kara and Rachel.

"Shut up. I'll apologize to her later. Or maybe I won't," deflected Jane.

"You should. She didn't deserve that," I suggested. She did deserve it and so much more. We all did. At that point it didn't matter. I was being accepted. If having friends meant picking on Jane, sorry Jane. I didn't want to go back to being a nobody.

Being popular seems to come from being rude and crass to others in a lot of cases. I knew it was wrong but this is funny. It gave me a creative outlet. Nice guys finish last but the nasty ones seem to finish first. If being an asshole is where it's at, I am going to be on the honor roll. Straight A's for me.

CHAPTER 13

· · · · · · · · ● ● ● ● ● · · · · · ·

It's time for another etiquette course. We waited with great anticipation as to what sort of bad behavior we exhibit that must be changed without hesitation. What as it this week? The anticipation was so thick you could cut it with a knife. We were so eager to learn the error of our ways and waited with baited breath. Yeah, I know I am I am being sarcastic. What better way to handle it than with the perfect amount of sarcasm? The things we do in a small town for entertainment. Ugh.

Deb and Josh's mom were standing at the front of the room while we sat in our chairs waiting for the rant of the week. People who look at others and criticize truly are never happy. I guess when you are the object of your own affection nobody ever will measure up to your stature. It apparently gives you the right to condescend to and demand others who you feel are less perfect than yourself.

"Tonight we are going to talk about phone etiquette," Josh's mom began. "I can't tell you how many times I have answered the phone only to get a 'Hello, is Josh there?' This is extremely rude. I am not a secretary. The proper thing to do is strike a conversation with the person who answers," she continued. This was of course directed at me. I rolled my eyes.

"What are we to talk about?" I asked. I couldn't resist. It isn't common to strike up a casual conversation with the receptionist at the dentist when you call. You book your appointment, thank him/ her and hang up.

"Well for one thing a 'How are you?' or 'It's a nice day outside today, isn't it?' A casual conversation so you don't make the person answering it feel like a secretary," she rambled.

"Oh, I get it. We're supposed to lie and be fake. Telephone etiquette is about lying and pretending to care. It's about striking up casual conversation with someone you normally wouldn't do that with because they were the first one to answer the telephone. Let's face it, our conversations have been 'Hello', 'Goodbye', and 'When will Josh be back?' We have never said much more than that face to face." I continued only to get a cold stare of contempt. If looks could kill, I'd be dead. There was a dead silence while our eyes met.

"Yes, of course. That is what etiquette is," chirped Deb. "You are showing you were raised properly and treat people with respect. It is the proper thing to do. You want respect, don't you? We all do. We get it by giving it. The favor is normally returned. It makes the world a better place." She was looking right at me. Behind that smile was a scolding and those eyes were saying plenty as well. How dare I question them and their teachings.

We spent the next half an hour improvising casual conversation. Mulling over the weather, and mindless conversations of "How are you?" Had they done their 'Research' properly, asking someone "How are You?" is one of the worst things you can ask in the business world or any world for that matter.

It leaves the conversation open to hearing about any and every personal problem with friends, family or relatives. You just opened the flood doors and there's no closing them now. They will ramble and pour out their emotions and dump all of their problems on you. You asked, right? Now you are being told. You may even get lucky enough to hear about personal body problems from bladder incontinence to constipation and even feelings of sexual inadequacies.

I made that mistake a few times at the restaurant and you can't shut them up or get rid of them. If you think walking away will help, you are sadly mistaken. They will follow you spewing their nonstop flood of raw emotions nobody they know wants to listen to. You are a perfect stranger and you asked and now you are going to know everything whether you want to or not. You are Dr. Phil. Congratulations and enjoy it. You asked. Suck it up, buttercup.

I have heard about drinking problems, ungrateful bastard children, hot flashes, lazy, useless husbands, bladder leakage, the inability to have a decent shit, infidelity, financial problems, PMS, irritated nipples, the need for sex and not getting any and the list goes on and on. Nothing is taboo. I asked.

We all ask and sometimes you get the proper etiquette based answers which are "fine", "splendid", "excellent", "good", "great" or any other word combinations of similar meaning. I have gotten the short version on the negative aspect as well. "Piss off!", "Like you give a rat's ass", "Fine (dripping in malice and sarcasm)", "Leave me alone (usually spat with venom)" To be honest I would prefer those than to have to role play Dr. Phil.

This one was the biggest waste of time and the most off based yet. Unfortunately there wasn't much else to do. It was winter and Josh got grounded for a month because he didn't make it home in time for his curfew during a really bad snow storm. He was staying at another friend's place and they own a farm. The snow storm came fast and dumped a lot of snow in a short period of time. His parents and siblings were away with the other vehicles and he was driven home in a tractor. He called ahead of time and explained the predicament. It didn't matter. Fifteen minutes will cost you a month.

Any other parent would have appreciated the fact that you called and made every reasonable attempt to get home on time. There was even inclement weather to contend with. Inclement weather gives a slight allowance to be tardy. Most employers will allow it in a snow storm. Not the McKay house. There are no excuses and no exceptions to the rules.

* * *

It was time for another bastardized rendition of Mother Goose. This one needed to be special as well. I drafted one and submitted it to Kara for approval.

Mary, Mary Quite contrary
How your crotch itches so
Not keeping tabs and got the crabs
You really need to say No

Kara was laughing out loud. Marissa, Rachel, Betty agreed it was my best yet. Clearly I was developing my talents. Fuck Andrew Dice Clay. His are juvenile by comparison.

I delivered it during lunch with my usual fast technique of slipping through the gap between the door and the frame. The envelope contained my poem and some information from the pharmacy on crabs in a nice little pamphlet. I thought it should be most helpful. After all, education is the key.

We had the timing down to an art as to when we should walk by Jane at her locker. This time we waited until lunch time. She would always wait to hand in the merchandise. there was a bit of an heir of drama to it. I was beginning to think she liked the attention. Jane almost went into convulsions when she was showing us this one. Kara was her friend and neighbor. There was incoherent gibberish coming from her, she could hardly speak. There must have been a breech in confidentiality. Don't you hate it when that happens?

"What the Hell is this?" she squeaked. "Who the hell keeps thinking I'm a slut? I don't have crabs!!"

"What?" I asked as innocently as I could while trying to show as much concern as I could.

"Here! You read it!" she squawked handing me the letter. I was almost in stitches on the inside. The pamphlet on crabs was an especially nice touch. I was fighting to contain my laughter. I handed it to Marissa and the others. Michelle was snickering and had to move away and turn her head.

"Stop scratching then," offered Marissa as she burst into laughter. "Then no one will think you have it," she howled. She totally blew it. She was in stitches. It was contagious. Within seconds we were all laughing. Everyone except Jane. She was livid.

"You're assholes! You're all assholes!" she shrieked.

"It's fucking hilarious!" I howled. The others nodded in agreement while laughing out loud. This seemed to settle Jane down a bit.

"I suppose it is funny if it weren't directed at me," she shyly admitted. "Marissa, you're a bitch!"

"Yup and damn proud of it," Marissa said folding her arms and looking directly at Jane with a smirk over her face.

* * *

When I got home from school, Jerry was there waiting for me. He was standing proud. It made me sick. His very presence nauseated me. I blame him for the Hell hole we lived in. He helped mom waste the money when we could have had something else to buy and move into. This dumb ass wasn't going to let that happen. It's trash like this that make me pro choice.

"Hi Jerry," I said to be polite while trying to mask my contempt for him.

"Hi Justin," he said smiling back at me. I could tell he was thinking 'you little bastard'. "Pick out something nice to wear tonight. I am taking everyone out for dinner," he said with a bit of arrogance.

I was surprised. I stood there like a deer in the headlights. He hardly ever paid for a damn thing. He was recently employed at a local farm that grew strawberries, corn, peaches and apples. It was a job and he was the only employee. It shouldn't be too hard to get along with everyone. The last job he worked on a farm he was fired for threatening another worker and I had to do his job. I did it for the summer along with mom.

The 3 of us were hired together. We finished the season and didn't go back. It was embarrassing to be associated with a hot-headed, immature jerk offs like him. The threat came over the fact that Jake (I think that was his name) was doing a job the Jerry wanted. Jake did it better and he couldn't handle it. Big sucky baby didn't get his own way and resorted to school yard threats. It didn't work and he got his ass fired for it and had to walk home. What a Loser.

I went and got dressed in black khakis and a light blue button down, short sleeve shirt. I left the top button open and put on black dress shoes and a leather belt. I even did my hair. I kept it short so I could wash, rinse and go. I used gel a lot to hold it in place. I loved the out-of-the-shower look. Kelly just got home and got dressed up as well. Mom looked great as always. Jerry not so much. He looked like a slob and in the restaurant, the staff will probably think we are doing our part as a good citizen and feeding a homeless person. To be honest I thought he was going to take us to a soup kitchen.

Everyone piled into his mother's van and we were off. We stopped to pick up his mother. He should. It's her vehicle and she doesn't drive. We arrived at the farm and he got out of the van. He walked over to the office in the small barn where the ATVs were kept and knocked on the small office door. The boss waved him in. A few minutes pass, still no Jerry. Mom got out and walked to the bard as soon as she saw Jerry and the boss emerge. The boss wasn't happy and neither was Jerry. I had a creeping suspicion I wasn't going to be either. No one was.

"He wants me to finish up what I started today before I get paid," announced jerry to the rest of us in the van. I could feel the vein start to bulge in the side of my temple near my forehead. My eye was twitching. I am about to lose it! I looked to his mother, she flung herself back in the bench seat with exasperation and contempt. The look of disgust on her face was predominant and she made no attempt to hide it. He left before either of us could say anything. However we did anyway. There was a discussion.

"Why am I not surprised?" said his mother with contempt and disgust. "That fat lazy bastard probably didn't do a goddamned thing all day. He can't hold a job to save his soul. We're going to be here all night. I like your mother but I don't know what the hell she sees in him. The best thing she did was leave him. She has a good heart but too bad it is wasted on the worthless." I nodded in agreement.

"You know I can't stand him but I like you. You tell it like it is and don't hold back any punches," I said in admiration.

"Most can't take it. Don't mince words Justin. Give to them as it is. Some will appreciate the honesty. Most will think you're a total jerk and those are the ones you don't want in your life anyway. True friends can handle you being blunt and honest. The rest can go to Hell."

"I like that. Jerry can go to Hell. What the Hell was he thinking making us get dressed up just so we can sit here and wait for him to finish his job?"

"Ugh. He probably didn't do a damn thing all day. Go find out from his boss how much longer it's going to be otherwise we will enjoy a night of fine dining with the crackers I have in my purse," she scoffed.

"Ok, I will," I said as I made my way over to the office. I had a bad feeling the night was going to get worse. The boss saw me coming towards him and stopped what he was doing. it was as if he was waiting for someone to ask what the Hell was going on. He waited until I got right up to him.

"I suppose you want to know what's going on," he suggested.

"Yes"

"Well let me tell you what he does all day. He comes here, stands around and smokes. If he isn't smoking, he is talking my ears off with random hokum. He gets next to no work done and then he probably told you guys he was taking you out for dinner with a paycheck he hasn't earned. I can't pay him to stand around and yap. He has a lot of work to do tonight before I even think of paying him. He has all of that sweet corn to pick and pack tonight and there's 20 rows of it," he said pointing to the corn beside the entrance laneway. My heart sank. I was going to be dining on crackers in a van and I was going to be up on murder charges. It's a farm, accidents happen in the fields all the time. It was an accident, yeah, an accident.

"Oh My God, are you serious?"

"I'm afraid so. Your dad is useless."

"HE is NOT MY DAD," I scoffed. Ugh I was insulted. "My dad can hold a job. That dead beat can't." I was absolutely disgusted and about to lose my mind.

"Sorry, your mom's boyfriend and she can do better. A lot better."

"I know and I am hoping this is the last straw," I turned my head to glare at Jerry while he fumbled at picking the corn. He was moving in 2 speeds. Slow and dead slow. I sneered at him. I wanted to hurt him badly.

I needed a machete. I saw Children of the Corn. I am so pissed off right now. I would probably get away with it. Hide the body. Cut it up nice and small for easy disposal. Let him work as fertilizer for next year's crops. Cut away the root system like sod and peel it back. Dig down more than 4 feet so the critters don't dig him up. Hit him in the head with a shovel. It's less messy. Push him in, toss the dirt back in, roll back the plants, water well and pat it down. No problem. His mother would help I am sure of it. Decisions, decisions. This douche brings out the primal urge to kill in everyone.

I went back and reported to Jerry's mother what I was just told. She could tell by the look on my face that she was right. Nothing done and dinner was bait and now we're trapped. Trapped like goddamned rats. She was livid and so was I. She shook her head and reached into her purse and pulled out a twin pack of crackers and opened it. She took one for herself and offered me the other.

"I told you, didn't I? He's a lazy son of a whore! Here you go Justin, it's dinner for two. Tonight's special is cat's ass and cabbage or the chef's surprise of fried farts and egg shells. " she said dripping in sarcasm. I took the cracker and we instantly took them and tapped them together as if we were drinking champagne and toasting a special occasion.

"That lazy cock sucker is in for a big surprise. I rewrote my will and he isn't getting a goddamned thing. My house would be repossessed because he won't pay the taxes. He lives hand to mouth and expects everyone else to pay his way. It will be just like his truck. That pathetic loser doesn't deserve squat. Oh wait. Yes he does. He deserves our contempt! You had better get out there and tell your mother or we are going to be here all night. Get out there and show him how it's done. When we get to the restaurant I want you to order the most expensive thing on the menu, you earned it. I know I always said order cheap when someone else is paying but in this case you are working for your own so go big or go home."

I looked at her and smiled. It was an evil smile. I was going to do just that. I could tell she was working on something of her own. I got out of the van and made my way to the field to find mom and Kelly. They were just going to love this.

I found mom and she was far enough away from the useless wonder that we could talk. She saw me coming and could tell the mood I was in wasn't good. She stopped what she was doing and waited for me to get close enough to talk to her.

"What is it, Justin?" she asked anticipating some bad news.

"I talked to his boss. He hasn't done anything all week except smoke and talk his ears off. He needs 20 rows picked before he will pay him. He tricked us. He lied once again! I hate his guts!" I was getting louder. I was hostile.

"It figures. Well, I don't have any money on me and it's their van so we are kind of stuck here. I need you to calm down and let's get this done. Getting upset isn't going to change it. Chanel your anger into getting this done and then we can go eat. I know you'll find a way to get him back. You always do. I will too," said mom while giving me the nod. I loved her passive aggressive ways. Take it now and let it build. When it's time to get even, let them have it so hard they won't know what hit them.

"His mother said we should order the most expensive thing on the menu. I am having a steak. A nice rare one. I'll make sure to tell them it has to be still dripping blood. He thinks I am a little psycho, I will show him one. If I was old enough to drink, I would get a nice rum and coke with it too. Raise my glass like I am toasting him when I am clearly saying 'Kiss my ass'. God, I hate that waste of skin," I sneered.

We laughed. It was an evil laugh. My tolerance for stupidity was diminishing quickly. Lesson learned. Once again it was the hard way. Always see the money first. That is unless you know the person is established and self sufficient. What I mean is employed and has their own vehicle and house or apartment. If not, have your own mode of transportation and cash and meet them there. You should always be prepared to pay for your own any way. Should lies and random falsehoods raise their ugly heads, you have an exit. Use it and run like hell. Never again will I be trapped in a web of lies nor will I let anyone else that I care about. Read the signs. If you think there is a chance the person isn't being totally honest, they aren't'.

We finished by 9 PM. It's amazing what you can get done when fueled by anger and hatred. These are still my driving forces today. Proving an adversary wrong and achieving a positive outcome for yourself is the best revenge. It's fun. It's the best 'Up Yours" you can deliver. Actions speak louder than words.

We finally got to the restaurant around 9:30 after having to go to the grocery store that cashed cheques. Yes 9:30 PM, the perfect time for dinner. Let it sit in your stomach like a rock before bed. I was starving and it didn't matter. This lying waste of skin was going to pay for it and I was going to enjoy it. It's either that or we resort to primal instincts and feast upon his flesh like rabid wolves. I would rather him be alive the whole time and listen to his delightful screams of agony. Ugh, he is repulsive. I will save him for the wolves. The things we think of when we are angry.

At the table, I sat as far away from him as possible. So did his mother, we were on the opposite side of the 6 seat table on the corner. Mom sat beside him while Kelly sat beside her across from me. The further we were away from him the better.

We all were ordering big. Mom had the fish and the most expensive she could find and washed it down with a nice tall boy of beer or 2. Who cares? She earned it. Kelly had the fried chicken and I ordered a rare 12 oz New York Strip with a loaded baked potato because there was an extra charge for the loaded and a coke. Jerry's mother ordered the most expensive fish on the menu and a rum and coke.

"You don't drink, mom..." Jerry pleaded.

"After your bullshit tonight, I am having one. Shut up and pay for it," she barked back at him. I looked at her and smirked through the side of my mouth.

When the drinks came and as soon as the waitress left the table, she quickly removed the lime wedge on the little plastic sword and place it in my coke and subtly switched the drinks. I now had the rum and coke while she had the coke. The drinks were side by side still so no one would notice. I felt a little kick on my leg from the right side. I knew what it meant. It's our secret. Shut up and enjoy it.

The food finally arrived and I dove into my rare New York Strip. It was still dripping blood. It was perfect. It cut like butter and I picked up the piece and raised it to my mouth with my fork tines straight up like a snobby foodie. I savored it like it was the best thing on Earth. I then raised my 'Coke' and took a nice sip as elegantly as I could and raised the glass to Jerry with a smirk on my face that would infuriate a priest. The rum flavor went down nice and smooth. The look of contempt I received from Jerry was priceless and so worth it. His own mother gave me a nod of appreciation and smiled at him.

To this day, I think that was one of the best meals I have ever had. I don't know if anyone ever remembered their first drink. I have to admit it was my first and best. I was 16 and the legal age is 21. So what. I earned that. Perhaps the splash of revenge the drink was served with made it taste that much better. In fact, it is one of my fondest memories seeing the look on that bastard's face. He figured it out and mentioned it later but it doesn't change anything. I'll drink to your misery any day. Cheers!

CHAPTER 14

$\bullet \cdots \bullet \bullet \bullet \bullet \bullet \bullet \bullet \bullet \bullet \cdots \bullet$

Kelly had run into some former friends from a few years ago when we lived in Derry the first time. Her name was Wendy. They used to be great friends when they were at the primary level in elementary school. They were now in the eighth grade.

Her parent s had a trailer at the local campground and Kelly spent a lot of time with her there as well. Wendy was popular with the out of town boys. I later learned she slept with just about every one of them and earned a lovely nickname of Welcome Wagon Wendy. She even got gonorrhea at 14. In a small town people talk and of course we all heard about it and it was suspected Kelly was involved in the same behavior. She denies it to this day. Thankfully.

Wendy's cousin, Sheila was known as Hoover. I don't think I need to go into details on that unless perhaps a suggestion of an etiquette class or two on why we shouldn't talk with our mouthful and the proper use of the napkin. Sorry, that was extremely rude but funny. Teen sex happens, education on safely doing it is required as well as discretion. Don't kiss and tell especially in a small town.

* * *

Jerry's mother, Brenda ended up in the hospital and we went to visit her before Christmas and we went to visit her. She was not happy and nor was her roommate in the semi-private ward. There was shouting and swearing coming from down the hall on her floor. I knew where it was coming from. We entered the room to find her sitting in her bed with the privacy partition drawn between the 2 beds. She sat there in her bed with a look of disgust on her face.

"Hello," I said to break the tension.

"Hello Justin. It's nice to see you. I have someone worthwhile talking to now. I don't have to listen to chronic bitching and complaining now. I heard of enough from her!" she scowled at the curtain with a look of disgust.

"Ok..." I said trying to get her to continue.

"All night she bitched and complained about my coughing. I am a sick person and I am not here for a fucking vacation. This stupid bitch in the next bed seems to think this is the Hilton. It's probably a step up from the dump she's used to living in," scoffed Brenda motioning her thumb at the curtain like a hitchhiker.

"I heard that," squeaked a quiet voice from behind the curtain. She sounded like a petite older woman.

"Yeah, I know you did. You hear everything! Then you bitch and complain!" barked Brenda.

BBBBBBBBBBBBBBBBBBBBBBBBBBBBBRRRRRRRRRRRR RRRRRRRRR! Brenda farted and it was vile.

"Complain about that Bitch! Better yet, you can fucking choke on it!" she barked and flipped her middle finger to the curtain.

"Oh my god!" squeaked the voice from behind the curtain.

It was bad. It stunk so bad mom and I left the room. We were laughing out loud. We were laughing so hard we were almost crying. Mom started coughing and continued to laugh. I thought she was going to choke. I still am not sure from the laughing or the toxic cloud of stench that was starting to work its way into the hallway at the hospital. You could hear Brenda chuckling in the room. Jerry was laughing hysterically but remained in the room. I guess living with her in the small house, he would be used to it.

I had to let the room clear before we went back in. It had some serious hang time. It was if it were sticking to everything in the room like when a skunk is hit by a car. The stench hangs around for days and seems to coat everything in the vicinity.

Needless to say, the visit was cut short as she was not in the mood for visitors. Jerry of course asked her for money. Brenda gave it to him as it was asked for regarding her personal finances. I think the figures were exaggerated.

I personally think it is the height of ignorance and rudeness to ask someone for money in the hospital. Apparently I need etiquette classes when Jerry was completely devoid of anything that included shame, class, manners, and compassion or empathy. A total twat by earlier definitions.

* * *

It was time for another special delivery to our dear friend Jane and after hearing how she did 3 guys in 2 hours at a bush party I figured it was time for something special. This is my finest work. I have to admit this definitely secures my spot in Hell. I presented t to Kara, Marissa, Rachel, Betty and Michelle. Hindsight it was a mistake doing it at Kara's locker. You'll see why.

The Whore's Prayer

Our whore who found Heaven
Who will scream out your name
His penis cums
Thy will be plugged with girth
In any position he asks
Give him head and your daily spread
And even take it in the ass
He may even let you finger his ass
He knows your filthy reputation
Working for a dollar a blow
For thine is the condom
The diaphragm and the foam
For preventing VD
Amen!

"Oh my God!" shrieked Kara. She was howling with laughter.
"You are so going to Hell!" squeaked Marissa in between fits of laughter.

132

"Ha!" squealed Michelle. She couldn't get anything else out as she was beat red and crying from laughing so hard. "Imagine Pastor McKay.." she managed to squeeze out before bursting back into laughter.

All of us were buckled over in laughter that people were starting to look at us. We were crying from laughing so hard. The onlookers looked at us and walked slowly by as if we were mental asylum escapees. 'You never saw us, we're completely sane... honest!' It was definitely a mistake to bring it out in public. Luckily no one snatched it from our hands. Clearly a work of art of this caliber must be shared.

I printed off a good copy, placed it in the envelope and delivered it. This time her locker was by the principal's office. I blended with the crowd gathered in the hall and slipped it in the crack between the door and the frame. I was fortunate not to be that popular as my actions were never noticed. The perfect messenger. Blend in, do your bidding and disappear.

It was around lunch time and Jane was in convulsions. How she never figured it out it was us was beyond me. After every delivery we were around to see the reaction. Every time. If you study psychological behavior, everyone likes to see the reaction to their handy work whether it is an arsonist, a bomber, a murderer, or a prankster like us. The common behavior is seeing the reaction. They usually show the most concern. It is an attempt to deflect the suspicion. Arsonist, bombers, thieves like to watch the police work and try to figure it out.

"I have had enough!"screamed Jane."I am so sick of everyone thinking I am a whore. Shut the Hell up Marissa. This isn't funny anymore!"

"Oh you admit it was funny?" asked Kara with her eyebrows slightly raised.

"Some of it was, now it's just annoying. The Whore's Prayer?! I am a Christian and this is just offensive. This person should burn in Hell forever! I have never seen such blasphemy!"Shrieked Jane.

She was completely flipping out. This was too funny. I took my masterpiece from her, pretended to read it and howled with laughter. I was red, crying and buckled over. Marissa, Kara and Michelle joined me. The fact Jane was flipping out made me laugh even harder. I wanted to mock her but didn't dare. I didn't want to blow my cover but holy shit this one is for the records. I know it is wrong on every level but hilarious due to its shock level. It's filthy and vulgar like the Aristocrats joke. I will let you look that up on your own.

* * *

The next day I got the news that Brenda had died first thing in the morning. I was upset. I loved her sarcasm and curt demeanor. Jerry was all but concerned. It was evident he was only concerned about the will and what he would be getting. He was transparent that way. A selfish, lazy bastard with sense of entitlement. Unfortunately this a trait we see more and more of every day.

Let me go on record and tell it straight up- Nobody owes you a goddamn thing. If you want something in life, you pay for it or earn it. Work for it. The accomplishment at the end of your hard work is the reward. If you think your employer owes you anything, it is up to and including the last minute you just worked. No more, no less. If you have any other expectations beyond that, you are delusional. That wage you work for is what was offered to you upon hiring and you accepted it as well as the terms of your employment such as holidays and weekends if applicable. You agreed to that wage when you started working for them. If you want anything in life, get off your lazy ass and work for it.

Anyway, Jerry was snooping through her house trying to find the will and she wasn't even in the ground yet. There were several copies as she changed it so many times. In one he was the executor and got the house, Jack got the van. In another he got nothing, his sisters from Maine got it all and Jack got the van. If that was any indicator, Jack should be happy he got the van.

Some seniors use their last will and testament as a toy and bartering tool. It is often changes at a whim to control family to get them to do things for them. Whoever pisses them off in the slightest is out of the will. It really is sad when you think about it. A pathetic manipulation ploy. By the time that comes, your children should be established in life with a house, a decent job, and a mode of transportation of their own. It's called independence. Jerry had neither nor did Jack. Both were in their 40s. They are pathetic in every way.

I am truly happy to say Brenda was no fool. She planned and prepaid her own funeral and gave strict orders to the funeral home how her final wishes were to be carried out. Those two idiots would have buried her in a card board box and cut every corner imaginable so they would get more money out of her estate. Too bad they didn't put that type of effort into a business venture but that would be too much like work and require ambition.

* * *

The day of the funeral came. Brenda was in her casket. It was open. There wasn't that many attendees. She was right about one things: You'll know who your friends are and most people can't handle honesty. When you are honest, you are a bitch or an asshole. It definitely showed at her funeral. It was small. Perhaps she was too blunt and crass for most but it doesn't matter, she was honest.

We were all mingling in the funeral and I got to meet Jerry's sister, she was nice and nothing like her brothers. She was happily married and they were successful in their business. Night and day by comparison. She had a very supportive husband and 3 children. In my opinion, she was successful. She was nice. Jerry was scum. If you put him in an AA meeting, they would be drinking again in no time. He could make the pope swear.

"Any donations to the family can be given to me," announced Jerry. I was utterly disgusted. I spun around and gave him a look of contempt and disgust. To pan handle and solicit donations at your own mother's funeral is contemptible. This time the dumb ass went too far. Luckily his little announcement netted nothing but dirty looks and eye rolling. My mother shot him a nasty look as well. Perfect.

As if I couldn't have any less respect for him from the previous announcement, the useless twat went and stole the money from the

American Cancer Society box. His mother gave to the American Cancer Society. He looked right at me while he did it and gave me the look of "shut your fucking mouth." I will but karma will kick your ass good and hard. I was so disgusted I couldn't even look at him for the rest of the day without shooting him the look of death. There is no level he wouldn't stop to now. I will even add the fact that he bought cigarettes with the money from the American Cancer Society box. It's scum like that that deserve to get the disease.

* * *

It turned out the will where he got nothing was right. The temper tantrum that followed was quite the show. I found it hilarious. Mom wasn't surprised and Kelly and I were smirking from ear to ear. We were loving it. Not even his own mother liked him and the proof was in the will. In her words, "He isn't getting dick all!" was resonating in my ears. Now all I needed was some popcorn. I chuckled to myself.

"What the fuck are you laughing at you little faggot? You're the reason I got nothing! She confided in you! You knew this was going to happen, you little cock sucker!" screamed Jerry as he grabbed me by the throat and pinned me to the wall.

"Are you really this stupid?! If I were to have manipulated her like you said, where's my cut?!" I screamed back right in his face looking cold and deep into his eyes. He paused and then let go of me.

"She probably didn't leave you the house because you don't have a job to afford the upkeep. Even though it's paid off, you would eventually lose it for not paying the property taxes. It'll be just like your truck! Repossessed!" I yelled back at him. I was pissed now and the gloves are off. "Before that happens, it'll be a dump in no time because you are too lazy to cut the grass or clean it! You didn't get the van because you can't drive! How many at fault accidents have you had?! Oh that's right, 3! She probably thought she'd be better off burning it than letting you have it and save the trouble for the insurance company. Oh wait, you have to have a job to pay that too! You're so broke, you can't even afford to pay attention!" I paused to let that one sink in. It was a good one.

"She clearly made the right choice to give a thankless loser like you a goddamned thing. Look at how you treated her or anyone else for that matter. How's your son. That's right you don't see him! He probably wants nothing to do with you! I wonder why. God knows how you treated him. If it's anything like the way you treat us or your own mother, it's no wonder isn't it asshole!?" I shouted.

He was like a deer in the headlights. I was loving it. When you go after someone hold nothing back. Use everything you have and Destroy! Check your conscience at the door. When you have to hurt them, make it sting and make it memorable. Nothing is sacred and nothing is taboo. At least not for scum like Jerry.

"Kiss my ass!" screamed back Jerry as he was holding back tears. I got him where it hurts. I gave him a malicious smile. I won. He lost.

"Did you earn your lesson? You can only bully so much and then you're going to get it back in spades." Mom said in her mothering voice.

"Yeah, remember that Jerry. Remember the story you told us about your dad being afraid you and Jack were getting big because of how he treated you? You didn't hit him, did you? You aren't my dad, are you?" I asked menacingly.

"Whatever Justin, you aren't big enough to take me," deflected Jerry.

"Not yet, but soon. I am patient," I said glaring at him.

"Enough you two! Enough!"scolded mom.

"Justin, show some respect to your elder and if you can't, leave the room," scolded Jerry.

"Heil mein Fuhrer," I shouted as I clicked my heels together and extended my right arm into the Nazi salute. I enjoyed the look of shock and disgust on his face before I turned and goose stepped out of the room. For those who don't understand the reference, it means 'Hail my Leader' in German and was a common salute for Adolph Hitler. I heard him call me a smart ass son of a bitch but I didn't care.

* * *

Within a few days of her body being in the ground, Jerry thought he was being haunted by his mother. I know, it's hilarious since there aren't any such things as ghost. There has been so solid scientific evidence to prove it. Forget about Paranormal Activity and the other ghost movies out there. I find them comedies more than anything. Call the Ghostbusters twat waffle. Complete nonsense in the same playing field as Santa Clause and the Easter Bunny.

Let's put all the scientific facts aside and play along. Even if there were such things as ghosts and poltergeists, I can think of two billion other people more deserving of the visitation and entertainment that will follow. Everything that goes bump in the night has a logical explanation. It could be an improperly closed gate or window that has the wind gusts causing things to bump. Oh no, you break out the holy water.

I will believe in such nonsense if I were to see it for myself in a sober state of mind in broad daylight where the walls bleed and furniture levitates and rearranges itself. The latter can't be too bad providing the poltergeist has a sense of style. It would save me from doing it later. Maybe through the Ouija board I can convince them to go into the furniture moving business with me and we can become famous and millionaires. I can single handedly move the grand piano to another room with my poltergeist friend without even scratching the floor. Miracle Movers. Let me call the Trademark Office. Look, I just found a career for the afterlife. I am set for eternity. I am a genius.

Back to the haunting of Mommy Dearest. He called us up at 8 PM and even called Pastor McKay. I was shocked to see Pastor McKay even entertain such nonsense. We all formed a circle and held hand while Pastor McKay prayed and cast out the evil spirit "In the name of Jesus Christ leave!" What a crock. Have ever seen the Exorcist? Pure entertainment. As if it were that easy. I was looking forward to the theatrics of at least a "Get Out" writing itself in blood on the wall. Life is full of disappointments isn't it?

"Thanks for coming out so late," I thanked Pastor McKay.

"You're welcome Justin. I am here to help," he replied with a smile.

"The truth is, he took the money from the American Cancer Society box at his own mother's funeral and all of the charades are from a guilty conscience, nothing more."

"That is between him and God," replied Pastor McKay.

"Yes, but he has to drag everyone else into it. So I figured let the truth be told," I said smiling. I think he knew I hated Jerry. I had no problem throwing him under the bus.

"Well goodnight," said Pastor McKay as he grabbed his hat and went out the door.

Luckily I never heard of the ghost thing again. If I were to have heard it again I can assure you I have plenty more sarcasm to go around. It is the only way to deal with stupid.

CHAPTER 15

· · · · · · ●●●● ● ●●●● · · · · ·

The church was now on another crusade. This one was aga world is flatty more sarcasm to go around.orite pass time.fe is full of disapoininst Rock & Roll and why we shouldn't be listening to it. It was a dangerous thing that opened the gateway for Satan to take over your life. The bands are mere marionettes for Satan and do his bidding to enslave the youth so we become Children of The Beast. I may have over dramatized it a bit but it is pretty close to that according to the religious based Hells Bells.

The religious right wing will convince you that KISS stands for Kids In Satan's Service. Rock and Roll is evil as well as all main stream music. It focuses on myths and misdirection on the relationship between rock and roll and sex, alcohol, violence, suicide, rebellion, miscegenation, the occult, and other events or activities deemed to be immoral by biblical standards. The website it encourages you to burn your music in a fire.

It suggests that rock music encourages sexual promiscuity and teenage sex. Teenagers need no encouragement in this category. How old were you when you lost your virginity? The average age is 16 according to Wikipedia and the Kinsey Institute. This has been going on for longer than rock and roll was around. Teenagers have multiple partners by the time they graduate high school. Look at Welcome Wagon Wendy and Hoover. They are typical teenage girls. They listened to rap. It wouldn't have mattered if they listened to Mozart.

Alcohol consumption predates rock and roll as well. Country music contains Alcohol related songs as well. As for violence, we are a violent species and have been doing unspeakable things to each other since the dawn of time. Suicide has unfortunately been happening for just as long, the main causes are depression, mental disorders, drug and alcohol abuse as well as financial difficulties and relationship problems.

Rebellion is a common human trait that has been with us since the beginning as well. War, riots, law breaking and other criminal activity is associated with rebellion. Miscegenation is basically multiracial mixing through sexual reproduction. we have evolved as a society enough where mixed races shouldn't be an issue. If it is for you, it is time to grow up.

The occult has been around for centuries and is often associated with pagan beliefs such as the use of alchemy, astrology, tarot, magic, spiritualism and divination. These have been around since the middle ages. Easter and Christmas both coincide with pagan holidays. You can reference those yourself. Search the Yule and the movable feast (Easter). Easter coincides with the first Sunday after the full moon that follows the Spring Equinox. Search out the origin of the Easter Bunny. It comes from a pagan belief.

These things have been happening long before rock and roll so to say it is the cause is nothing short of lying and using it as a scapegoat. Ozzy bit the head off of a bat. It was supposed to be a rubber bat and it was maliciously switched for a real one. The person who did it was fired and Ozzy was subjected to rabies shots. That is definitely not something anyone would want to subject themselves too on purpose. Rock and Roll has stage productions with special effects and pyrotechnics as well as props like any other staged event. Alice Cooper uses mannequins and theatric props such as guillotines into his medieval house of horror style show. I love it.

The fact is music is written to reflect life events. We all go through feelings of worthlessness, despair, loneliness, anger, hatred, love, happiness, and screw you. This is why it is so popular. Rock and Roll All Night is having a good time. It makes us feel good. It's about having a good time with friends and family and the music is to relate to the audience whatever the subject matter. It's also a lot about storytelling, an art Bon Jovi excels at.

Anyway, it didn't take long for the church to want to have a music burning with the teens CDs. I refused. I can differentiate between right and wrong. I can also tell the difference between fantasy and reality. Today it's video games too. First hand shooter games that are creating serial killers and mass shooters. Total nonsense. Video games show consequences for your actions. the police always get you in Grand Theft Auto.

Josh McKay was the first. Pastor McKay would not have that devil music in his house. He even broke his stereo. The CDs were to be burned. Josh took them out of the sleeves and I hawked them at a pawn shop for him. Only the sleeves were burned. They tried on several occasions to get me to do it and I refused.

"Justin are you going to get rid of that heavy metal you listen to?" asked Deb.

"Not ever. It's Rock & Roll," I responded condescendingly with a smile.

"It's sinful and wrong. You watched Hells Bells," she shot back.

"It's misinformation. The artist they are talking about in there not all devil worshipers. The songs are about life. Life is full of ups and downs. Not everyone can love in the Ivory Tower," I said with my voice dripping in sarcasm. Here we go with the Holier than Thou crap again.

"It is warping our mind," she persisted.

"Yes and other things are too. Why upset the balance?" I asked.

"You need focus and direction and that music will only distract you. Josh burned his and now his focused more than ever," she persisted even more.

"It wasn't his choice. He was forced to do so. In your opinion he is doing better. We start with burning CDs, what's next? Movies? Books?" I challenged.

"What exactly is that supposed to mean?" she challenged me back.

"Well, we are doing World War 2 history and it sounds awfully familiar, doesn't it? Hitler burned books that didn't reflect on his views or Germany's. American and Jewish authors, liberalist, anarchist, propaganda were top of the list. Cleansing the nation by fire. I feel that you want to do the same. If it isn't Christian or support the Christian agenda, it must be incinerated. I feel we are substituting a 'Seig Heil" with an "Amen"' I said to her looking her straight in the face. I was right. I knew it.

"That is blasphemy!" she was starting to freak out.

"How is that blasphemy? You want to burn CDs, Hitler burned books. If American music were in CD form, he would have burned that too. The director of Hells Bells is off base. His opinion is bigoted against Rock & Roll from the start. The backwards messages is 80s and I can't clearly make out what he was showing us on Queen's song. "Smoke Marijuana" is by spinning a vinyl at various speeds to get it sound like that. I will bet he can do it with another one and make up something else there too. Highway to Hell is a fun song. It's an anthem and everyone knows it. It's called satire. The whole premise of that set is to promote his own agenda. It's propaganda and full of misinformation," I told her putting my own spin on things.

"I will have a chat with your mother about your attitude and the music you listen to," Deb said in a scolding tone.

"Go ahead. She bought some of it for me and listens to some of it as well," I responded smiling at her.

"You would not be listening to that in my house. You would not be working Sundays or driving to wherever you please either in my house," she said trying to show authority.

"I don't live in your house and for that I am eternally grateful. My mom is awesome and I respect her. She has rules and boundaries and I respect those too. If I had to live with you, I would leave the second you weren't looking. I couldn't live like that. That isn't living. It's survival," I said to challenge her again.

"What is that supposed to mean?" she demanded.

"I won't live under the fear of repercussions for my musical and cinematic tastes or art. I did that before with my dad, the only difference was it was alcohol and lots of yelling and swearing. Life with Jerry is the same way except we had less. He has made our lives even more miserable and I hate his guts for it. I was afraid to put a toe out of line in both cases and I will not live like that again," I affirmed.

I didn't care is she was done talking or not. I left. I was sure next week was a book burning.

* * *

The following Monday Kara was waiting for us at her locker as usual. Today she didn't look too smug. She was concerned. I will never forget that April morning. I looked at Michelle and she looked at me. We instantly knew something was wrong.

"Spill it," I said looking right at her. She knew she couldn't hide it.

"Jane is a neighbor of mine and her sister overheard my sister and I talking about the poetry. She overheard me say I knew who it was," said Kara slowly without any emotion.

"And...?" I asked. It was like pulling teeth.

"Well, I had to do something. Michelle, they took your books out of your locker," she said trying not to cry.

"Are you fucking serious?!" I shouted. Son of a bitch. Stupid, big mouth, fat, dumb ass twat. I was losing my mind. How could she be so stupid? It was her idea. She was throwing Michelle under the bus. Spineless bitch! I was being consumed by rage. I wanted to knock her out. Michelle and I ran to her locker and upon opening it, sure enough. Her notebooks were missing. Damn It!

"I say we throw her under the bus too and the rest of them. Maybe they will easier on us." I suggested.

"So far I am the only one that is caught and there is no guarantee they have anything," suggested Michelle. Just then the other girls came up to us. I think they heard us. They all had the deer in the headlights look.

"You can't. My parents will kick me out," pleaded Kara. She was almost begging.

"Mine too," piped up Marissa.

"And mine," added Rachel.

"I wasn't involved," reiterated Betty. This was true. She really didn't do anything. She laughed and kept it a secret. That isn't worth ruining her for.

"Don't worry, Betty. You are safe. You laughed and you knew who was responsible but you didn't participate," I reassured her.

"What about us?" asked the others in unison.

"You were active and willing participants too. Don't think you are getting off like Betty." I shot back.

"We'll get kicked out," pleaded Kara.

"You should have thought about that in the first place. You should have that about that before you opened your big mouth and not look to see who the fuck was around! What the Hell were you thinking?!" I was raising my voice. I was livid. Stupid bitch. Ugh! I was advancing on her and looked her dead in the eyes. I stared an icy cold stare into her eyes.

"Justin, please," begged Kara.

"Justin, we don't rat on friends," reminded Michelle.

"That's right, we don't rat do we, Kara?" I asked with malice in my voice. I was calling that fat bitch out. She rolled over on Michelle. She is a fat, rat ass bitch.

"I didn't rat you out, honest," pleaded Kara.

"Yeah, why are Michelle's books missing then? Because you are a fucking snitch and a liar! It was your idea!" I blasted. Kara stood there emotionless and looked at me. It took all I had not to punch her face in. I really don't think I could have made her bleed enough. It was her and Marissa who had the idea. She was the one who told us where the locker was as well as the combination. She gave me the resources for the poetry as for what happened. She was probably friends with Jane at the same time since they were neighbors as well. Kara is a fat, two-faced, back-stabbing, lying bitch. Whore. Ditch pig. Slut. Twat.

We separated and went to our first class. By the time it was over I was called to the office and I am sure you know what happened. Rolled over in the clover. I was having a great time with the vice principal Donald Hammer and Aiden Lynch. I would have rather had my ball sack glued to my leg. Yeah funny names but whatever.

Mr. Hammer was a shorter man around 5'8" with a small build and a graying receding hairline with glasses. He was a bit of a sharp dresser and I kind of liked him. Mr. Lynch was over 6' tall and that mustache he wore, I wanted to wax it off his face. I found him to be condescending. He was a bit of a sharp dresser but wore dark clothing to try and cover the fact he had a belly. It wasn't working. The light colored shirts he wore did not help. The fact that he tried was laughable. It was if they were playing good cop, bad cop but in this case I will go with bad cop, bad cop.

"I am so disappointed in you! Do you know how much trouble you are in?!" scolded Hammer.

"Do you have any idea what you have done to that poor girl!!" scolded Lynch.

"We have been looking for you for quite some time. Your friend Michelle turned you in. I know you didn't act alone and this is your chance to turn in the others. Your friends are letting you take the fall. They are great friends. You fall, they get away scot free. Think long and hard but don't take too long," Hammer was in full interrogation mode.

"Do you know where she lives?" demanded Lynch.

"No, why do you ask?" I asked quietly.

"Really? You don't know about the stuff happening at her house?" interrogated Lynch.

"What stuff? What are you talking about?" I asked. Now I was concerned. Kara really made it bigger than I knew. The fact we agreed to not turn her in was pissing me off. What a twat! She needed to be turned in and get her ass kicked. I kept my word and didn't turn them in and I regret doing it. They should have burned too. A true friend will be right there with you. Not these spineless twats. If you are ever in this situation, make a note of that. Better yet, learn from this and don't put yourself in this situation.

"You don't know about the flaming dog crap bags and the toilet papering or the late night window knocking?" asked Lynch in disbelief. Kara is the biggest twat there is.

"No, I don't."

"Ok. I believe you on this one. I need you to clean out your locker. You are out of here. Both of you. You will never be allowed back. There is no room for that behavior and it is unforgivable and inexcusable."

I am going to abbreviate everything in a cliff note version. We both got expelled. Mom recruited Pastor McKay to help and he did, I am grateful for that. Michelle went to another school in Paisley after taking a year off. I went to another 40 minutes travel away in Mavis but I always has to connect with another bus in Palmer for another 45 minute ride home with those with learning disabilities. Lynch made sure life was as difficult for me as possible. Jerry couldn't help but throw his two cents in how Michelle was ruining my life and how stupid I was. The usual gibberish you would expect from the peanut gallery.

Within a few months of the expulsion, my girlfriend and the manager of the restaurant I worked at got into an argument and I got fired for it. That's fair, right? I had no part of the argument. They later changed the discharge papers to not being punctual. That was made up too. Can't get her way one way, make something up to get it another. Funny how we all know someone like that. Politicians are good at it. It closed a few years later and became a daycare and car rental place as it was divided in two.

As a precaution, mom sent me to psychiatrist referred from my family doctor. The only thing I think I needed it for was because I couldn't believe I let those bitches off the hook. Of course they didn't have the guts to go and admit their part. They are spineless, cut throat, back stabbing, two faced bitches for sure. Kara is the worst. It was her idea and handy work and she rolls over on us. Snitches get stitches. Snitches end up in ditches.

I met the doctor at the county Mental Health Unit. He was a middle aged Asian man barely over 5 feet tall with a heavier medium build. he wore glasses and had a grandfather hair ring. Nothing on top, but lots on the side of his head that wrapped all the way ears.

"Hello Justin. I am Dr. Tao. Yes, it is like the chicken dish at your favorite Chinese restaurant." he said as I sat in the chair next to his desk. He smiled. This wasn't our typical psychiatrist office you find in the comics or on TV. It was a regular style doctors office without the instruments. Instead of stackable metal chairs with a little bit of padding, they were recliners you find in the average living room.

"Hi," I answered sheepishly as I didn't know what to expect.

"I went over your file. You really don't need to be seeing me. You pulled a prank and got caught. You probably took the rap for some of your friends or people you thought were your friends. You are a teenage boy and this happens all the time. It wasn't very nice as I am sure you already know. You thought it was funny and tried to fit in. How am I doing so far?" he asked.

"Right on the money," I replied. He's good. I'll give him that.

"The fact is you are being made an example of. It stinks, I know but Mr. Lynch wants to appear tough to the other students. If he were to let you back, anything else that happens will pretty much be blamed on you. I highly doubt you will do anything like this again but it a hard lesson to learn. My question to you is why you didn't turn the others in? Was it because they gave you a story as to what would happen to them to try and con you?"

"Yes they did and I fell for it," I answered. I was pissed. The fact that it was something so pathetic and the fact that Michelle didn't want to throw them under the bus. I wanted to burn the bitches. The disgust and contempt I hold for them is severe.

"It is classic human behavior to con someone into taking the fall. I am sure this was a harsh lesson. If there is some way of selling another person out to 'get away with it' if you will, they will do so. It is also sad to say you will probably not hear from them for a long time to come as they wouldn't want to associate themselves with you and their guilt. You are far better off without people like that in your life anyway. As for the recommendation of Mr. Lynch you see a regular psychiatrist on a continual basis, I don't see it. However you are scheduled for 12 visits so we will deal with some of the anger and hostility you must be feeling over it and your life changes instead. I will not waste any of our time together rubbing your face in this mistake. It has no benefit to either party. I am seeing here in the file they are going to send you one of their own to visit you in Mavis on a weekly basis. This is just a reporting tool for the school board and to rub more mud in your face. Tell them nothing personal. Tell them how you are adjusting fine and reiterate you learned your lesson and everything is fine. Pick your new friends more carefully. Am I making sense?" he asked. His delivery was like reading a textbook but also like a friend too. Weird.

"Ok. I will. Yes you are making sense. I will tell the school psychiatrist nothing. Mr. Lynch loves rubbing shit in my face, doesn't he," I answered.

"Yes he does. those who constantly rub others faces in it are usually doing it to cover up person deficiencies they may be having of their own. He also may just like bullying people around too. It's hard to say. In this case I would assume both by the lengths he's going to do it. The psychiatrist would be a sign that he actually cared about your wellbeing if you were to remain be at his school. This is clearly not the case," report Dr. Tao.

"Nope. I guess not."

"Ok, enough about that. Tell me about your home life," enquired Dr. Tao.

"My mom is awesome. My dad is out of my life as he is a selfish drunk. My brother and sister-in-law won't let me see the kids since they say my mom is a bitch. Yes, that's the reason. My sister is cool and has a whore for a best friend. She sleeps with every guy from out of town and got the nickname Welcome Wagon and her cousin is Hoover because of her oral skills. My mom's boyfriend is the biggest loser piece of garbage that ever lived and I wish he would just die. I hate his guts so much I would like to kill him. He has made our lives a living Hell for the last two years. we even moved out on him. He won't take the hint and still comes around. We already discussed my friends suck," I reported to him as if reading an essay in bullet form.

"Ok. I can't help you with your sisters friends other than to say if you are going to engage in sexual activity with them, be protected. As for your mom's boyfriend, tell me more about him and why you hate him so much. Your brother and his girlfriend are childish and shouldn't be concerned, hopefully they will grow up," said Dr. Tao. He was clearly interested in my anger issues.

I went through the whole spiel on how he was given a key to watch the house and then decided to move himself in, the dump of a house where I didn't have a bedroom, the bullying, dictatorship, name calling and other forms of abuse. I mentioned the fact he can't hold a job and the dinner evening or picking corn. I told him how we moved out on him and the stalking. I couldn't pass on the opportunity to show what he was like at his own mother's funeral. Needless to say, Dr. Tao was disgusted and shocked.

"He sounds like a real piece of work. It must drive you crazy you can't get rid of him," he suggested.

"You have no idea. The loser won't go. We moved out on him. You would think that would be a hint. The fact I am constantly rude to him is another but he keeps coming around. In cases like that, murder should be legal," I scoffed.

"It's never ok to murder but I get what you mean. You can't even restrict him from the property?" asked Dr. Tao.

"No, he is taking the front unit of the house," I groaned.

"Why is that?"

"His sisters are selling the house and he has to get out," I replied with disgust.

"You are in a really difficult spot. Does your mother want him around?" asked Dr. Tao.

"No, just keeps coming around. He now goes to the same church and we just can't get rid of him," I was getting angry just thinking about it.

"You are working yourself up. The answer will present itself. just do not do anything that you will regret or get yourself in trouble. You made a mistake and if you do anything whether it's fighting or otherwise, the chances are they will not take your side if you are right or not. I must advise caution in everything you do for a while especially at school. You will already be branded a 'Troublemaker' and that is how you will be perceived. You have to change that perception no matter what and it will take work. Lots of work," advised Dr. Tao.

"I know and if it gets out there, I am going to be pushed around even more to see if I snap, aren't they?" I asked already knowing the answer.

"I think you already know the answer. The answer is yes. So no matter how much you want to fight back, I suggest not doing so. That is unless you are in danger," he advised.

"I got it," I said. I wasn't happy but I got it.

"Ok, I think we are good until next time. I think I will see you on a monthly basis. just book it on your way out," suggested Dr. Tao.

"I will. See you next month," I said as I shook his hand and left his office.

CHAPTER 16

· · · · · · ●●●● ● ●●● · · · · · · ·

The last etiquette program was on abstinence. Who didn't see that coming? Now we get to sit through the biblical reason why sexual organs are decorative body ornaments until marriage where they will become magic vessels of fulfillment. These abstinence advocates seem to think that you're going to be good at it the first time. Here's the reality, the male will be lucky not to cream in his pants or make a mess the second it gets out of his underwear if he's never done anything with it. Reading this paragraph will take longer. It's like riding a bike for the first time with the unrealistic expectations of finishing first in the Tour de France. It's just not happening. Sorry.

"Tonight we are talking about teen sex. This is the last of our etiquette series," began Deb. There was applause. We were so sick of these programs. She saved the worst for last.

"We all see what happens when teenagers have sex. There are pregnancies, Sexually Transmitted Infections and can be harmful to your health mentally and physically," she continued. The scare tactics have begun I thought.

"God made you pure and to give away the purity in an ungodly way is sin. Sex is for marriage. No exceptions. As for having premarital sex, it has been known to destroy the relationship. How many of the 'couples' stay together after sex in your high schools?" she asked and paused. There was silence. "As I thought, none." She was standing superior like an insufferable know-it-all. I had to take her down a few pegs.

"I am sorry. I don't make it my business to know what other students are doing sexually. I know of a few couples who have been together since they were in grade 9 that are now in 11 or 12. They are still together. I assume they have had some sort of sexual experience but I will not ask them. It's rude. This is assumption." All eyes were on me and a few heads were nodding in agreement.

"Whether they are or not is irrelevant. They are a minority. Why must you try and undermine me every time Justin?" she screeched.

"I'm not. There are lots cases of people marrying their high school sweetheart. You can bet they had sex in high school. What you are saying isn't accurate. Yes, some don't make it and some do," I protested.

"Are you saying you should have sex?!" She was freaking out.

"When did I say that?" I glared at her in the face. I was pissed. I hate it when people try to put words in my mouth. "I didn't. I said your generalization wasn't entirely accurate. It isn't. Some cases people make it. To say otherwise is false. In fact some marriages don't even make it. People change." She looked at me with contempt and disbelief.

"You shouldn't base it on your parents. That situation isn't normal," stated Deb.

"The situation wasn't normal from the start. Neither is yours. Not everyone gets along like you and your husband. In a perfect world, wouldn't it be great if everyone did? It's nice but not normal either. People disagree and fight. It's a way of life. Put two people together and there will eventually be conflict. That's just the way it is. Let's leave sex out of it. They will fight. Life isn't a 'Happily Ever After' fairytale. Trust me on this one."

"I can agree to that, we can discuss this later. I want to get this lesson done and it will go much faster without interruptions." Deb was pissed and here goes her Queen Bee persona.

"Oh forgive me. Please continue," I said dripping in sarcasm as I put my leg over my lap and reclined in my seat. I folded my arms and rolled my eyes back in my head. Pure steaming pile of crap. Grab me a shovel.

"Anyway..." she began with tones of judgment and contempt as she looked right at me."The best sex you will ever have is when you are married. you will have more respect for yourself knowing you were pure and right in God's eyes. The night of your wedding will be the most magical night of your life," she said beaming and grinning ear to ear. I'll bet it was over in 2 minutes or less I thought to myself and chuckled. Bipidy Bopity Boo. Then it's over. A magical experience like no other. I chuckle to myself again.

"Who did the comparison? You can't lose your virginity in high school, grow it back and then do it again when you are married. So how would you do the comparison?" I heard someone ask. It was a girl. I was impressed and so happy the skepticism was spreading. Another person listening to their internal lie detector. I looked over and it was Donna. You could have heard a pin drop. Eyes were going back from me to Donna to Deb. It was priceless.

"You're right. You can't grow it back, Donna. This is based on how many make it after marriage versus high school or unmarried couples. Married couples overwhelmingly stay married longer than those who aren't. It's what God wants. You shouldn't question it. Just do it." said Deb with her usual tone of judgment. That was it. Shut the Hell up and do as you are told.

Had they done their research, teens have been having sex since the dawn of time. The average age for losing your virginity is 16. Kinsey Institute research since 1950s and is ongoing. Abstinence doesn't work. Trying to fight nature is impossible. Once you hit puberty, sexual urges are there and get stronger throughout your teens. Just saying no isn't going to work nor is prayer. Telling someone what do in this case judgmental and condescending. Discouraging sexual education on the premise of telling them to say 'no' is education enough makes you delusional. Educate them on all aspects of sexual behavior and let them make up their own minds on their own time. Saying sex destroys relationships and the first time will be amazing is misinformation.

Time to be cynical. Here's the truth to that, divorce is expensive and once the lawyers are in, everyone loses. Lawyers win. Some generally love each other to the end. The rest don't. They have affairs and ride it out hoping the other will die first. Death is cheaper than divorce. Murder gets you prison or worse. Being married is often compared to prison. Damned if you do, damned if you don't. At least being married you aren't passed around for cigarettes. The only one who cries during sex are inmates.

You don't even have to have sex after marriage. I actually heard a newlywed bride say this. Don't go crying when he's getting it from someone else, bitch. When Target doesn't suit your needs, there's Wal-Mart or the other way around. Happily ever after is a fairy tale like the Easter Bunny and Santa Clause. Up yours Disney. Piss off, Snow White. Cinderella can kiss my ass. Ok, that was my rant.

"Ok. Are there any more questions?" Deb asked reluctantly. She was dreading it and you could tell by the tone of her voice. She had me and now Donna. I am sure we were Hell to deal with. Too bad, you want to push your nonsense? That is what you get, skeptics.

"I have one," I said. Now it's my turn to splay stump the bigot. "Where does the bible stand on masturbation? We can't have sex and biology has a mind of its own." Again, you could have heard a pin drop.

"It doesn't. It depends on who you talk to. I am not touching that one. that is between you and God," she replied with her hand up in the stop position.

"I will. I am going with that it is ok. That's where the saying 'God helps those who help themselves' comes from." I joked. Deb was shocked and before I knew it she was right up in my face.

Slap The bitch actually slapped my face.

"That is for blasphemy! Don't ever do that again," she said with her voice raised and her finger in my face.

"What? You haven't heard that?" I shot back.

"Yes, that is NOT what it means! It means you should take initiative and not expect Him to do it all for you," she shrieked.

"That's exactly what I meant. We are made in His image, right?" I continued. She nodded. "So there is no accident we have perfect reach for that area, is there? Because sometimes you need to take matters into your own hands." I asked. Her jaw dropped. I was waiting for another slap but it never came. She just walked away shaking her head.

Another rant. Masturbation is natural. Fetuses touch themselves in the womb as do babies. We live the feeling of our genitals being touched. When you have religious twit like Focus on the Family and other idiots saying masturbation is bad. It can cause problems with development. It is as natural and beautiful thing. Your hand has perfect reach to that region and it is no mistake. What more proof do you need that you are intended to do so?

Circumcision was intended to stop boys from masturbating. A little spit or lotion and problem solved. For women, a good dildo and/ or vibrator is a must. Practice makes perfect. It is proven to release stress and can raise self esteem. In men, it can reduce the risk of prostate cancer. In 2008, at Tabriz University a study showed it can reduce nasal blood vessels from swelling thus enabling the airway to be more free for breathing. The climax can put you in a relaxed state and can help you fall asleep when you do it in bed.

Pornography is associated with masturbation as well. The internet is full of every legal fetish you may have. Bigots will say they show rape and torture. This is completely false. Pornography is willing couples doing things they enjoy and pleasuring each other. Everyone is satisfied and happy. They usually act out fantasies. These fantasies may be a little rough but never enough where someone is begging for mercy or requires medical attention. That is violence and it not only illegal but uncalled for. It is role playing. Whatever your fetish from screwing the delivery man to the naughty, dominatrix nurse is available. Feel free to explore. Fantasies are free. We all have them.

Just stay away from child pornography, you sick bastards. It's illegal and you should be beaten for seeking it out. Rape is a violent crime and illegal. There is nothing pleasurable about torturing and violently defiling another person, especially children, if you disagree, seek professional help.

* * *

The entire etiquette program was so we could go eat a buffet which we were overdressed for. We were dressed Semi-formal. Needless to say Donna was my date. There was a connection through skepticism but a connection anyway. We are still friends.

Unfortunately she was kicked out of the church shortly after "asking too many questions" .

After dinner, it was off to a ballet where we as teenagers spent the entire time looking at cleavage and cock pieces or support belts through binoculars. There was a lot of leering on these items. We are teenagers with raging hormones watching the tits, cock and ass. So much for the abstinence speech.

Too bad the girls and the bisexually curious didn't do their homework on the dance belt first. It is like an athletic supporter and a thong in one. It is designed to hold the genitalia in place to prevent injury and pinching which could cause serious damage through some of the dance moves. An issue no man want to endure. The second reason is to prevent the audience from seeing the entire contour, shape and size of his member while he wears those white see-through tights. This could be a distraction for sure. Wear a skin tight white pair of shorts to the pool and get them wet or even a pair of tighty whiteys at a pool party. Same effect. All eyes on your member. The dancers might as well go naked without it.

After a titillating look at the ballet, we were off for horse drawn carriage rides and desserts. Conversations were usually sexually charged or an exchange of dirty jokes. Lots of mocking the stay away from sex and why you shouldn't pleasure yourself topics of the previous week. I love abstinence. It's very helpful especially for comedic material. Masturbation is nature's way of saying go fuck yourself. It's ok because God helps those who help themselves.

* * *

New school, long commute, no friends and a bad reputation that already proceeds me. This should be fun I thought. It was. Either people are oblivious to their surroundings or they just don't care. It took two weeks before anyone would even talk to me. I got the odd 'Hello" but I usually had to say it first. Mavis seemed really stuck up. I couldn't believe it. I can at least say they weren't rude and would respond when you talk to them. It's that whole etiquette thing again. Always respond politely and keep the conversations small if you don't like or want to talk to the person. This way you don't look like a stuck up twat. Amazing. Ok, I will admit it. Some of it was useful however the condescending manner it was force fed was not.

I eventually made a few friends. One guy named Allen, a girl named Jen and another named Mary. Allen was the same age as me and roughly the same build. We were both kind of lanky and geeky looking. I will go with average build and looks as I hate labels. Labels belong on clothes and food products not on people. Jen was out of school before and returned to school as an adult. She had a infant son. She was homely looking and around 5' 3" and slightly overweight with long brown hair that had no body or volume to it. She was very plain.

Mary was fairly attractive. She tall and slender and had wavy blonde hair. The 4 of us would hang out at lunch but it wasn't long before our personalities would collide. Jen was sitting across from me one day and we were all smoking in the local coffee shop and I exhaled the same time the door opened and the smoke went right in her face. She had a complete bitch fit.

"What the fuck are you doing blowing smoke in my face? It's rude. You are such an asshole. Do you know what that means? It means you want to fuck me!" she said with her voice raised.

"It was an accident. I don't want to fuck you. You are making a scene over nothing." I protested. I forgot to apologize for it but to her, everything is intentional. As for sex with her...ewww. I could just throw up in my mouth. Picture her naked. Ugh!

"No, you did it on purpose. You know better than that. You are such a liar," she shouted back.

"Oh really and you are the expert on human behavior. A single mom on welfare but you're the expert," I said sarcastically with my eyes rolling.

"Don't roll your eyes at me!" she said staring me coldly in the face.

"I'll tell you what. When you learn to accept an accident as such and stop being such a bitch, I'll stop," I shot back.

"So I am a fucking bitch?!" she shrieked. She was pissed now and I honestly thought the table would flip over any second. Allen and Mary sat there looking at each other and didn't say a word.

"I said you were acting like one. I didn't call you one. Learn the difference," I said condescendingly.

"Don't you talk down to me!"

"Ok mom," I sassed back.

"Oh you are such an asshole. No wonder you got kicked out of your old school. I swear to God, I am going to kick your ass," she shot back.

"Bring it on bitch. I was taught not to hit women but you are a whore. Whore's get smacked around regularly. Where's your baby's daddy or do you even know who it is?" I fired back. This one was too evil but in the circumstances, I make no apology.

"Fuck You!"

"What's the matter? Does the truth hurt?" I taunted in a condescending, sassy tone.

"I hate you!" she screamed. She was ready to cry. Awesome. That will teach you to fly off the handle for no reason.

"Lunch is over, we need to head back," reported Allen sheepishly.

I glared at Jen and she glared at me right back. The four of us walked down the road back to school. I looked over at Jen and made the devil horns with my left hand and extended across Mary who was standing between us and growled like a demon. I thought it was a proper greeting for Satan's mistress. Allen was beside me on my right.

"Don't shoot Jen the finger, Justin," joked Mary. Jen wasn't having it. She looked over an d glared right at me.

"If you have something to say, say to my face," Justin.

"It was devil horns. That is how you greet evil. Did you hear me growl?"I said condescendingly.

"You lied to my face. I hate you. Don't talk to me again or I am going to kick your ass," she said staring me in the face.

"You have threatened that three times now. Let's see what you got. I don't think you will because you are all talk, no action. If you were really going to do it, you would have done it by now. You know I will hit you back and that scares you, " I challenged and taunted.

She glared at me and walked away from us by quickening her pace to almost a jog. This of course after shooting me a dirty look.

"Don't go away mad," I taunted. Allen and Mary gave me a sideways glace in disbelief. I'm not sure if it was in disgust or disbelief and I didn't give a flying care. The high and mighty white trash slam pig had to be called out. She didn't talk to me for quite some time after that. Every day she didn't was a blessing. I should really count those blessings.

* * *

Jerry's uncle was now blind and the house was sold. Jerry as living in the other half of our duplex and his uncle was in a home. He was losing his mind as well. Unfortunately he died quickly within a week. Another funeral for Jerry and company. The cleaned out his account and gave him the cheapest funeral ever. The casket was something I would expect to go in the incinerator for cremation but there it as on display.

Pastor McKay oversaw the funeral and of course the American Cancer Society box was cleaned out again. As if I couldn't lose any more respect for him, he even removed his shoes and wallet. My disgust for him was overwhelming. Vile cockroach!

The grave didn't get a tombstone. They were too cheap to pay for one. The tablet marker that sets in the ground was $225 and they wouldn't spend it. They had no problem cleaning out his wallet and account but not pay for a marker with his last few dollars made me sick. If there ever was a reason to support preplanning your own funeral, this is it.

* * *

Jerry stopped bathing shortly after that, he stunk. It was disgusting to be around him and he kept coming over to visit. He was like a stray. Feed it once and it keeps coming back or it stays. He wore the same dumpy jeans and dirty t-shirts that you find in the underwear section at the department store. Not to be worn in public. If it wasn't that, it was dirty jogging pants. All of his clothes had stains. He had no washer and was too lazy to go to the laundry mat because it was too far. It was 6 blocks. Exercise would do him some good. Walk some of that fat off of his ass.

"Do you think I can do my laundry here?" he asked Mom.

"Use the laundry mat. We are not together and you need to do things for yourself," she replied.

"It's too far and I don't have a car," he whined.

"You would have one if you paid your bills and kept a job," she shot back.

"Are you going to keep throwing that in my face?" he snarled.

"Have you learned from it?" Mom fired back in a split second as if she was waiting for that snarly remark.

"Everyone is against me. You all are too," he whined and bitched.

"You brought that on yourself. You are a prick to everyone. You reap what you sow, in your case it's shit because that s what you smell like," Mom said in a matter of a fact tone. I was smirking.

"I can help both of you right now," I said. I had picked up a can of Lysol. "Look it kills 99.9% of viruses and bacteria." I sprayed him with the can. I was shocked he stood there and let me. I was impressed. I sprayed him from head to toe and front to back.

"Justin, you are a smart ass but if it helps..."

"You just had to be the .1%, didn't you? " I scoffed at him sarcastically cutting him off in mid speech. Mom started howling with laughter. She was turning red and nearly buckling over. I joined her. You shouldn't laugh at your own jokes but this was too funny. He stormed off out of our house. Mom and I were still laughing. Kelly missed a good one, she was still hanging out with Welcome Wagon.

CHAPTER 17

I had my driver's license and was going to take the car to visit a friend. It was old and had the crank windows but it worked. Jerry came running out of the his apartment towards the car. I had the window down and was reversing out of the driveway.

"Where the fuck do you think you're going?" he asked. I applied the brake and stooped. I put the car in park.

"None of your business. It isn't your car and I sure as hell don't need your permission to drive it," I snapped back.

"You're going to that little cunt Michelle's aren't you?" he demanded.

"Yeah, I am. What the fuck are you going to do about it?" I taunted.

He reached into the window for the keys to try to turn off the ignition. Without thinking I locked the door and cranked the window as fast as I could until his arm was now pinched in between the glass and the door frame while I swatted his hand away from the ignition. I smiled at him and put the car in reverse and gunned the engine. I let go of the window crank and he was able to get his arm free before I could drag him down the gravel driveway. Goddamnit! So close. I slammed on the brakes and put it in drive. I glared at him again and gunned the engine and steered right it where he was standing. The lucky waste of space ran back into the house before I could reach him.

That dung pile would have been fun to drag down the driveway. I would have put in drive and drove over him a couple of times. Then the fun part of taking a tire iron and smashing him in the head. I am sure Mom or one of the neighbors would have helped me stuff him in the trunk. I'd be a hero. Mom and Kelly wouldn't roll on me. The guy is such as prick, I don't think anyone would.

I was then going to take him to Michelle's and have her come with me to the place of disposal. The swamp, an orchard or some other remote place and bury him below the critter line. That is the depth that most animals will dig to find food and unearth things. It is usually 3 feet or less. If you go deeper than that, you are safe from that any way. With only one cop in town and nobody to really file a missing persons report, it was perfect and the ass-hat ruined it.

I always cleaned Mom's car so that wouldn't be out of the ordinary. Bleach for the blood stained tire iron and no problem. Burn the carpet liner from the trunk, it was old and it may have gotten wrecked over the years anyway. Get an newer one from the scrap yard and good as new. Since he didn't own much, it could have been taken in one load to the dump and he would have been merely a bad memory. But no, the son of a bitch had to go and ruin it. Wow, that was psycho. Understandable to vent but psycho.

* * *

A few day late, after the smoke cleared so to speak. I decided to do some more evil. That meant playing nice. It sickened me. I ended up apologizing to him for the driveway incident. I was sorry it didn't work out the way I planned. But nonetheless I was sorry. He was receptive or scared to death of what I was plotting next.

I was going out with friends a few nights later and Mom was soaking in the bath tub. I needed a shower. The filthy pig had one and I needed it if I was going out. He came over right on cue since it was close to dinner time and he was always looking for a free meal. I was pacing.

"Justin, why are you pacing?" he asked.

"I am supposed to meet some friends and go to the movies but Mom is in the tub and I need a shower, "I whined. I was putting it on thick.

"Go use mine. Have fun," he suggested. I jumped at the chance.

"Thank you. I really appreciate that," I said before grabbing a towel and new change of clothes and running to his apartment.

I got undressed and turned on the hot water. I stared at the vanity and his toothbrush was in my vision filed and I couldn't stop looking at it. I shut the water off. I sat on the toilet and squashed one out. It was nasty and it stunk. It was the type of shit that still had lasting effect on your asshole. No matter how much you wipe, it had the smear factor. I could feel it on the inside of my ass cheeks. Not today. I flushed and didn't wipe. I had something better. I could only think of his lies, the yelling, the bullying and the belittling remarks as well as his Nazi, fascist, dictatorship style rules I had to put up with for the last 3 years. It was a Reach toothbrush and it was designed for the hard to reach areas.

I slid the shower door open, turned on the water and reached for the toothbrush. I eased it down my crack and went for the sphincter or my asshole if you will. I gave it a gentle circular motion. I was thinking of those instructions from the dentist to make sure to scrub the area well. A few small chunks fell to the tub floor with their leaching brown into the water while they broke apart and rinsed down the drain. Back and forth, back and forth but not too hard. You never want to cause bleeding. Another small drop of watching brown water go clear. Circular motion is best. I raised a leg on to the lip of the tub. Gentle circular motion to make sure the area is well scrubbed. I pulled my knee into my chest to widen the opening and gave it a good scrub. A couple of rinses later and I made sure the water was clear between the final scrubbings. I rinsed the toothbrush under the shower head and I put it back on the rack. Good as new. Nice and tasty for him.

I had to put up with his shit over the years and now he can have a taste of mine. Hopefully a good mouthful of it too. Please let him be a molar man and start at the back. Flood that mouth full of flavor. If he doesn't like it, he can kiss my ass. I assure you it was minty fresh now. Pucker up.

* * *

A couple of nights later Mom had a bit too much to drink and Jerry was over for a social call or in his case a drop in problem. The free loading bastard had no clue when his welcome was wore out. Clearly. I looked over at Mom and she was sitting on his lap straddling him. Clothes on, you filthy minded freak. Gross.

Anyway, she had him by the throat with her left hand and was staring him right in the face only inches away.

"Do you remember when you said you would be my best friend or my worst enemy?!" she growled and hissed.

"Yes," he answered sheepishly.

"Well I fucking hate you!!!" she screamed digging her nails into his cheeks and ripping them downwards. There was blood. It was awesome to watch. That abusive waste of skin was bleeding. I thought about all the times he yelled, swore and smacked us around. Yeah, I left that out but with everything else I figured you would assume there was physical abuse as well. It was nice to see him bleed. There were 5 bloody trails on each cheek where she dug her nails into his face. That is going scar. Perfect. Everyone needs a reminder or a memento.

"Oww! I'm bleeding," he whined.

"Well yes you are! It looks good on you too! After everything you put us through I should just kill you!" growled Mom. Damn straight. I would help her cut him up into little pieces and put him out in the trash.

Slap! Mom bitch slapped him across the face and had her index finger poised over his left eye. I was so hoping she was going to ram it in his eye socket. Oh, ok. I have hatred issues and anger issues too. This is well deserved. He looked over at me as if I was supposed to help him. Are you kidding me?! The only way I would help him is if he were drowning, I would toss him a cinder block and help him drown. If he were on fire I would get the gasoline and then maybe some marshmallows or hot dogs.

"Don't look to me for help. The only thing I will do is grab the salt or the lemon juice for those nice cuts you have on your face. I will even give you a choice of which one," I scoffed at him in my most mocking tone as I made my way over to the kitchen. I even did it with a most menacing smile. I reached into the cupboard for the salt and then to the refrigerator for the lemon juice. He couldn't take us both. I was 16 now and had my own demons to help with the cause.

"So what's t going to be? A?" I asked in my taunting voice raising the salt with my left hand and giving it a shake. "Or B?" raising my right hand holding up the lemon juice. I smiled again. "Or maybe you want both and a little vinegar and baking soda to go with it for the bubbly effect?" I taunted with a chuckle. "I don't give a rat's ass, I just want to hear you fucking scream!" I shouted with my eyes narrowing o his bleeding face with a sinister sneer across mine. I advanced on him with the salt and lemon juice.

"Justin!" shouted Mom. I stopped dead in my tracks and glared at him. "I've got this, go to one of your friends places. I'll be fine. We are going to spend some quality time together, aren't we?" she hissed turning her head towards him and taunting him. She now had him by the throat with her lift hand again. "As you can see, we all hate you and wish you were dead. Should I let him rub the salt and lemon juice in those cuts? I want to hear you scream too."

I found out a couple of days earlier he punched her in the mouth downtown on the sidewalk. Someone called the cops on him and Mom didn't press charges. She obviously had something special planned and this was it. She was going to make him hurt. Good. He deserves everything he gets. I wondered if he even noticed I used his toothbrush to clean my asshole. Who cares? I did as I was told and went out with friends. Let Mom have some fun.

* * *

Within a couple of days after Mom's fight with him, he was leaving for the east coast. Maine, I think. Then again, I really don't care. One way tickets are always best. It meant he wasn't coming back. If only he would let me help him pack because I really would have enjoyed it. Garbage bags are perfect for getting rid of useless crap you don't want. Unfortunately they don't make them for 6' piles of shit. Before he left, he pulled me aside on my way to the bus stop.

"Justin, do you have a minute?" he asked. I stopped.

"Sure, "I responded.

"You don't like me very much do you?" he asked. I was taken back for a second. what a keen observation. I am shocked. Whatever gave him the first clue?

"Let me put it this way for you. I wouldn't let you eat my shit if you were starving. Does that sum it up for you? Or how about this one? The next time I want to see you is in a casket" I shot back at him with voice dripping in sarcasm and contempt.

"Wow. I guess that does it," he answered in shock.

"Good, Is there anything else you want to know?" I asked sarcastically.

"Just wondering why you would say something like that," he asked. Wow, talk about a stupid quiff.

"Really?! You don't know?! Let me shed some light on the subject. You are a liar. You made our lives an absolute hell. You're a bully and a useless waste of space. The fact is my dad kicked your ass years ago and you took it out on us for the last 3 years. You have to pick on women and kids. Big man. You didn't deliver on a single thing! I especially loved the dinner for picking corn the most. The sooner you are gone, the better. I hope the train derails and you are the only casualty. Let me put it this way, the only way I want to see you again is in a fucking casket!" I couldn't help it. Was he really this stupid? I glared at him and put my hand up to his face and marched to the bus stop. Dumb ass! Shut up and don't put that image in my head!

He left while I was at school. It was the best day of my life in quite some time. To be finally rid of a lying, controlling, blood sucking leach, freeloading, abusive, baby-talking, obnoxious oblivious tyrant. Hallelujah!! People were looking at me. I was too happy. Even that pathetic slut couldn't bring me down. Woo Who!!!

Ironically I met with the board psychiatrist that day and I was actually glad to talk with him and just vented everything I went through with that twat. He keep t looking at me like I had a stunt double or evil twin. I was talkative and cooperative. This time I could share and release pent up aggression and the joy as well as the relief I was feeling.

"Wow," he said. "You finally opened up. I am glad. It took a while. I am glad you feel better."

"Thanks, I can't wait to get home and go through whatever he left behind. I know there's more lies buried in there. I know I will find something to prove it all. Too many lies and too many questions. Even his own mother hated him. Obviously. I can't even begin to tell you my disgust over the way his uncle's funeral was handled," I replied.

"You have been through a lot. They just want to make sure you aren't a risk to yourself or anyone else," he assured me.

"These session aren't out of concern. We already know that. It's condescending and demeaning," I shot back.

"Yes. However, I have my own concerns.." he started.

"As long as they aren't shared with Lynch, I will share. I don't give a rat's ass what that useless quiff thinks and I don't want him knowing my business. If he were so concerned, I wouldn't be here, right?" I asked. He nodded.

I went on to tell about the fight and the salt and lemon juice. I did leave out the car incident and the thoughts I had at the time. That would be something he would report and then I would be in therapy for the rest of my life. No thanks. I kept the talk small from then on and concentrated on my relief and happiness. It's always best to be happy and positive with those people. However, if you really need help, get it. If you aren't comfortable with one, get another. We all need it sometimes even if it is to vent.

* * *

When I got home, he was truly gone. Another celebratory meal coming my way. Mom was all smiles. Something I haven't seen in a while. I couldn't wait to go through his apartment and see what lies I could expose. I wouldn't be disappointed.

In the bedroom, there was his mattress on the floor with no blankets and a black greasy spot on the wall where he put his head at night. Gross!. The blankets were ours but they were getting tossed in the trash. I was thinking there bed bugs and some other virus or parasites that multiplied in filth. Luckily they were old and ready for the dump any way. At least Mom saw that coming and didn't give him the good ones.

I looked in the closet to find a few old jackets that were going straight to the trash as well. First I was checking them for money. My expectations were low on that front but I had to check anyway. Nothing. Just as I suspected. There was a pile of paperback novels on the floor and I couldn't help but notice that some of the pages were dog eared and there were little slips of paper sticking out them like I do with some textbooks when I was studying for an exam.

The first one "The secrets of the Ninja." I picked it up and opened to the first dog eared page. He took notes! There were hand written phrases on Never Be Seen and other notes on covert operations of the ancient Japanese sect. I was sure this was going to be another one of his stories of actually being trained by them. I could hear it now. Like they would waste their time on a fat, lazy slob , mouthpiece like him.

The next one was of course on the Vietnam War and with no surprise, I found notes and multiple dog eared pages and the after reading some of them, it was a well rehearsed script. Absurd and unbelievable in its entirety. He was taking claims for someone else's valor. A disgrace to the military and everyone who fought in it. Way to go Rambo. He deserves a firing squad. Forget about putting any blanks in the rifles. Make them all live rounds and give them multiple rounds as well. Slash him with a samurai for insulting the Japanese as well. I was disgusted and ran over to show Mom.

"Mom, Look what I found. The source of his lies," I reported as I showed her the novels I found. I had the Ninja book open. She looked at the page and rolled her eyes.

"I'm not surprised. Just get rid of those and toss out everything else as well. The less I see to remind me of him the better. Just put everything in the garbage and the recycle unless it's ours. Burn the blankets is you must." There was no emotion in her speech. It was as if she didn't care and the sooner he was a memory altogether, the better.

I ran back over without a word and carried out the clean up. The clothes went in the garbage, the books were recycled and the blankets were burned. I had to. It was the only true way to purge filth and disease. Cleansed by fire. I sprayed the entire apartment down with Lysol. I sprayed every surface until I nearly choked on the fumes. In the bathroom, was his Reach toothbrush. The same one I cleaned my asshole with. I chuckled and then tossed it in the trash. There was one order of business to attend to and that was the greasy spot on the wall. I am sorry but that was for the landlord to do. Ugh. Disgusting. Did you really think I was going to get out the degreaser and scrub it? Better yet, are you nuts?

CHAPTER 18

• • • • • • ● • • • • • •

We were enjoying the "No more Jerry" days. It really is amazing how good getting rid of someone can make you feel. The proverb of "People always bring joy to your life, some when they stay and others when they leave" rings true. We went out for a celebratory meal. Free at last. The joy of never seeing his face again was overwhelming. I was all smiles. The only thing that would have made it better was if he were dead. Oh I know. It's bad. I would be a damned shame, wouldn't it? The world would be rid of another abusive prick. Oh what a sad day that would be.

It was towards the end of the school year and I have had just about enough of the psychiatric evaluations and Jen's crap. Luckily for me we started talking again and I was pretending to have changed to her liking and she was starting to tell me her personal things. They tell you to keep your friends close and enemies closer. Her son's father was retired and they met after a few drinks. One thing led to another and here he is. Wow. Can you say "daddy issues"? And they say I'm screwed up?

I waited until the opportunity to let the bitch have it and I didn't have to wait long. It was the last day of school and she was in my marketing class. Things were going fine until it came down to the usual summer plans conversation. There were lots of travel and beach comments.

"I am going to find a part time job and maybe go camping." I responded. Today, I hate the idea. What was I thinking? Camping isn't happening unless there is a camper or cabin involved. My idea of "roughing it" is Motel 6 or Super 8. The only way I will ever pitch a tent is in my pants.

"Good luck with that," piped up Jen in her usual judgmental, snotty tone.

"And what are your plans? Sleeping with the rest of the rest of the town or have you already done that?" I shot back. It was on now.

"You are broke ass poor and nobody will hire an asshole like you," fired back Jen. This got the class giving out "oohs".

"Says the pathetic slut on welfare with daddy issues. That's why you fuck the retired, older men or is that a grandpa fetish? Do you missing sitting on his lap?" I said returning fire with my voice dripping in malice and sarcasm. There were "ouch' and "ow" comments. To Hell with being on my best behavior! I wasn't coming back to this place and now the bitch must die. The gloves are off!

"Fuck you!" she shouted back. The look on her face was intense and the vein in her temple was starting to bulge.

"I am too young for you. I don't require a walker. Besides, it would be like throwing a hot dog down the hallway. The hallway is tighter. Ghetto Whore!" I scoffed at her. I was on a roll. I looked over at her and her jaw was dropped. Speechless. Awesome. This of course elicited laughter.

"Your baby's daddy is retired. I am actually surprised you got more than sawdust out of that old piece of wood. Tell me, did he put his teeth in the glass by the bed? " I hissed. The class was laughing out loud now.

"Justin, you're a fucking jerk!" yelled Jen. I was really getting to her now. Stupid bitch wants to try and humiliate me? She is going down.

"And you're a filthy slut. A white trash ghetto whore. Seriously, that pussy of yours has been passed around more than the common cold." The guys were laughing hysterically at her. Some were buckled over and the teacher was even laughing at her. I couldn't help it. I was pissed right off. This was too easy. "By the way Jen, those shorts have turned me off cottage cheese for life. You are supposed to let yourself go after you get married, not before. No wonder you are reduced to sleeping with the elderly. Tell me how are you going to get to pay for your son's college tuition or are you going to wait for the estate sale?" This erupted even more laughter.

"You can lick my pussy!" screamed Jen.

"If I wanted all-you-can-eat crabs with cheese dip, I would go to the crab shack." I shot back. The class was dying from laughter and a few "ewww's" were mixed in with it. Jen made a move from her desk like she wanted to fight. I mimicked her fighting stance and glared at her. "Throw a punch bitch. I fucking dare you . Hit me, then I can hit you. I will slap you around like the filthy, white trash whore that you are," I sneered. Jen was red in the face and almost in tears. I had my right hand in a fist cocked near my chest to the side and ready to go. My piercing, evil stare was ripping right through her. She cracked like an egg and started bawling and left the room. "Don't go away mad..." I taunted. The room was silent. "Was it something I said?" I asked sarcastically.

"You did good. it was about time someone put that bitch in her place. That was impressive." complimented one guy who I hardly spoke to all year. Several others nodded in agreement.

"Yeah but it should never have happened. I really don't like getting like that. It's not cool. It's mean." I responded. I wasn't very proud of myself as it was overkill.

"She deserved it," he replied.

"Yes, she did and hopefully she will think twice before insulting someone else for no reason. Big tough bawl baby." I scoffed.

"If I only knew you were this cool..." he started but I cut him off.

"Well, you should have go to know me. I tried to be nice and was looking for friends. I found 3 and only one was worth a damn. That slut was supposedly one of them. One of my old neighbors is here and she said 'Hi" to me and that was about it. I never saw her again." I explained.

"If you come back next year, it will be better for you," he said with sincerity.

"No it won't. I am not coming back here. I have had enough. I have been subjected to enough and I really can't take any more. It took me verbally and publicly slam someone to get anyone to talk to me. It doesn't matter if she deserved it or not. I was sent here for a prank and subjected to weekly psychiatric visits and a short leash because of it. I took the blame and found out my so-called friends were done with me. I got it. I can't do this anymore. If I come back next year, I will get more of the same. No thanks." I needed to clean up my image so I decided to enroll in the Catholic school system. I stayed friends with Allen over the years and we still remain friends to this day.

* * *

The Catholic school contacted my last school and it was determined I had problems getting along with my peers and since it was my last year and I was turning over a new leaf, they let me in under conditions where if I was to be an issue or a problem I would voluntarily withdrawal from school. The problem I had with getting along with others is the fact I stood up for myself and I wasn't going to be intimidated, pushed around or dumped on by anyone. The only persons who should take shit run mushroom farms. They take it by the truck load.

It was a different scene for me for sure. I had a few friends who went to this school so it made life easier and it was back in Palmer and of course I had to stay out of trouble too. Having friends that are quiet and keep to themselves is the way to go.

I was having issues with faith, religion as well so I stopped going to church altogether. I figured I was having enough religion in the Catholic schools. This confused me even more. I never understood what purgatory was and it came up in a class subject.

"What is purgatory?" I asked.

"A place where you go for purification after judgment before you are allowed to enter Heaven," answered one female student.

"I never saw it in the bible so I would like to read up on it," I answered.

"You will have to find it yourself. It's in there, you just have to look," she replied. I found this to be very condescending and rude. If you know where something is that someone is asking for, show them or at least point them in the right direction. I believe she was being a total bitch about it since I have not been able to find the reference at all. I also feel she didn't know either and was trying to make me look stupid. It backfired.

She reminds me of those people who like to tell you took it out of context. Out of context is when you don't understand what you just read or what you were told. Usually by reading the proceeding sentences as wells the following sentence will clarify the sentence in question.

Another problem is the misuse of words when we don't really know the definition but use it anyway. My favorite example of this is when someone calls a child "a little bugger". The true definition of bugger is one who practices sodomy. An ass fucker in layman's terms. Point that out to the parent and watch the look of horror. It's quite funny.

Another definition always misused is "humbug". Most believe it is a word that is used at Christmas to show hatred for the season. It really means a person or item that deceives, dishonest, false, a hoax. It also means nonsense or in layman's terms Bullshit.

Now for out of context. I think it's crap and words have meanings. if you know the right meanings out of context doesn't apply. It is a copout to say you misunderstood. Ezekiel 23: 19-21 New International Version states: "[19] Yet she became more and more promiscuous as she recalled the days of her youth, when she was a prostitute in Egypt. [20] There she lusted after her lovers, whose genitals were like those of donkeys and whose emission was like that of horses. [21] So you longed for the lewdness of your youth, when in Egypt your bosom was caressed and your young breasts fondled."

Out of context is pure rubbish. It means she likes her men with big dicks that shoot large amounts of cum. If you got the same interpretation of that, you are right on the money. In this case, it's the money shot.

What I found most interesting about this passage is the fact they won't use the word in penis in the translations. It is called a member, genitals or flesh. P-E-N-I-S penis. The proper term for the male genitals. A great big, fully erect, vein laced, throbbing penis. Phallus is the proper term to an erect penis. Phallic symbols such as the Washington monument seems to resemble an erect penis. Fellatio is the act of sucking a phallus. A blow job, sucking off, or giving head or fellatio.

Rather than using semen, it is referred to as issue. S-E-M-E-N semen or ejaculate is the proper terminology. A thick, creamy yogurt like substance that comes from the penis during orgasm. Horses shoot large loads whereas a human will shoot around a teaspoon per ejaculation on average. I often wonder the comparison. Bestiality or also known as sex with animals?

I always had the issue as to why people fight over religion so much. If the bible were actually written by an all-knowing, all-powerful god, don't you think he/she would have seen this issue arising and set us straight right from the get-go? Let's face it we don't fight and argue over the encyclopedias and the dictionary because we know it's true. We only add to them as words become modernized such as "selfie" or "twerk". Just a couple points to ponder.

* * *

I was hanging around Josh and a few others who all had girlfriends. I was tired of being lonely and I made the mistake of mentioning I would even settle for a boyfriend. Big mistake. I might as well have pissed in the wine challis, take a steaming shit on the alter and wiped my ass with its tablecloth. A few days later I got a letter from the church on its official stationary.

Dear Justin Williamson

We 're writing you to inform you that we have become aware of your recent behavior. It is extremely alarming and not becoming of a Christian. We understand that young men such as yourself go through many trials and tribulations. We understand the presence of peer pressure in schools, however being a member of this church, we expect you to behave more responsibly.

It has been brought to our attention that
you have been experiencing some homosexual
relations and these are an abomination to the
Lord as stated in Leviticus 20:13. "If a man also
lie with mankind, as he lieth with a woman, both
of them have committed an abomination: they
shall surely be put to death; their blood shall be
upon them."

Therefore this leaves us no choice but to
suspend your membership until your behavior
improves. For the sake of your salvation, I would
do it soon.

Sincerely
Derry Baptist Church

My belief in God was nearly diminished at this time. This letter
was the icing on the cake. They couldn't say it to my face and took the
coward's way out. A goddamn letter accusing me of being the faggot
version of the Whore of Babylon. It's funny that Leviticus 20:13 is
always the go to. Forget the fact of Josh's Disrespect of his parents on
the CD issue or freaking out when his stereo was smashed. Leviticus
20:9 " For every one that curseth his father or his mother shall be
surely put to death: he hath cursed his father or his mother; his blood
shall be upon him." let us not forget how many people sleep around
and extra marital affairs where the next verse clearly states. " And the
man that committeth adultery with another man's wife, even he that
committeth adultery with his neighbor's wife, the adulterer and the
adulteress shall surely be put to death." Get fucked! Here's the truth:
MY first heterosexual sexual experience was at 19 years old and my
first gay experience was at 22.

Shorty after this letter, I had to leave that place for good. I sat in
the teen Sunday School room and stewed. I looked around the room
and tried to read their faces. It was clear to me I wasn't very welcome.
I heard them talking an as soon as I got close to the door and as soon
as walked in, it went quiet. I am sure I was the subject of discussion.

177

"Ok today we will be discussing our next trip to Kentucky." started Josh. Keep in mind Kentucky is about 10 hours away. This was a full weekend. Thursday night to Monday.

"I am sorry but these trips are too expensive and it is almost as if it is done on purpose to keep some people from going," I stated.

"I am sorry you feel this way," replied Josh.. What they really mean is I am sorry it took you this long to figure it out. Really?! You ran your mouth to daddy I was a promiscuous homosexual. You learn who your friends are. Come to think of it I should have saw this coming. Here he is a friend. At school it was like pulling teeth to get a word out of him let alone 30 seconds of his time. At school I was an embarrassment. Typical behavior. How many times I saw it and let it go as he was busy and doing other things. It is a friendship of convenience. No one else around so it was like doing a good deed. Condescending and fake! Looking back, there were lots of people like that.

"Well I do and I don't think I can be part of this anymore. I have things I need to work on and this isn't helping. I definitely don't think this has any answers for me. So see you later. Enjoy your trip" I said as I got up from my chair and walked towards the door.

I took one last look at everyone in the room. Their faces were emotionless and you could have heard a pin drop. Were they shocked or were they relieved and hopeful I meant it? I opened the door, walked out and gently closed it behind me. I stood by the door and waited a second and listened to the dead silence on the other side. I made my way to the old wooden stairs and walked out the door. I turned around and took one last look and waited a minute. Nobody was coming out after me. Confirmed. I wasn't welcome and they were glad to get rid of me. It's funny how when your gut tells you something it's always right. If you feel a certain way, you can bet your ass it is the case. Hind sight is always 20/20. They were not my friends.

Unfortunately Mom learned the same way from a bible class a few weeks later. She felt she wasn't really a part of it and left as well. Once again nobody followed. We always learn who our friends are when the chips are down. It's hard to tell who is a two-faced prick until it is too late. I have gotten better at it.

It's also funny that after going to a Catholic school and learning about things like purgatory that conveniently aren't in the bible or if they were nobody had the decency to show me. I was having so many issues with the fact that my experiences have been condescending and having the feeling of alienation from those who I thought were my friends. The friends that leave without saying goodbye.

I wasn't around for all the carnage at the church and it made me believe I made the right decision in quitting. It also seemed that anybody we prayed for either died or didn't get better. I didn't appreciate the judgment or the fact that no matter how much prayer we did, things never got better. I am still here getting disrespected and hating every minute of it. My observations right now are that prayer was about as useless as it gets. I would get the same results from wishing on a star or a visit from Santa Clause.

It's funny how Christ is the last thing to go. We learn that Santa Clause, the Easter Bunny, the Tooth Fairy are all figments of the imagination at a younger age and hang onto a deity. We hang onto that so tight as if it were the last thing to hang onto. The doubts of the truth in the whole scheme of things and the promise of a glorious afterlife. We are told he loves us all very much and we see the inequality of life where some are blessed with a loving family while the rest of us have to bear the brunt of alcoholism, addiction, abuse, neglect, starvation, and poverty.

We are told to pray and it will get better. At this point in my life I have to toss the towel in and say "Bullshit" After having go through this with dear old dad who only cares about himself. The "I love you" I have been told are nothing but lies. Each and every one of them. No cards or calls for birthdays or Christmas from anyone. I might as well not even exist. Pray. "I Love you." Piss off! Kiss my ass!

Those words are so empty and meaningless lies. We struggle every goddamned day to pay for the basics and no matter what we can't catch a break. Mom gets a decent job and it's snatched from us like pulling a rug out from under us. Delivering the ad mail was great but there was an issue with the union or management and it was no longer outsourced. Gone in a second. Having that useless loser Jerry around, the two-faced friends I have had, the hypocrites at church and family that doesn't give a rat's ass whether I live or die or any of the other stuff I've been through so far. What a crock! "Pray and it will get better" my aching ass. Suck my ass! Jesus Christ!

Oh yes, pray for the poor, the starving, and the sick just to watch them suffer and die in the end. The ones that do make it, it's a miracle. My ass. It's a placebo. The doctors never get the credit for helping them, it's divine intervention. And I am Mickey Mouse.

My personal favorite is "God's punishing you." For what? What the Hell did I do? What the Hell did that starving child do in Africa that will die next week? What did that small child that gets beaten every time he makes a sound do to get parents like that? Punishment for being born into those situations all across the world. "God loves us all the same." Really?! You really believe this crap? You're a judgmental twat!

I had enough. There will be no more religion for me ever again. I really don't know why I was so upset. It's not like the signs weren't there and the whole thing was an exercise in futility. I don't even think I was this upset over Santa Clause or any of the other mythological characters. In fact, I will bet I wasn't. I was upset this time because it was the last one and now there was nothing left. If I wanted anything I was going to have to do it for myself and not rely on nonsense. I was more angry about the time I wasted believing the lies. Let's face it, from my point of view, it was. I had nothing to convince me otherwise.

This was also around the same time the church congregating pretty much imploded. Pastor McKay and Pastor Tim left to broaden their horizons if you will. Of course I never got a phone call from Josh or even a visit at the restaurant. They had a huge fight and the congregation was split. The organist was asked to leave because of a divorce and she had a boyfriend afterwards. They terminated the secretary's employment and spread rumors about her stealing money.

She was an honest woman who put in extra time and hours to help out anyone who needed her. I have seen her pick up found money and put it in the donation box. The rumors were completely made up as usual. I would think that people who are supposed to be your friends would support you when you are going through a rather difficult time and be grateful for years of service in both cases. Both were really nice and didn't deserve to be treated in such a despicable manner. I guess conditions apply. Perhaps the word "friend" was taken out of context?

In Catholic School, two of the girls I didn't get along with was on the yearbook committee and they deliberately left my photo out of the yearbook and graduating class poster that goes with the diploma. They thought they were God's gift to the world. Stuck up and rude. It's funny now that one is an accountant and a simple $120 software application can pretty much replace her. As for the other, I really don't care what she does.

* * *

Kelly found a boy friend and they moved in together. This was after I found out she was pregnant. Teen pregnancies happen and she should have known Mom and I would have been supportive. It's like anything else when life throws a curveball your way, it's how you react. I will admit it was a challenge but like any relationship with another person, you will have your ups, downs and challenges. As long as all parties can work at it, it's never that bad. When you reach impasse or show the other person no regard for their feelings it becomes personal, hurtful and bad blood is inevitable. Just ask dad.

* * *

Within a couple of months (6) of my breakdown, I was working when I ran into Cindy Smith when I was getting out of my car to go to work. She looked at me and you could tell she had something on her mind.

"Justin, do you have a minute?" she asked as she approached my car.

"Sure. What's up?" I asked.

"I haven't seen you in church for a while. Is everything ok?" she asked.

"I haven't been there in over six months and you are the first person to notice. It's really sad isn't it? The fact is, I have been having issues with the whole thing and no matter what we do, nothing gets better. I have been taking a break. A nice long one so I can sort things out," I explained.

"Don't take too long. You're life is going to Hell and you need to find your way back," she said with sincerity and concern in her voice. I burst out laughing. I couldn't help it.

"Really? My life is going to Hell? I hate to inform you it's been Hell for the longest time. It's been Hell going to church and it's been Hell without it. I have to thank you though. You clarified everything for me with that statement alone. I am never going back. It makes no difference whatsoever. Damned if you do, damned if you don't. Isn't that right?" I scoffed.

"That's not what I meant..." she started to say.

"Too late. That was the icing on the cake for me. Do me a favor and never bring up God, Jesus or anything else that has to do with religion again. I don't want to hear it. I am going to burn my bible tonight. It's all lies. Thank you for clearing that up with me," I said with utmost sincerity.

"Why are you going to do that?" she asked in shock.

"The church taught me that. Burn what poisons the mind. They wanted me to burn my music and movies so I shall burn that instead," I said flashing a malicious smile across my face.

"I'm leaving. Good day, Justin," she said before she walked away from me. She was hurt by my words but I didn't care. I was insulted by hers but also glad she confirmed everything I was feeling at the same time. Amazing how many people still live life thinking they can judge, condescend and mistreat people in this life based on your beliefs to be rewarded in an afterlife. It makes perfect sense. Really?!

That night after work, I did carry out my cleansing. I grabbed some logs and matches along with the bible and set the logs in a pyramid in an upright position. I tore the cover off and placed it at the base. I began ripping out more pages and crumpling them as I went to fill in the cavity left at the base of the logs. I lit the entire book of matches from a local restaurant on fire and tossed it in at the base. The paper caught immediately and it was a full bonfire in no time.

I looked down at my hands to what remained of the book and shredded it some more. I kept ripping and tossing it in the fire until I was left with a few pages and the back cover. I tossed it in and watched it burn the whole time thinking of the previous conversation on how my life as going to Hell. I laughed. What a crock. I stayed with my fire until it was a pile of glowing embers and ash. At this time, I grabbed the hose and put it out. It was time to start living for me and stop trying to be what others wanted me to be. No one was going to run my life any more but me.

CHAPTER 19

B etween going to school out of town and working at the restaurant
and going to school, I pretty much had no life. If I wanted
anything, I had to get tit myself. Money was tight. I was hanging
around some local teens and there was one in particular that still
stands out. Her name was Dianne. She had hair that looked like it
never saw a brush. It was all over the place and she didn't care. She
wore ripped jeans all the time and baggy t-shirts. A pure tomboy. I
liked her as a friend but her attitude really sucked. She had no self
esteem and she seemed cool with it. The more I think about it, the
was something amiss.

Your typical conversation went kind of like the following:

"Hi Dianne"

"Hi," usually had a 'what the Hell do you want' underlying to
it. She was stone cold. Her defenses always seemed to be up and had
a mental wall.

"How you doing today?"

"Like you fucking care, don't ask." She always had tone with it.
A sense of 'Piss off."

"Well I do, otherwise I wouldn't ask."

"Well you know how I am, I was shitty the last time we talked
and shitty again this time and I will be shitty the next time too."

"What's wrong?"

"Nothing, I am perfectly fucking happy. Can't you see me
dancing with joy?" Her voice was dripping with sarcasm and a hint
of malice.

"Ok then, good to know." She was a buzz kill. She wasn't fine.
Not by any stretch of the imagination. It was like she wanted to reach

out but was afraid to let any emotions show whatsoever. I knew the feeling to be miserable inside and it seemed like there wasn't a person in the world who gave a rat's ass. I think she needed help but it wasn't going to come easy, not while she kept rejecting it. Then again she was probably your typical teenager with a bad attitude and full of angst. Who knew? It's not like she was letting anyone in any time soon.

* * *

It was a couple of months of that behavior when it started to make sense. A local boy who drove an old black station wagon. It was flat black and he obviously spray painted it himself. Globs of paint from where he held the can too close. There were waves in the paint blotch. It was obvious he held the spray paint there too long. His name was Jason. He wore ripped jeans, had a braided belt that was semi tied with the excess hanging down just after his buckle. He waved and started walking over to us. Dianne scowled.

"Hi Justin, What are you doing hanging around with this loser? It's bad for your reputation. Trash will drag you down." he said so calmly with sneaking in a sneer at Dianne. "Trash like this," he sneered and pushed her backwards knocking her on her ass.

"What the Hell?" I barked.

"What?! This is how you treat trash. Look at her. On her back like the filthy, dyke slut she is." He scoffed looking at her with total contempt. Hccckkkkk He cleared his throat and spit a thick wad of phlegm laced spit right in her face.

Dianne jumped up and slapped him right across her face. Smack!! There was impact and you could hear the sting. She was so angry she was shaking and crying with his spit still running down her cheek.

"You stupid, filthy cunt!" he screamed. He cocked his arm back and made a fist and was about to punch her when another guy, Bob grabbed his arm and put him in a full Nelson.

"We don't punch girls! It's bad enough you pushed her and spit in her face. What the Hell did she ever do to you?!" screamed Bob.

185

"Nothing. I hate trash!" Jason was yelling and turning red. The veins were bulging in his temples. He glared at her. He despised her with every ounce of his being. Bob let him go.

"If you can't be civilized, leave. And I don't ever want to see that again." Bob calmly told Jason.

"You seriously need to stop, Jason and you need to stop now." I stated. Jason shrugged it off and got one at glare in at Dianne before he got in his car and left but not without kicking up some gravel with his tires first.

"Thanks. I can take care of myself. I don't need you guys." Shrieked Dianne as she finally wiped the spit off of her face. She stormed off. It turns out Jason had been bullying her for quite some time.

* * *

The next time I saw Dianne, she was more miserable than ever. She was almost in tears. My first thought was Jason was bullying her again. I liked Jason. His bullying was uncalled for. I thought after we talked to him, it was over but deep down I knew it wasn't.

"What's wrong Dianne? Please talk to me." I pleaded.

"Jason and his friends. Don't worry he isn't hitting me. He pushes me and calls me dyke, bitch, and trash like always. I can't take it anymore. I know you are friends with him too. So you'll probably take his side." She started to cry.

"We have told him to stop..."

"It didn't do any good. He is still bothering me," she snapped.

"Is it just him?" I asked.

"No. I hate my life and I just wish it were over." she pouted.

"You don't mean that, do you?" I asked with concern. I couldn't help but think of the asshole I was in my first high school. It wasn't funny. It was mean and hurtful. I mean I did what I was asked to by a so called friend. It was supposed to be a joke. It was mean. I get it now. I mean I really get it. I was sorry.

"I do sometimes. Mom is more concerned about the store and is always there. I get it, it's our livelihood. I wish sometimes she would get a job and sell it. She cares more about the store than me."

"I don't think you mean that. She is trying to build a better life and that is how she's going to do it. She cares that much to make it a success so you don't have to worry. Everyone in town knows her. She is well liked," I stated.

"I know but sometimes I think she forgets I am here. I am hardly home now. One day she'll wake up but I'll be gone," said Dianne. She was calm and emotionless.

"It gets better. I promise." I regret saying that the second it came out of my mouth. It is a cliché and over used.

"When?! When the fuck does it get better, Justin? When?! Answer me!" She was actually yelling at me. What the Hell did I do? I am trying to be supportive here.

"I don't have all the answers, Dianne. You know that. After high school I guess. When we grow up. We have to learn I guess... Sometimes the hard way. Trust me on that one." I explained.

"I have had enough of the hard way. Someone else can deal with the hard way. Like that ass-hat Jason," she stated.

"It would be nice for all the bullies to have things the hard way, wouldn't it?" I asked.

"You're damn right. Ok, I got to go. Nice talking to you as always," she said. She didn't wait for a response and left. Little did I realize, I wouldn't see her again.

* * *

It was about 2 days later I got the news. Dianne killed herself. She got dressed in black with a hoodie and curled up in a ball in the highway in the county. She was hit by a car and killed almost instantly. It was 55 mile per hour zone. Even more bizarre and ironic was the fact it was Jason's car and he was driving it.

I am told he got out of the car to see what he hit and pulled back the hoodie to see Dianne's face and she died right there in front of him. I can't begin to tell you how he felt. Like a sack of shit I am sure. He killed the girl he bullied accidently of course but you know there was guilt in how he treated her. The town felt sorry for him. I delivered free food to his house that someone bought. He wouldn't leave his room. I saw him for a brief second at the delivery and his face as red from crying. He felt awful and he should.

In the wake of the tragedy, Dianne's mother sold the store and left town without saying where she was going. The store never reopened after the funeral. It was quickly sold and she was gone. I can't say I blame her. Jason's family were customers. People talk. I am sure she heard how Jason treated her daughter. I wouldn't be able to face them either. The worst part is a suicide effects so many others. I may be over for the person who decides to end their life but the ripples it leaves are far reaching. You may not think your life matters but it most certainly does. A few months later Jason ended up taking his own life too.

* * *

A few months later towards the end of the school year, tragedy would strike again. The girl at the locker next to me had died in a single car accident while running late to her job at Circle K. Her name was Kristen. She lost control, flipped over in a ditch filled with water and drowned.

Let me tell you what she was like from that couple of minutes I saw her every morning. She was a sweetheart. You could be having a bad morning and she would say something nice to you to try and brighten the morning. Whether it was a friendly" hello" or "it's ok, things will be better later today," or anything nice. She was genuine. Her boyfriend Tom was tall, lean and handsome.

I went to school that morning and found him crying while placing a rose at the base of her locker on the floor. There were already some teddy bears, cards and other flowers stuffed in the ventilation slots. I went over to try and comfort him. I already knew what happened. She cheered me up a few times so it was the least I could do.

"I am so sorry for your loss," I said with the deepest sympathy.

"Thank you, Justin," he said between sobs.

"She was a good person..." I started to say.

"But you hardly knew her." he said and started crying again. I put my hand on his shoulders and tried to comfort him. He shrugged my arm off.

"I knew her for a few moments a day and I could tell she was a really nice girl. She always had nice things to say. She was great to be next to in the morning. She was always smiling and happy. This is what I know and saw," I stated trying to recover from what we both knew. He was right, I hardly knew her.

"I miss her so much...." he said crying even harder now. I looked at him and couldn't help but think of Dianne.

"Are you thinking of hurting yourself?" I flatly asked. I couldn't help it. It just came right out.

"I don't know," he choked out between sobs.

"Don't do it man. She loved you a ton and this is not what she would want for you. Live your life and honor her. Name your first daughter after her. There is no way anyone with half a heart would object. Live your days and die an old man content and warm in your bed. You know that is what she wanted with you," I said sternly with compassion. I didn't want to hear he killed himself or hurt himself. He looked at me and nodded. I think I reached him. The warning bell rang.

"Thanks. You need to get to class," he said in a matter of a fact tone. He stopped crying. I really hope I reached him.

* * *

The next morning people were talking about Tom. I heard his name and rushed over to friends. Yes, it was true. Tom hung himself last night. Goddamnit! I was so pissed off. I was kicking myself. I should have told someone. I didn't. What the Hell was I thinking? I am no therapist. Why was I acting like one? We talked. I tried to comfort him and give him goals. I wanted him to live. I hardly knew him but Jesus Christ, why? 17 years old and gone. What a waste. He was good looking. He had so much potential. This one still haunts me to this day. It is still upsetting. I really tried to help. I really did.

CHAPTER 20

• • • • • • • • ● • • • • • • • •

I was still working at the restaurant and it really is amazing how
many people will try and stiff you on delivery. Not having enough
money and being a few dollars short, or conveniently having exact
change and any other excuse you can come up with. The ruder they
were, the more I made them wait. It reached the point where I didn't
give a damn when they ordered. If a customer that actually tipped
and was decent was after some rude prick that wouldn't tip or tried to
stiff me ordered, they were delivered first. I didn't give a rat's ass. You
went to the bottom of the pile as your level of rudeness warranted.

Don't judge, this is the way it is in the service industry. A known
cheapskate in a restaurant or bar that doesn't tip, waits. Why should
anyone rush over to someone who doesn't appreciate good service?
Good luck with that. Try this experiment: Go to a busy club on the
weekend and pay the bartender exact change on your first order and
see how fast he/ she is on getting to you for your next order. It's busy
and it gets real hard to see who's next at a crowded bar. You showed
that person you don't appreciate their service or that it was worthless.
Enjoy your wait. Don't be surprised if you don't get served at all and
have to rely on someone else. Complain to management. It's busy
and they are serving everyone as fast as they can.

If you were a total douche, you were dead last. Really, why should
I rush to you? You don't tip, you're rude and/ or condescending or
you try to get free stuff? You're a dead beat and dead beats wait until
the very end. I will give my best to people who appreciate it. Traffic
can be a real pain in the ass, can't it? Sometimes it all boils down to
what is the "best and fastest" way to deliver in an efficient manner.
Don't forget the fact I plan the route. I designed my routes around

who was pleasant and tipped in the most efficient manner. If you were a rude cheapskate, you waited.

I had one customer who had a $39.97 order and the quiff gave me a $0.03 tip and she was 1/4 mile out of delivery area. Really?! How rude! She actually handed me the $40 and said "You can keep the change" like she was doing me a favor. I glared at her and reached in my pocket to give her the 3 cents.

"No, that's for you," was her response and the funny part was it was a large house with acreage worth over $300,000 and you want to tip me 3 goddamned cents? Call me an asshole if you want to insult me, twat. I was on time. I was actually early and you give me 3 cents?! It was in the blowing snow just before Christmas. 3 cents?! 3 whopping cents ?! Panhandlers get more than that!! I threw it at her feet and left in disgust. I threw it at her feet like a cheap whore that you violated in a back alley. Keep the change bitch! 3 goddamn cents?! Every time that bitch ordered after that you can bet your ass she waited until the very end. Merry fucking Christmas.

If you want another favorite thing I like to do, it's called crop dusting. This is when you deliberately fart near a rude customer or someone who doesn't tip. Baked beans, cabbage rolls and gas giving vegetables like broccoli are wonderful meals to have for this purpose. It is best to drop the bomb upon receiving payment and walk away as fast as you can. It works best in a dining room setting but ok to do at someone's door or preferably in the door. Bask in the ambiance bitch.

I delivered to factories and got there 5 minutes before their lunch time. Food was ready and orders were set up for fast and easy payment. I even picked up cigarettes from the corner store for some and beverages like chocolate milk. I did the same in Palmer and they tipped extra, saved them time and they were grateful for me doing them a favor. Not in Derry. One person in particular was short almost every time. Short $2 one day $1 another and it was always "I will get you next time" until I got fed up and it went down a little like this:

"I am sorry I am $2 short today," said the usual male customer. This is for an extra stop of cigarettes and chocolate milk.

"Then decide what you are getting. I am sick and tired of you being conveniently short every time I do extra things for you. In fact if you want cigarettes and drinks, you can get in your car and drive the 3 miles and get them yourself. Your favors are done. You never have enough money and you don't tip so I will no longer waste my time doing them for you. I'm sick of it. Now decide what is more important. I am not letting you off this time."

"But I need it all," he persisted. He used to be a neighbor and tries hustling me for money as a kid. He thought it was still working.

"I don't care. Make a decision or I will make one for you," I shot back. I glared him right in the eye.

"I guess the cigarettes and milk."

"Good. Then I guess you're going hungry. I am going to enjoy this as my lunch when I get back to the restaurant. Enjoy your lunch" I said with malice and sarcasm. This is when another one of his coworkers gave him a $20 bill.

"Good, you owe her $20. Your lunch comes to $7.50, cigarettes and milk brings it to $14 plus the $2 you stiffed me on Monday and the $1.50 on Thursday brings it to $17.50 plus tip. We're square. Enjoy." I said in rapid fire progression putting the $20 in my pocket before grabbing my delivery bags and headed to the door.

"You can't have it all," protested his coworker.

"Take it up with him. I am done with this crap. Have a nice day," I shot back. No more favors for thankless ingrates. Yes, I crop dusted their break room every time after that. Blowing them a kiss.

* * *

I got a knock on the door at 10 AM on a Sunday morning and after until 11 PM the night before like I did every Friday and Saturday night. Yeah, I had no life. Anyway, it was the cops. I opened the door to two officers.

"Hello, can I help you?" I asked still trying to figure out what the hell was going on.

"Yes you can. You delivered a pizza last night and we believe it was to a friend of yours that broke into someone's house," stated the first officer. I was completely taken off guard and stood there like a deer in the headlights of an oncoming car. A moment passed and my jaw was still dropped in shock. I was trying to remember all of the orders I took out the night before.

"I didn't deliver to any friends last night," I replied still trying to put it together.

"We'd like you to come with us," he said. Holy Shit!! Are you kidding me?! I was freaking out. I looked over at Mom and she was just as surprised and shocked as I was. "You aren't under arrest. There's some writing on the box and we were told it's yours and we want you to come and see it with the home owner. Maybe you can remember who took the order from you," he reassured me. He must have seen the panic in my eyes. I can breathe again. I wasn't made for prison. I am not into being gang banged and sold for cigarettes. Sorry for the stereotype.

I grabbed my jacket and went with the officers. I got in the back seat of the cruiser and I am sure my neighbors were watching thinking I really fucked up this time. People in small towns are nosy and have no problem running their mouths with the slightest bit of information and make the rest up as they go along. The truth is relative and unimportant. A juicy story, however, is what makes the world go round. Improvise.

We got to the house in question and as soon as I walked in the door I was getting dirty looks. The owner, a woman in her late 40s was standing there glaring at me as soon as I came in the door with her arms folded in a standoffish pose. Her scraggly brown hair looked as if it hadn't seen a brush in days. She had a slim figure and continued to try and stare me down. I looked past that and looked at the floor. the place had been ransacked. Movies strewn about the floor, the TV, movie player and stereo equipment was gone, only empty shelves and a few bare wires remained. The drawers to the cabinets were open and obviously searched.

"Do you like what one of your little buddies did to my house?" She asked in an accusing manner.

"Excuse me," I shot back in a don't blame me tone.

"Yeah, I know your game. You deliver and then tell your hoodlum friends which houses have the nicer stuff. Then they break in and order pizza and you deliver to split the loot. Like that box over there," she said pointing to the pizza box on the kitchen counter.

"Nobody is accusing him of everything," shot back one of the officers. "We checked him out, he's clean and he has never been in trouble with us. His boss will even confirm that."

"If that were the case, I deliver to houses worth 10 times what this one is. They don't get broken into. It's probably because they are nice people. Besides I really don't think my crime ring would be wasting their time here. Oh, I forgot your last name was 'Rockefeller'. Keep trying to solve the case, Nancy Drew," I threw in with my best sarcastic tone. When people are this stupid, they deserve my best sarcasm underlined with just the right amount of condescension to go with it. If looks could kill, I'd be dead but it was so worth it. I swear I heard the cops snicker. Yup, I am a sarcastic bastard. Awesome.

"That doesn't help," said one of the officers. He had his hand over his mouth. He was hiding his smile. I did hear him snicker. I was quite proud of myself. The bitch was still speechless. Amazing.

I went over to the pizza box on the counter after shooting her a dirty look of "Shut the Hell up" and "told you so" all in one. Twat. I then gave her a quick smile. The counter had a few days worth of crumbs on it and the dishes looked as if they had been sitting there a while, possibly 2 or 3 days. I looked at the box. There was writing on it.

HAW
No Mush

The writing looked a lot like mine when I mark a box before either putting it on the top of the oven to keep warm for pick up orders or putting the bag for delivery. I grabbed a pen off the counter and wrote on the box.

HAW
No Mush

It matched. I looked at it again. I was trying to remember that order. I knew that order. It was a regular order. It was a Hawaiian pizza with no mushrooms. We put ham, pineapple, mushroom and extra cheese on the Hawaiian.

We use shorthand writing. In the food industry, it's a requirement and you had better get used to quick or you are dead. There isn't time to write "Hawaiian, " it's "Haw." You have to rely on initials like "GP" for green peppers and "pep" for pepperoni. When a customer orders, they talk fast and you had better be fast too.

"I know this order. It's my writing on the box. I know this order. It's a regular one. I can't think of it right now," I said while scratching my head.

"You should know it! It's one of your friends! You probably stayed and had a slice while they trashed my place!" shouted the homeowner.

"We already covered this! If he doesn't want to help you, I don't blame him," snapped the officer that chuckled and told her off earlier.

"Oh I will help with it. It isn't for her. It's for you," I said to the officer and shot the homeowner a nasty look.

"Is there anything else?" he asked the bitch.

"No, get him out of here before he finds something his friends missed," she shot back. On that note, we left. I got back in the patrol car with the officers and we drove away.

"She's going to be a problem for you," stated the nice officer who stood up for me. the quiet one nodded in agreement.

"You think?" I asked sarcastically.

"We're on your side. Just give us a call when you come across that order again," he instructed me.

"Oh I will. I am just more curious than anything as to who's it is. I am leaning heavily towards her own. I hope it is. that will be funny. too bad I can't be there to see the stupid, vacant look on her face if it is. What a bitch," I said relishing the thought. Like I could be that lucky. At that point we were in my driveway. I couldn't wait to tell Mom about my new friend in town.

* * *

Within a week. I got the order I was waiting for. Large Hawaiian no mushrooms. Guess who's it was. The bitch. She even had the gall to say she'll pick it up. There was tons of sarcasm and blame in her voice but she can get off her raggedy ass and pick it up. As soon as I hung up with her, I called the police and told them it was her order. They laughed. My accuser was a pig. Two to 3 days off dirty dishes and a pizza box on the counter and couldn't remember her own order. What a stupid, lazy bitch.

I also learned she was running her trailer trash mouth around town about my crime ring. I couldn't wait to ring in this sale. Most people didn't believe her but I am sure the ones who did will love it when I tell them it was her pizza and imply how stupid she is. Two can play this game. Twenty minutes later she was there at the counter and I looked at her and smiled.

I placed the pizza down on the counter towards her with the usual writing on the box.

HAW
No Mush

"I guess we solved the pizza mystery didn't we, Nancy Drew? It was yours. The world is now safe. Way to go Scooby Doo." My voice was dripping in sarcasm, malice and condescension. I was still smiling. No, I was grinning like the Cheshire cat. She hung her head. She didn't even have the guts to look at me. I stared her down grinning. She looked stupid and pathetic. I was loving it.

"By the way I love you had no problem running your mouth about my alleged crime ring and you can't even remember your own order. How hilarious is that? I already took the liberty of telling the cops it was your own order. They laughed too. I just thought you'd like to know. That will be $16.95 please," I reported still grinning ear to ear.

She threw $17 on the counter, snatched her pizza and left without making eye contact once.

"Thank you. Come again" I shouted after her in my delightful tone. As soon as the door closed I broke down in laughter. Oh yes!!!

It was a friend of a friend who broke into her house. It was also her neighbor. I couldn't stand him. So much for Nancy Drew's theory. Better luck next time, Nancy. Realistically she was Scooby Doo. She looked like a mutt anyway.

* * *

There was one other customer I couldn't stand. This one had that snotty, condescending tone whenever she called. "Don't burn it." was her catch phrase. I absolutely despise that tone and it takes all I have not to punch the person right in the snot box when they use it. It was always for a small personal size pizza to be shared with her husband. I know she did it just to be a pain in the ass. The boss knew it too. To bring you up to speed . There was a small burn mark the size of a dime on her pizza that was made a few years before I even started and this snotty, condescending bitch hasn't let it go since then and has to be a condescending whore every time she called her pain in the ass order in. She got off on it in some holier than thou, my shit don't stink way. The boss tried to appease her by under cooking it every time and with no avail, the same thing every week. I was getting pissed.

The owners were on their honeymoon and I was in charge of the restaurant and like clockwork, the snotty bitch called.

"Hello, I would like a baby deluxe pizza. Don't burn it," said that irritating, snotty, condescending voice I grew to hate with every ounce of my being.

"You won't have to worry about that because I am not making it." I instinctually said and hung up the phone on her. Take that bitch!

Twenty minutes later, she shows up. Seriously?! People in this town are stubborn and stupid. That is the worse combination anyone can have. They can't take the hint. I am going to have to get out the crayons and draw them a picture every time.

"Baby pizza," she said in her usual snotty, condescending tone. My turn bitch!

"What part of "I am not making it' didn't you get? Do I have to draw you a picture? I am sick of your lies and crap and so is everyone else," I was letting her have it in her same condescending, snotty tone. "Don't burn it, Don't burn it" I mocked her. It took all I had not to punch her right in the smug, lying bitch face. Stuck up, condescending whore. My nostrils were flaring and I glared at her staring her down.

"Well, I'm not leaving here until you do," she said in a spoiled brat tone like I would expect from a 3 year old.

"Oh, is that so? Sit down bitch. You're going to be here a while. I am afraid it's going to take all night," I scoffed and sneered at her. I pointed to the chairs we had by the wall for waiting. They were very uncomfortable and this was going to be fun.

I made her sit there for 3 1/2 hours. Every time she asked where her pizza was, I made her wait even longer. Customers came and went. She sat there the whole time. It was a battle of wits on who could wear the other down. I was up for the challenge. I hated her guts and now she knew it too.

"What about her? She was her first," stated one customer.

"Oh. She's waiting," I replied back in my best customer service voice and smiled over at the condescending bitch. It was my most evil smile.

"Ok then. I am here for my large pizza. For Jones," replied the customer.

"It just came out Mrs. Jones. You timing is perfect," I smiled and was in perfect customer service mode again. I flashed my evil smile to the bitch again before going to get Mrs. Jones' pizza.

When I returned, Mrs. Hones already had her money ready and even a $2 tip. She was really nice.

"Keep the change, Justin," said Mrs. Jones as she took her pizza out the door. She turned and gave a small wave as she closed the glass door.

" Thank you and take care," I replied back to her. I looked over to the bitch and smirked at her. She was still waiting. She didn't say a damn to me. She wouldn't dare. Justin is psycho.

I let her wait enough. I made her pizza. I cut it and boxed it and was back in customer service mode. I placed it on the counter.

"Your baby pizza is ready. I am sorry for the wait. It's been crazy in here, hasn't it. Thank you for being so patient ," I said to her in my friendliest, sarcastic tone. I opened the box to show her a smoldering, charred briquette of a pizza. You could barely make out the toppings. She looked at it shock and then up at me in disbelief. I smiled at her.

"Now you know the difference between burnt and what you were getting. Don't you?" I hissed. She looked at me and then the pizza. "Is there a problem? I can make you another one but I am not sure how long it will take," I hissed

"No, this is fine," she said quietly.

"Good, that's $4.95 please." I said smiling at her. She paid me $5 and waited for her change.

"Your boss is going to hear about this," she said quietly in disgust.

"Yes he is, because I am going to tell him. This should teach you to be rude," I shot back.

"I hope you get fired!" she shouted.

"It was worth it. Putting you in your place. Have a good night and enjoy your pizza," I scoffed at her.

I didn't get fired, luckily, but we did have a long discussion about it and he had one with her as well. She agreed not to be rude any more. No hard feelings. However, whenever I answered the phone after that she always asked for someone else. Once in a while I would refuse and make her give me the order just for fun. I never heard that snotty condescending tone from her again for some reason. It's a blessing all the same.

* * *

The guy from the factory that wouldn't tip actually asked me to pick him up cigarettes again on another order. Unfortunately I didn't take the order and it was on the chit. I explained what happened to the boss and his favors are over. I even wrote a note that said," No more favors for Jones Manufacturing" and stuck it by the phone. I grabbed the food and went to do the delivery.

"Where's my cigarettes?" he asked.

"At the convenience store 3 miles up the road." I answered in my smartass tone.

"I told you to get me cigarettes," he said as if he were my boss.

"And I told you 'No more favors'. What part of that didn't you get?" I shot back in the same holier than thou tone.

"I didn't think you were serious..."

"Well now you know. If you want a smoke, you'd better get a move on it. The clock is ticking," I interrupted him and pointed for the door. I smiled. "Never take advantage of people because they get sick and tired of it."

He grabbed his jacket and keys muttering some nasty things under his breath and almost sprinted to his car. The tires spun and gravel flew in the parking lot. He was pissed and I was laughing. Serves him right. Watch who you step on. Don't anger those who serve you or take advantage of people or take them for granted. You will lose in the end.

I did find it interesting how those who didn't tip called me a tight ass when I didn't give them a discount. Isn't it supposed to be the other way around? My disgust for the rude and cheap was at critical mass. Here's a note for you to ponder on: If you have money for delivery or eating out, you have money to tip. You can't mistreat the serviceperson and expect optimal customer service at the same time. If you are the type to take all kinds of abuse and mistreatment and still go back for more with a smile, seek therapy and get your dignity back.

The only thing I will ever take out of the book of lies is "Doing unto others as you would have them do unto you." The reality is treating others the same way you want to be treated and it isn't just a religious thing because places where religion doesn't exist have the same principals. An example would be an Amazon village that has never seen a bible. How do they get along? Do they need a bible or religion to get them to treat each other with respect and share responsibilities or have they been doing it all along? Of course they have, they wouldn't be here otherwise.

I am not a slave and you are not my taskmaster who can whip, beat and berate me at will. It gives the person a superiority complex to do so. You sure as hell are not going to get favors from me after doing so. I will take so much and the you can fuck right off and die. I despise the rude. Loathe entirely.

It's typical Passive Aggressive behavior. The most dangerous kind. I am just as guilty as per the stories I have told so far. A husband catches Hell from the boss but can't stand up to the boss in fear of losing his job. He goes home and berates and abuses his wife for whatever reason he can find such as the dishes not being done. She takes it out on the kids and the kids take it out on each other or the pets or another kid. A bully is usually mistreated at home so in order to make themselves feel better, they do it to someone else. I did. I am not proud and am truly sorry for those actions.

CHAPTER 21

I got some news about a week later from Mom. She called the restaurant to inform me that dad's wife had passed away. He had the gall to ask her to sign over her plot. She did it willingly telling him she didn't want to be buried anywhere near him. When they were married, they had adjoining plots. Side by side. I was laughing. After all the years of being neglected by him. No birthday or Christmas cards from him or anyone else on that side of the family. They didn't even call. The blessed gifts of disrespect and neglect. Thanks for showing me how much you care.

I found it really ironic he ran to her when he needed to bury his whore. I broke out in song. Ding Dong The witch is dead. I was happy. She made the comment of "Let's kill the bitch" about Mom and her ass is dead instead. Ha! Bitch!

I know this wrong on every level imaginable but I definitely had my reasons. I felt even less guilty when the obituary came out he next day. I wasn't even mentioned. Nothing like showing you how much you mean and the entire town as well as the readership of the newspaper. Ding Dong the witch is dead. If I was going to Hell, I might as well go all the way. I decided to take Mom out for dinner and celebrate. Since he wanted to go out of his way to show I didn't matter or exist, I will toast your misery. Anthony called and asked if I was going to the funeral?

"Are you high?" I asked

"What do you mean?" he asked.

"Did you not see the obituary? I wasn't even mentioned. So if I don't exist to the son of a bitch, why ask? Also why would I go to the funeral of a person I couldn't stand? Think about it." I scoffed.

"I guess you're right...."

"If you were me, would you go?" I asked.

"Probably not."

"Why did you ask?" I had to ask. I mean, really?!

"I thought you would want to be the better person..."

"I am. I'm not going because if I went I know I would say something really nasty. So in a way I am the bigger person. I would be all smiles and it's best I stay away. I never liked the bitch and I sure as Hell am not going to her funeral pretending I liked her or about to lie about what a nice person she was. I am not a fraud." I explained.

"I guess you're right." agreed Anthony. He couldn't help it. It's painfully obvious. Actions speak louder than words. The conversation was over and I hung up the phone. Ironically her family ever calls or visits him after she was buried. They were never to be seen or heard from again. I wonder why.

* * *

I had to do something for myself and saw a dermatologist for my facial complexion. I was put on Accutane and with a few weeks my problem was pretty much gone. I will tell you how shallow some people really are. I couldn't get a second look and as soon as my face was cleared up I got a nice look from someone now and then. The best was when I got it from a girl who wouldn't give me the time of day. She actually asked me out. I turned her down flat and it felt good.

I wanted to feel even better so I went to an open audition for a modeling and talent. I was stunned when I got accepted. I even got a call to try out for a furniture store commercial! I was so excited. I couldn't wait to do it. I drove 3 hours to get there and it was set up in a hotel banquet room. The guys were outside in a waiting area and there were about twelve us in total. Pretty good odds I thought.

Within an hour, it was my turn. I went in the meeting room to find a set up of a sofa, a lamp at one end of the room. At the other end of the room was a desk with a computer, office style chair and a lamp. Interesting. There was a white back screen for each area and lots of lights, a camera on a tripod with more lights and white umbrellas around them. The only other people in the room were a director, a camera guy and another guy in a suit.

"Hello and welcome to the set," said the guy in the suit extending his hand to shake mine. We shook hands. "Ok, Justin is it?"

"Yes sir," I responded.

"Great. I suppose you are wondering about the set up," he continued. I nodded. "Ok, we want someone around college age and you are to sit on the sofa and pretend to watch TV and make yourself comfortable. I am going to give the command 'Here comes mom' and at that point I want you to jump up and run around the sofa over the computer desk. I want you to turn on the light and give the 'Ok' hand sign and sit down like you are doing homework. "

"That sounds easy enough," I responded as I was calculating how I was going to react. I figured just go natural. How hard could it be?

I kicked my shoes off and took my place on the sofa and slightly reclined with my left foot resting on my right knee and let my arm rest on the arm rest letting my fingers dangle off the end. All I needed was a remote control and I was at home. I then shifted my legs so they were beside me on the sofa in an L-shaped pattern. Now I was really comfortable.

"Here comes mom," said the director as if in a panic.

I sprang up and went to vault over the arm of the sofa. I had to run around the back of it and my foot got caught on the lamp cord. As I was rounding the corner, the cord ran out of slack and I tripped bringing the floor lamp with me right over the opposite end of the sofa and did a face plant right into the cushion before rolling off on the floor. This caused the entire room to erupt in laughter. In order to maintain my dignity all I could do was stand up and take a bow as well as laugh at myself. It's funny how you know we were all hoping the other would trip and fall on the set and it just had to be me. Damn.

Luckily I got to try the shoot again but they were still chuckling at me. I did it without incident but it was too late. The first impression and folly was what mattered. Needless to say I didn't get the part but it was an experience all the same.

Mom met someone new and this time she was helping him out. Of course he had a down-on-his-luck story that a mutual friend of hers verified and vouched for him. He was homeless. His name was Ron. he had shoulder length dirty brown hair and a thin beard with a mustache. Mom was a caring and giving person but unfortunately she got taken from granted too many times. I was skeptical but kept my mouth shut. He seemed ok but they always do when they want or need something from someone else. It's a total facade and it's only a matter of time before the mask falls off.

One thing we learned really quick was that he liked to drink and party. In fact, that is pretty much what he did. I can see now why he was homeless. Probably drank himself out of house and home. He was obnoxious as a drunk like most are. He was a know-it-all and knew absolutely jack shit. It was fun to prove him wrong and effortless.

He had no problem eating the groceries and drinking away his pay check. It turned out he was accepting collect calls from one of his friends in jail and driving up the phone bill. He of course didn't pay for it. It got to the point when I was taking away the phone and putting it in the trunk of the car when we left the house.

One night while I was at work, Mom and Ron went away for the weekend to Niagara Falls with another couple. When I got home, the groceries weren't purchased and I had a large crock pot of white rice. There were condiments and few frozen vegetables and sauces but not much of anything else. I was pissed right off. I knew they were going out to eat and I get to enjoy what was left. Awesome. Nice to know that after carting his ass around to work every day, I was even considered. What a selfish twat.

Mom at least had the decency to call and tell me. She had no idea where they were going when she got in the car. She has apologized profusely for it. I accepted it because I know she wouldn't do that to someone intentionally. I am grateful that I worked at a restaurant and had recently got paid to get me through the weekend.

* * *

One night, we heard him stumbling in the door late at night. I believe it was around 3 AM. He fell on the floor with a loud crash that woke me up. I jumped out of bed and turned on the light to find him with multiple facial lacerations and bleeding from the nose, lip and pretty much the rest of his face.

"Get your mom! I'm beat up!" he barked while he dragged his worthless ass in and bled on the living room carpet. I looked at him in disgust and for some reason I wasn't the slightest bit surprised. Mom came out of her room and looked at him, then back at me. We had the same look of disgust on our faces.

"What the Hell happened to you?" I asked. I still was standing with my arms crossed. I wasn't helping him. I will bet he deserved it for sticking his nose in where it didn't belong or being his loud and obnoxious self. Mom got him a wet facecloth and tossed it to him.

"I got jumped by an entire hockey team," he whined.

"Nobody does something for nothing. What did you do or say?" I asked.

"Are you saying I deserved it?!" he shouted getting up trying to act macho and intimidating. I chuckled. As you can see, his macho bravado really pays off.

"Sit down before you fall down or have you had enough already tonight? Now, what the Hell did you do and do we need to worry about someone coming to the door because of your big fucking mouth?!" I shouted back.

"They aren't coming. They know you and your mother. You probably set it up." he accused.

"Wrong answer! What the fuck did you do? You say I know them and the people I know don't randomly attack people for no reason. You got drunk and shot your fucking mouth off, didn't you? Did you pretend to be the new big boy on the block? It worked out great, didn't it?!" I fired back. Now I am pissed this dumb ass is going to answer me.

"The were picking on a friend of mine and I asked them to stop. They kept on going and then they jumped me outside," he whined.

"Did they tell you to 'Shut the Hell up'?" I asked.

"Yes, several times," he replied.

"Can't you take a hint?! When someone says 'Shut the fuck up' or 'Mind your own business', here's a clue... Do it!" I scolded him.

"I am going to get them all..."

"Sure you are. You look like you got a lot of good hits in. Let me guess..." I scoffed. "We should see the other guys." I said mocking him with my voice dripping in sarcasm as I waved my hands making the quotations signal with my fingers.

"Fuck you Justin. I will kick your ass," he said trying to be intimidating. I laughed as he was still on the floor in pain.

"Really?! You aren't even strong enough to stand up right now. As for kicking anyone's ass, it will be yours. Don't even think about trying that crap with anyone as you can see it doesn't work out well for you or would you like me to get you a mirror?" I asked him sarcastically. Mom chuckled again. "And another thing, if you drag me into this, I assure you I do not have your back. You had better not have anything start around here or you are history. Are we clear?" I asked with my malice in my voice. I was totally disgusted. Learn to shut the Hell up.

"That's right. We don't have problems here and you will not be bringing them," confirmed Mom as she was still trying to clean him up. He looked at her and then back at me and it somehow sunk in to not say another word. I went back to bad. I had enough!

* * *

Ron got invited to a wedding where he worked and I was to drop him off. The wedding was in Palmer at the Waterfront Banquet Hall which was built on the pier with a small lighthouse at the end. The banquet hall was huge. Maybe about half the size of that on Navy Pier in Chicago. I dropped him off and went to work.

My night was uneventful until I went to pick him up. I quickly learned what his problem was, alcohol abuse. The stupid ass didn't know when to quit drinking. I was instantly notified of his abhorrent behavior the second I arrived and how "I had better get him out of here." It turns out he had been drinking out of other people's glasses when they cut him off as well had been confrontational and rude to other guests. There's one at every wedding and I had the privilege of being there to pick him up.

If looks could kill, I would have been dead too. Luckily a couple of his coworkers helped me get to him and of course he wouldn't leave on his own. He even took a swing at his boss's son and then he was picked up by four family members and carried out of the hall with disgusted guests watching his display of repulsive behavior. It was embarrassing.

On the way out I was asked several times why I brought him. I could only respond, "Ask his boss. It's his daughter's wedding." When I go to wedding or formal events, I have class. I may talk too much at times but I know my limits. Nobody is trying to punch me in the face and I sure as hell won't be carried out for alcohol abuse. No wonder the hockey team kicked his ass. I want to kick his ass.

The nearly threw him in the lake and it was churning really good, water was splashing off the pier and spraying my car. I talked them out of it. I will regret that decision before the night is over. I opened the back door to the sedan and he was thrown in and the door closed. I apologized for his behavior only to get a few shouting "Get the fuck out of here!"

I got in the car and drove off and heard something break and watched the groom return his foot from the kicking position. The son-of-a-bitch kicked in my tail light. I bought a computer off of him a few months before and he kicks in my tail light. He never admitted to me or offered to pay for it. That's one customer who won't come back.

I was maybe a mile out of Palmer and Ron reached around the back of my seat and grabbed me by the throat while I was driving 55 mph. "You set me up and I am going to get you for this," he slurred.

"Sit down and take your arm off my neck or you're going to fucking regret it. As for you "you set me up theory', let's look at that. Why kept pouring drinks down your throat? You did! Who doesn't know when to shut the fuck up and stop dinking so much? You! Who got their ass kicked again and thrown in the back of a car? You! Who's probably fired for their behavior tonight? You!" I was yelling and let him have it. My voice was accusing and sarcastic. I hate drunks! He quickly removed his arm from my throat.

A couple of minutes later, he grabbed my hair and reefed back on it causing me to tip my head back. I immediately slammed on the brakes, swerved to the right and elbowed him in the face when his head was close to my right shoulder. Crack! Direct hit! Right in the beak. He wasn't wearing his seatbelt and I was. I started driving erratically to keep him off balance and could hear him fumbling around and falling in the back seat and on the floor. What a stupid twit.

I grabbed my 4 cell Maglite flashlight I kept under the seat for special occasions like this. I held it by the light end and now it was a stainless steel baton and it now has a date with Ron's face. I was now speeding 65 mph in a 50 zone but didn't care. I had to get home and warn Mom the night was going to get interesting. Every time I saw him move in the rearview mirror, I would make a sudden swerve of jam on the brakes to let him hit the back of my seat. I will admit at times I did it for my own amusement since he didn't have the mental capacity to put on a seatbelt.

I turned hard and fast into my driveway and jammed the brakes causing some skidding action on the gravel narrowly missing the concrete porch. I slammed it in park and removed me seatbelt at the same time, grabbed my Maglite and took the keys from the ignition. I opened the door and got out as quickly as I could to warn Mom. I slammed the car door and bolted in the house.

"What's wrong?" she asked. She could tell by my behavior and the look on my face.

"I picked up Ron and he's drunk as hell. they had to throw him in the car," I explained.

"Why the hell did you go and get him?! You know he can't handle his alcohol.." she began.

"I thought you said get him after work, so I did.." I began to explain.

"No. I said 'Don't get him after work' How bad is he?" asked Mom cutting me off.

"Bad," I said. Just then the front door was thrown open and there was Ron glaring at me in the door space. He took a couple steps in the living room and closed the door. I was in the kitchen, the next room over standing by the archway near the refrigerator on the right side of me. Beside the refrigerator was the furnace room. That was all that separated us.

"You're fucking dead! I am going to kill you and you're mother is next! You made this happen!" shouted Ron advancing on me. He was charging like a bull. I put my flashlight in my left hand and threw a punch forward with my right hand catching him right on the chin before both of us fell back and into the wall separating the bathroom from the kitchen.

I punched him in the head again and flung him face first into the wall while I pulled myself from it. He fell to the ground and I bunted him in the back of the head with the Maglite in my left hand. I pushed Mom into the living room towards the door.

"I'm going to slit your throat, Justin," He said as he got up and went for the kitchen drawer where we kept the knives. He opened it with his left and started reaching for a knife with his right hand.

"Bull-shit!" I said as I took the heel of my palm and slammed it into the drawer face as hard as I could slamming his right hand in the drawer. I threw my entire body on to it as well in a hockey style body check. He let out a gut wrenching scream. I elbowed him in the face with my right elbow again since the drawer brought him to his knees. This time I took the flashlight and put it in my right hand and clobbered him in the back across the shoulder blades. Whack! He screamed again.

I released the drawer and he fell back with no knife in hand hitting the back of his head off the edge of the dining room table. He glared at me and sneered as he got to his feet. I let him. I was standing at the other side of the refrigerator with my left hand resting on the freezer door. He of course started to charge me again and I threw open the freezer door which flung around and cracked him in the face before slamming shut again. Bull's-eye!

"You asshole!" he screamed as he covered his face. Mom grabbed the phone to call 911. The operator answered immediately. She saw me coming and handed me the receiver.

"911 what is your emergency" asked the female voice on the other end.

"I am being attacked! Send the cops!" I shouted into the receiver. From my peripheral vision I could see Ron advancing again. I swung back with the receiver in my hand and caught him in the jaw. Wham! He fell back again into the archway separating the living room from the kitchen.

"Is he in the house with you?! What was that noise?!" asked the operator in shock.

"Yes! I cracked him in the jaw with the phone," I replied.

"Get out of the house! The police are on their way!" she said in alarm.

"I can hold him," I replied while I grabbed my Maglite and crowned him with it on top of the head with my left hand. Crack! Ron fell to the floor.

I turned to watch Mom go out the door, she was getting some help from the neighbors or going to try to. I felt a hard blow to my lower back and fell forward. I made the mistake of taking my eyes off my enemy. Damn it! I managed to break my fall with my knees and my left hand. Ron was already grabbing my from behind. I still had may jacket on and he as grabbing on to it rather than me. I took a couple of sucker punches to the back of the head while I wiggled my way free from the jacket. Ron looked surprised when he was left holding the jacket. I punched him right in the face as hard as I could before it registered knocking him backwards.

He went for the flashlight I dropped and we wrestled over it. He had it with both hands when I came around behind him and put him in a half nelson and leaned over his back forming a 90 degree angle. I then reached around the front and grabbed the flashlight. He dug his teeth right into the soft tissue of my hand between my thumb and index finger.

"You fucking bit me asshole! You want to bite? I'll bite too, try this," I yelled before digging my teeth into the back of his neck and clamped down with all I could muster. I ground my teeth together on his flesh and clamped down harder. He screamed and released my hand. I removed the flashlight and flung it behind me. I grabbed his exposed right ear with the hand he bit, pinched pulled and twisted it while I sunk my teeth back into his neck a second time grinding my teeth back and forth in seesaw action until I could taste blood. I released.

"That's how you bite!" I growled and hissed. I flipped him over by pulling on his right ear and reefing on his right shoulder. I slammed the back of his head on the floor and sneered at him while I repositioned myself where I was now sitting on his chest using my knees as a clamp on his shoulders. I wrapped my fingers around his neck and started to choke him while leaning forward to put more of my weight on his neck.

"I.. can't... breathe," he gasped.

"That's the whole idea," I hissed. "Now how about I bite that ugly fucking face of yours and see if it bleeds easier than the back of your neck?" I taunted. "Does that sound like fun to you?" It does to me!" I leaned over and snapped my jaw within an inch of his eye. I bared my teeth and sneered the most evil sneer I could while a wave of panic rode over him as he tried to get out of my choking grasp. I pulled my head back far enough to see the panicked look on his face.

"I'll bet you would rather the hockey team right now, wouldn't you?" I hissed glaring him right in the face. "Oh, this didn't turn out as well as you hoped, did it?" I mocked him in a condescending soft voice. "Now you know not to fuck with me too, don't you?" I hissed. "This is far from over, we still have a little play time before the cops get here and if I were you, I would hope it's soon," I sneered and laughed.

I let go of his throat and grabbed a fistful of his hair and twisted, pulled back with my right hand punched him right in the face throwing my body weight into it. His head banged off the floor with a loud thud. I grabbed both of his ears and lifted his head off the floor and slammed it down several times throwing my body into it each time. I pulled back and punched him in the jaw again. He was starting to wrestle free, I lost my balance and fell over to the left. He was starting to get up. I sprung to my feet and kicked him right in the ribs with my right foot knocking him over on his back.

"Stay down!" I screamed kicking him in the ribs again. I put my foot right on his throat and glared down on him. "All I have to do is stomp and you're dead! It's the best thing for you really. Your life is going nowhere. Nobody likes you and it really is hard for me to imagine why you were homeless.... Oh, that's right, it's because you're a thankless twat, and an abusive fucking drunk, aren't you?" I scoffed.

I pulled my foot off and dropped my body on his chest with my elbow hitting him first. He howled in pain as I repositioned myself back in position with my knees pinning down his shoulders while I went back to choking him.

"Die Asshole! Just fucking die!" I screamed while I choked him again. He bucked me off and I flipped over his head. He rolled over on his stomach and started coming at me. I kicked him in the face with the bottom of my foot before springing up and pouncing on his back like a mountain lion. I then threw my left arm under his chin and laid across his back, locked my lingers together and reefed back on his head using his back as a lever. I dug my feet in and braced them off the heavy entertainment unit's base. I squeezed his neck between my bicep and forearm reefing back on his head at the same time listening to him gasp for breath. I squeezed harder and tighter like a python.

A few minutes later the police arrived, Mom brought them in the house. There were two officers and they were large and built. They came in the door and looked over at me and my python grip on Ron.

"We'll take over from here," one said while they advanced on us. I let go and got off of Ron. They helped him to his feet and then he made the mistake of throwing a punch at one of them. The officer punched him square in the jaw and threw him up against the wall.

"Don't even think about it! You're in enough trouble already!" he barked at Ron. I stood behind the officers and smiled at Ron maliciously.

Ron was handcuffed and escorted out the door by the first officer while the other that punched him took my statement. I went over the events of the evening from the pick up at the banquet hall to the ride home and the violent fight at our house.

"I have to hand it to you, usually when we attend these calls it's the sober person that gets beat up. You did a good number on him. You did very well," complimented the officer.

"Thanks. He just wouldn't stay down so I got a little rough with him. I will admit he is damn lucky we don't keep fire arms in the house, otherwise you would be picking up the body. I would have shot him without hesitation. He threatened to kill us," I replied coldly.

"That reminds me, does he have a place to come home to?" he asked with doubt in his voice.

"No. I don't want him back here." I said flatly.

"Nor do I," replied Mom. Awesome. , I thought. I looked at her and flashed a slight smile. I was done with drunks and losers. I was done with this goddamned town too.

Within 3 months we were moving back to Palmer with no intentions of ever returning to Derry. It turns out that the landlord was harassing Mom. He actually masturbated in front of her in the foyer just inside the door on 3 separate occasions. I found this out towards the end of our stay there. No wonder Mom had me home or pay the rent. What a pig.

A short time after that, I took a job over 60 miles away at a hotel/ convention centre. I accepted it without hesitation as it was my ticket out of Hell. I was free to leave. It was as if I had a huge burden lifted off my shoulders and I would never have to see these people again or deal with their rudeness and blatant lies. I was free! Free to start a new life and have new friends. My fondest memory of Derry was watching it disappear in my rearview mirror. I drove out of town with my right middle finger fully extended and over my shoulder.

CHAPTER 22

I was adjusting to my new job very well. We would go out for drinks after work and it was great when nobody knew who I was. It was a fresh start and I was loving it. If I knew that starting a new life was so cool, I would have done it years ago. People were nicer and gave me a fair shot. I can honestly appreciate that because let's face it, that's all we really want is a chance. I didn't get the usual nasty remarks or jabs I got in Derry. They were nice here. It was like night and day.

I was shocked at how open people were about things that were taboo in Derry. I met openly gay people, bisexuals and everyone seemed to be cool with it. In Derry, you would get your ass kicked for the second you came out of the closet. I was even asked by some coworker to go to the gay bar after work so I thought, why not and went .

Once inside, I was expecting to see drag queens and the usual stereotypical show you would find in a movie or television show. the fact is, it was nothing like that at all. It appeared to be a regular bar with the exception of same sex couples making out. The coolest thing was I had drinks bought for me. I was extremely flattered. Nobody ever bought me a drink unless it there time to buy a round. I even got asked out and groped a couple of times as I walked by. I am not going to lie, it felt awesome since I couldn't get a date in Derry if I begged.

I made some great friends whom I have kept over the years. I decided to go with it and stop lying to myself. I wasn't sure what I was but these people were accepting. Was I gay, bi or an ally? Whatever, let things run its course and let me find out for myself. The fact is your twenties are for discovering who you are. It was a road of discovery. Rather than getting into intimate and graphic details, I will take the highroad and let you figure things out for yourself.

I started hanging with a guy named Ryan and his friends. I liked him, he let me crash at his place and I was really starting to like him even more. He would entertain other guys too. I found this out the hard way when it was brought to my attention he was seeing two of us at the same time and wanted to know who made more money. The whole thing is on honesty and not playing games with people's emotions. Of course I got angry and spiteful. Ryan needed to be taught a lesson.

The fact is I was helping him do some renovations on his apartment. I was giving him rides and I even let him borrow my car one day while I was working because he needed to get somewhere and had no other person to help him. I was pissed and understandably so. I got used enough in Derry by so-called friends for rides. Take me here, take me there and barely pay for anything. In this case I am more pissed because I thought I was seeing him and now he has someone else?!

I went to the club we frequented and with my luck, he was there and so was the other guy. I will call him Andrew for the purpose of this story. Ryan was not happy to see me. He was with Andrew tonight and I apparently wasn't supposed to be there. This made Ryan very uncomfortable. Good, as he should be.

I went and sat at the bar while Ryan and Andrew socialized and drank. I pondered heavily how I was going to handle this one. This needed to be addressed. It is not ok to play one off on the other. It is not ok to be a gold digger and base a potential relationship on earnings or potential earnings. Ryan needs to get the message loud and clear. I sipped on my drink and contemplated my move. I sipped and thought while the bar filled up with more patrons. Ryan went outside for some air and I followed him.

"Hello, Ryan" I said as politely as I could.

"Hey Justin," he replied trying to remain professional.

"Is that all you have is 'Hey'? I see you have a new friend," I shot at him.

"Yeah. You were going to find out sooner or later. The fact is I like you both and I am not sure which one I want," Ryan answered. I didn't like the tone of his voice. It was without emotion and made me believe it was who had the bigger paycheck.

"Or is it who makes more money?" I scoffed. The look on his face confirmed it. Deer in the headlights. Game on. I work at hotel/convention centre and Andrew was a nurse. We know exactly how this is going to go. 'Fuck you Justin.' Nope. Fuck you Ryan. I walked away and went outside where I found Andrew sitting on the bench having a smoke. I lit up a smoke and walked over to him. He looked at me like I was about to attack him. His guard was up. It was very evident.

"Hi Andrew. I need to talk to you if you have a minute," I said quietly. I was doing my best to contain my anger. It wasn't his fault and I wasn't going to lash out at him. I needed him. "I know what this is about. It's about Ryan, isn't it?" he asked softly. I could tell he was anticipating a fight.

"It is. However, I want to make it clear I don't have any issues with you. You probably didn't know until tonight I was seeing him too. Is that correct?" I asked. He nodded. "I thought so. I will also assume you don't appreciate the fact that he is seeing both of us at the same time either." He nodded in agreement again. Perfect. "I will also put it out there that he is out to see which of us makes more money as well. I just found that out and I am not happy about it and he needs to be taught a lesson, doesn't he?" Andrew nodded in agreement.

"Follow my lead and play along. I think we should make up his mind for him. He gets neither one of us. Are you willing to have to some fun?" I asked and gave him an evil smirk.

"Yes he does," he said smirking in agreement.

"Let's go 'talk' to him," I said grabbing his hand and leading him over to where Ryan and his fag hag were standing. They were standing at the drink ledge that surrounded the dance floor. A fag hag is a girl that hangs around gay men. They are usually sexually attracted to gay men either openly or secretly as a stereotype but usually in a relationship of their own. This pig would fit the stereotype.

Completely fat and unattractive in every way. She uses to gay men to make herself look more popular and desirable surrounding herself with slim or muscular men. The talk was she would perform fellatio in the alley or in a car in order to get the money she needed for drinks for the evening. A real cum dumpster.

"Hi Ryan," I said as we walked up to him on the dance floor separating us with the drink ledge. Without missing a beat I grabbed Andrew with both hands on the side of the head by the cheeks and planted a wet, sloppy kiss and he responded by French kissing me driving his tongue right in my mouth.

"Oh my god, this is just wrong," whined Ryan. I could see the look of disgust I was getting from him out of my peripheral vision. I kissed Andrew even harder to which he responded. "This is disgusting," continued Ryan. I released Andrew.

"Oh I'm sorry, did you want some too?" I asked condescendingly with a menacing grin. I glared at him while grinning like the Cheshire cat.

"Evil!!" screamed Ryan "You evil fucking asshole!" Ryan was pissed. I enjoyed seeing the hurt in his eyes. He was almost crying.

"What's the matter Ryan? Did you not expect to get hurt instead? You were going to do it to one of us. We beat you to it. You aren't getting either of us," I hissed. "I guess you're going home alone, aren't you?"

"Asshole!" he screamed. "Justin, you're a fucking asshole!" he screamed again stomping his feet on his way out of the bar. There was laughter from all direction. "I hope you fucking die!" he screamed. I followed.

"What's the matter, Ryan? Are you having a bad day?" I taunted. "I'll bet you would really like to take a swing at me now, wouldn't you?" I hissed still walking after him outside. "Do it, then I can kick your ass for dessert, bitch!" I challenged.

"Fuck you Justin! Fuck You!" screamed Ryan while he stomped his feet some more. We were outside now. He stopped and glared at me a few feet away on the sidewalk.

"It hurts to lose, doesn't it?" I sneered at him. "Maybe this will teach you not to play with people's feelings again. It doesn't feel so good, does it?" I snarled at him. "Here's your chance bitch, take a swing. I dare you." I said cracking my knuckles and then started punching my left hand with my right fist. He gave me the deer in the headlights look again.

"That's right, you get the first punch. Take it! Then I am going to kick your ass. Self defense, bitch. There's nothing you can do about it. Take a swing. I dare you!" I challenged.

"Fuck you Justin! " he screamed.

"Just as I thought, you're chicken shit. By the way, we already tried the 'Fuck you" thing and I had better. I just thought you'd like to know that too," I taunted with malice. I gave him another menacing grin.

"Arghh! I hate you! I hope you die!" he screamed again before running across the street. His fag hag was standing next to me.

"I hope you're happy," she said looking at me in disgust.

"I am. He learned a valuable lesson tonight, didn't he?" I asked her condescendingly.

"You're a real asshole, Justin. You know that?" she asked.

"Yup. Tonight I am damn proud of it too. Look at him carry on and have a tantrum. He did it in front of the whole bar too. Now everyone knows what kind of little bitch he is. Never play with people's emotions," I said glaring her in the eye. "Now you can teach him how to suck cock for drink money. I don't expect anyone will be buying him any for a while. You can show him your business plan. It's pretty good since you don't work and I never see you without a drink in your hand," I sneered in a condescending tone. The look on her face was priceless. Shock, horror, and anger all in one.

"Ahhhh!" she shrieked before running across the street after Ryan who was standing on the opposite sidewalk glaring at me. I stood there and chuckled to myself as I watched her run her fat ass across the street.

"Oh and one more thing Ryan," I shouted across the street.

"What's that?" he shouted back while his fruit fly was still giving me the look of death.

"Don't go away mad," I taunted. The two of them stormed off down the road and I went back into the bar to applause. I even had someone hand me a drink. Awesome.

"You're a Class 10 evil cunt. I meant that with love. That took balls. Really big balls. I'm really impressed and also afraid to get on your bad side at the same time. Wow," said a friend from work who was with his boyfriend.

"No offense taken, Will. Thanks for the drink, and the compliment. I think that just made my cock bigger too." I said patting him on the shoulder in appreciation. The funny thing is nobody let my drinks go empty that night. Apparently they were waiting for someone to put him in his place.

I am proud of the fact I stood up for myself in doing it but also I have to admit it really shouldn't have happened either. It is sad as well. The fact that someone will lend you their car means they care about you and trust you. They think the world of you. To go and play one off over the other is just wrong. It makes you a total douche and you deserve whatever happens to you.

Would you believe that Ryan actually expected me to finish helping him renovate his apartment after this event? I laughed in his face. Really?! Are you kidding me?! I grabbed my tools and left. There is no way in Hell I would help someone after that. Tough. It sucks to be you.

* * *

There was one guy I met who I liked and still like to this day. His name is Dylan. He is my height, build and works as a nurse. I know it's the stereotype of the gay nurse but whatever. Not all male nurses are gay. I don't know if he really knows how much I liked him then. He was really nice to talk to and someone I would have been proud to bring home to meet Mom. I was very comfortable around him.

The problem he was looking for the dream guy. I wasn't the whole package. He needed attention or something. I couldn't give. This not to be insulting since we all like to get attention but some of us need more. He needs more for some reason. I don't understand the reason since he has a profession he can be proud of and is likeable. I worked at a convention centre. Boring by comparison. The truth is we only know what they let us.

I can attest to the fact that I didn't have a lot of friends growing up so I kind of grasp on to any attention I get as well. That explains my need for it. I never got it. Maybe he's the same way. I never got any from family from the age of 13 and on. I can still remember all of those lonely holidays and birthdays without even a card or a lousy phone call. Thanks for caring.

I watched him go off with others only to end up single again and again. It really sucks because I would never have left. We are all human and come with our own flaws and baggage. It takes a real special person who can still care for you and see the real you past your flaws and baggage. I felt like more of an acquaintance than a friend and still do. He wouldn't go out with me if I begged it seemed. Oh well, one can dream. We still remain friends to this day but don't hang out much.

* * *

I did meet one guy that I really liked who lived half way between my new job and Palmer. It was a remote farm house. I liked the idea of being in the middle of nowhere. His name was Alex and he had a daughter. This was new territory for me and I wasn't sure what to think of it. I gave it a shot. Luckily his daughter liked me and she was actually ok. This relationship was short lived because he was fresh off of a breakup and still had feelings for the ex.

It may have been short but it was fun. Both of us had a high sex drive. Think mink. We had 2 days off together and I don't think we got dressed once. His daughter was at her grandparents. When the cat is out the mice will play. We only stopped to eat, sleep or shower. Correction: we didn't stop except to eat or sleep. I will tell you the Kama Sutra could have been written that weekend.

It hurt me to do it but I had to let him go and find out for himself about the "what ifs" running through his head. What if they made a mistake in breaking up? What if it doesn't work out with me? What if we move and start over somewhere else? You name it.

I decided I couldn't spend the rest of our time together with him wondering what would have happened if... I had no choice but to remove myself from the equation and let him figure it out for himself. I knew it was the best decision and hopefully it would work out best for him and his daughter too.

Within a couple of months they were moved away and I didn't find him until Facebook came out. He is a 5 hour drive away. I have to admit I love social media. To this day we are still friends and communicate regularly. He is still grateful for what I did. It didn't work out with the ex but he did find someone new and is quite happy. That's what we want for our friends whether we could provide that or not.

* * *

One night I went out to the bar and was hoping to meet up with some friends and hopefully Dylan but fate had other plans I guess. I went on my usual rounds of "Hellos" with friends and drinking excessively. Yes I admit it. I drank heavily then. Maybe Dylan saw that and didn't like it. If that were the case, I would have cut back if it were brought to my attention. Who knows?

Anyway, one guy did catch my eye. He was good looking and I liked to find something to start a conversation on them. I would usually find something to compliment or something I could use to strike up conversation with them rather than just a lame ass "hello" that would have some awkward silence after that while we each looked for something to talk about. Yeah, you know those conversations. Lots of "ah" and "so" or "um" in between to try and cover the fact you have no idea what the hell you are doing. It's like a fumbling virgin on prom night in the back seat of their parents sedan or minivan with their date.

Being a gay man can be very dangerous when you are looking for a hook up or a date. There are straight men out there who will pretend to be gay and get you to go with them so they can take you some place and beat the Hell out of you or worse. Google Matthew Shepherd. It's a sad story and very tragic. If you are gay, use your head and be safe. Pay attention to the safety tips on the apps and websites.

Anyway, in this case I struck up conversation with him based on the hoop earring he had in his helix part of his ear. The helix is the outer shell ridge of the ear that goes from the connection to your head and arches to your lobe. The inside of the helix in the upper part is the scapha. To learn more on the human ear please consult your biology textbook or your favorite search engine. Thank you.

I walked around him a few times while he was on the dance floor. I of course was with drink in hand. I looked him over and then pretended to see a friend at the other side of the dance floor when he returned the look. I put my index finger up to indicate to 'give me a minute' and took off. I didn't want to be a total snob. I just needed to make sure I was ready to talk and not sound like a babbling idiot. I let a few minutes pass and then went over again.

"Hi. I have to ask you if that hurt. It looks cool," I asked pointing to the earring in his helix.

"Not really. Maybe a little bit," he replied while playing with the hoop in his helix. "I'm Cody."

"Justin," I responded holding out my hand for a handshake. We shook. He had a decent grip and it wasn't wet and clammy. That's a good sign. A firm handshake utilizing the whole hand shows they are interested and sincere. A limp, finger tip only handshake usually indicates the person is doing it with little or no interest and only for show so they don't look like a total snob. However, it still means to "go away, you are bothering me."

We had a few more drinks and I was in no shape to drive home to Palmer. I was making the commute of 60 miles each way, 5 days a week. Sometimes 6. Cody was nice enough to let me crash at his place since he lived nearby and wasn't drinking nearly as much as I was.

He had a modest one bedroom apartment on top of a bank. The building was really old with radiant heat and no elevator. Luckily it was only 3 floors and he lived on the 2nd. Once in the apartment, you were at the living room. To the left was the bathroom and bedroom and the kitchen was to the right. The bedroom was the size of the living room. It was quite large.

I took my shoes off and sat on the sofa. I immediately heard growling coming from a covered coffee table from across the room. I looked at him and then the growling, angry coffee table across the room and back and forth a few times before he said anything.

"That's my cat Xavier. She doesn't like company much. Don't worry, she'll stay under there and eventually stop growling," he assured me.

"Eventually? Should I sleep with one eye open in case Demon Kitty attacks me in my sleep? This is the only cat that I have ever met that doesn't like me," I asked with concern and sarcasm in my voice. Cody laughed.

"Relax. She doesn't have a taste for human flesh. She will come out eventually and check you out. She may even like you. Give her a chance," he assured me.

"Ok. That's reassuring. Demon Kitty doesn't like human flesh. For some reason I was waiting for a 'yet' with that," I joked.

"You're funny," replied Cody with sarcasm in his voice. Awesome. He is another sarcastic bastard like me.

Just then a scrawny, long haired black cat came out from under the coffee table and jumped up on the sofa next to me. She sniffed me and then sat down beside me and started to purr. I pet her for a couple of minutes and without warning the little bitch bit me right in the hand and ran back under the coffee table.

"Yup. Friendly cat. Lets you pet her and then attacks you," I scoffed.

"Usually it takes more than one visit for that. She won't come out when my sister comes over She pees on the floor, growls and hisses before she comes in the door and then hides," explained Cody.

"I should feel lucky I guess," I said with some sarcasm in my voice masked with a touch of sincerity.

"Give her time," suggested Cody. "She'll come around."

"I will. But if she bites me again, I'll bite her back," I threatened.

It wasn't much longer after that we were ready for bed. The bedroom was huge. The bed was at the far end of the room and I swear you could have put in a small dance floor in there and not touch the bed. It's not anything we tried although I am sure we could have. I would have preferred a wrestling ring but I am sure the person below would start banging on their ceiling with a broom stick and/or call the cops for creating a disturbance. It doesn't matter, I was tired and I needed sleep. Luckily I kept an overnight bag in my car and got it out before we came here. Travelling 60 miles each day, you need to be prepared for that just in case.

I thanked Cody for the night's stay and we exchanged numbers. I couldn't wait to tell my coworkers about him. they made me promise not to call him for 3 days to let the high of being together wear off. They were there when I let Alex go and how upset I was for doing what I knew was right.

CHAPTER 23

· · · · · · · ●●● ● ●●● · · · · · ·

Cody and I decided to continue seeing each other. It wasn't long before I left Palmer permanently. No more small town mentality for me. It is very important o broaden your horizons no matter where you are. Experience life and learn there is more than what you are accustomed to especially if you are influenced by myopic, bigoted, prejudiced religious idiots that have about as much understanding of the real world comparable to that of a 5 year old.

There are different people from different countries who have different food and a different outlook on life. It's called culture and I strongly suggest you get exposed to as much of it as possible especially if you were raised in a similar environment as I was. The more you learn about other people, the less prejudiced you become. It's an unlearning process.

Travel and see it for yourself. Visit Mexico, Cuba, Brazil, the Caribbean and anywhere your heart desires. Go to a big city and spend the day in Chinatown, Mexican town, the Italian district, the Middle Eastern district or even the gay district. Always keep an open mind and you will see people are not all that different from yourself. Eat the food, drink the beer and wine. Take in the sights and enjoy them.

Cody and I love to travel. We have been to Las Vegas several times, Chicago, Toronto, Atlanta, Tampa, Curacao, Jamaica, Mexico and Cuba. We have done road trips to see where the highway or freeway will take us. Life is an adventure, embrace it.

My dad came back into my life after 17 years. I was reluctant and agreed to see him again after Mom asked me to. He wanted the family back together. Unfortunately it was short lived but I will admit I wasn't expecting much out of it. After 17 years there really isn't much point, is there? Trying to rebuild something that just isn't there. After that long let's face it you don't know each other anymore. Trying to make up for lost time is a waste of time.

We were talking to him because he ran into problems with the latest wife, Eva. I never met her but I am told she is literally nuts. Eva Insane. She even had him arrested for assault after giving herself a black eye and a few bruises assuming from the stairs. She even vandalized her own car and tried to blame Anthony for it.

All four tires were slashed, every window and mirror were smashed to the point there was only a trace of glass around the frames if you were lucky. The seats were slashed and stabbed as if Freddy Krueger went on a psychotic, razor happy binge while high on speed. There were more holes than a brick of Swiss cheese.

It turns out she has done this on 3 separate accessions in 3 separate towns and blamed somebody different each time. What a twit. If it were different persons involved, why would there be identical damage each and every time? Like all cars are vandalized the same way by every vandal. She got busted by the insurance company. Dumb ass.

She claims to be disabled but it's funny we all now or heard of someone on disability leave that has been caught moving furniture even though they were off work due to a bad back. It takes time to do that kind of damage and privacy too. Only one was done in town while the others were in a rural area. All were done late at night. Probably around 3 or 4 AM when most are asleep and probably won't hear the glass breaking or the tires popping. There would be lots of time to vent her frustrations with a knife wielding psychotic rage on helpless upholstery.

There was an inevitable divorce and she of course took half the house and whatever she could carry out of the house when he wasn't home. The gold digger worked part time at a convenience store first. Way to go Eva Insane.

He still drinks and I watched him go through several girlfriends who all left for the same reason. Alcoholism. The message doesn't get through. They were all wrong. After all it is never the person's fault that drinks or uses drugs fault is it. It's always everyone else.

I can't tell you how many times I have drunk dialed to hear the same old sob stories at all hours of the night. We could discuss how I am expected to drop everything including my job to go over and do everything he asks like I am 12 years old again. When I did go over, there was always drinking and little work got done.

We went over to his place for a Thanksgiving dinner and sat with his new girlfriend and her family as well as a few of her friends. I enjoyed the fact that it was my birthday and of course that it was overlooked as usual. I will not remind someone of that. A family member or friend should know your birthday and mention it. If you can't remember a person's birthday, there is a problem. Case dismissed.

This Thanksgiving was as joke. Watching dad's girlfriend and her friends cook and smoke at the same time is something else. I am a chef and if you were to smoke in my kitchen, you would find yourself unemployed so fast you wouldn't know whether to shit or go blind. It is unsanitary and inexcusable. I took pleasure in kicking them out of the kitchen if they had a cigarette going. It's disgusting. It's almost as bad as those who don't wash their hands after going to the bathroom. Now let's think of them handling food. Filthy, disgusting pigs.

We ate and were gone shortly after. It was Cody's idea. He couldn't stand the fact that out of all of the people there, not one of them could wish me a happy birthday. In fact, he was disgusted. From that moment on, we blew family off and took a vacation for Thanksgiving. For a few years we went to Las Vegas and then to Chicago, Niagara falls or Toronto in the following years. It took him over a year to ask Mom why I don't go to family events. She told me her response to that question.

"You want to know why he doesn't come around or go to these family events you have. The reason is simple. Let's talk about what he knows. He grew up without you around. You never sent a card for his birthday or Christmas or any other time for that matter. You ignored him even as a kid because he had different interests than you. The only reason you remembered his birthday when we were together was because I reminded you. I will bet you don't even know how old he is any more.

All you wanted to do is get out of paying child support and you showed no interest in his grades or anything else for that matter. He may as well have not existed in your opinion. All of those actions showed him you didn't give a damn one way or another. He sat at your dinner table on Thanksgiving which was his birthday and you couldn't even acknowledge that. I have had the privilege of seeing that over the last 17 years. He even tried to talk you at Kelly's grade 8 graduation and you totally snubbed him like he was nothing. You went to Anthony's and Kelly's graduations but you couldn't be bothered with any of his.

That proved to him you didn't give a flying care about him. All of those birthdays and Christmas's he would mock you and sarcastically ask what you got him this year. It was always nothing but he'd say 'Wow! He outdid himself again'. When your slut died you didn't even have the decency of putting his name in the obituary. That was more proof you didn't give a damn and you liked shoving it in his face. The funny part was you actually expected him to go to the funeral. Were you drinking more than usual then or have you lost your mind completely?

You haven't shown him any love or appreciation or anything for over 17 years. I take that back. He's 30. You can't make up for any of that. You lost him years ago. He didn't even want to talk to you but I pushed him to and little has changed. I don't blame him and I am sorry I pushed him in your direction just to get the same shit you've shown him most of his life. Maybe you should have just let him suffocate when you're god damned ice shanty fell on him. Remember that? It took you long enough to get out of bed and get it off of him., didn't it?

That's what he knows. You don't care. Never have. Never will. That slut and her kids were more important. Your beer is more important or any other whore you see than your own kid. Great dad you are. Father of the year! The only thing you gave him was the cold shoulder and neglect and you wonder why he doesn't come around. You fucked up. You fucked up huge and you won't ever be able to repair it. He gets more love and appreciation from total strangers and Cody's family than he will ever get from you.

Cody is the best thing to happen to him. It got him out of Derry and Palmer. You weren't around for all of the crap he went through there either. There were days I was wondering if he was going to kill himself and if I was going to find him dead. Thanks for the support. Does that answer your question?"

From what I was told afterwards, the subject was dropped. There really isn't anything you can say to that other than "Ouch". I think everyone has the thoughts of killing themselves at one point or another. The quicker that idea is put in the scrap pile, the better.

I can even tell you dad put a rope in a tree on 2 separate occasions for attention. He got it and not the positive outcome he was looking for. Police intervention and psychiatric evaluations are not positive things. If you are looking for attention do it another way that doesn't put yourself at risk or anyone else for that matter.

After the suicide attempts I just got fed up with the drama and the constant need for control from dad. The ties were once again severed and I do not seeing them mended in the near future. Unfortunately the definition of insanity is doing the same thing over and expecting a different outcome. Alcohol and selfishness are what relations with him have been a priority and will remain that way. I can't be around that any longer. I have my own life to live and will not be told how to live it by anyone.

The fact is, he is the last person to say how I should live it since he was away for more than half of it. From 13 to 30 is no comparison and you can't say you know the person any more. At 13 it's sports, games and school whereas at 30 it's careers, homes, relationships and adult interests. You can't base knowing someone on their childhood when they are an adult 17 years later. That time in between has had lots happen and there was no interest in it on their part. Therefore no comments can be made with any relevance. To even try to say otherwise is only going to end up embarrassing yourself.

I moved Mom away from Palmer and she couldn't be happier. A whole new start for her as well. Family we have lost contact with is gone and have made no attempts to find us either. We had an incident where a family member was dying of cancer and we were asked to reach out to them as a way of mending fences for closure. I highly recommend not even bothering.

It was met with rudeness and even the assumption we wanted a handout from the estate. Some people never change and it was the most awkward incident I have ever been put in. If they want to mend fences, let them come to you. Ironically the person died 3 days later and the obituary was worded only friends and colleagues were welcome to the celebration event on their life. After the rude manner in which we were treated, I would never think of attending. When someone has that type of mindset, you are better off without them.

Kelly has moved on and has a great relationship with her new fiancé and four children. They are nowhere near Palmer or Derry either. She has never been happier. As for Anthony, we have put the past behind us and build on it every day. Lots has happened and we All of the crap we went through was another lifetime ago and will not be repeated for any of us.

I am happy to say that I now do the things I enjoy. I scuba dive and have seen some really cool things. I am fortunate enough to do some of the things I enjoy and will continue to do so as I should. Negative influences are removed from my life since I really have no interest in those types of people any more. It's a blessing.

CHAPTER 24

• • • • • • • • • ● • • • • • • • • • •

I enjoyed working at the hotel and convention centre. It was a resort as well. It has lots of great amenities. It was a unionized job. It had its moments like any place of employment. It has its challenges too. There was a drop in attendance seasonally and there were lay-offs. It seems to go with the unionized territory.

Without glorifying what happened because it is not to be glorified in any way. It is a tragedy and we will handle it as such. Sarah was a good person at heart with 2 kids and had a warped sense of humor. It goes with the territory in hospitality and retail or any customer service industry for that matter. The humor can be dark and morbid as well as sarcastic.

She joked about jumping off the parking garage. It is not funny and we told her this. She persisted. There were 2 others in the group at this time. We all stated this isn't funny. The subject was dropped.

Thanksgiving came around and on Friday morning we started our shift to some pretty insensitive comments about a jumper the night before. An emergency meeting was called only to find out Sarah had ended her life the night before by jumping off the parking garage.

I am not including dialogue in this story. I have dealt with enough suicides and now we must face the demon head on. The ripples are deep and effect a lot more than the victim. Yes they are a victim. They didn't get the help they needed whether not knowing how to ask for it and afraid of the stigmatism of being weak or attention seeking.

Let's make this very clear. it takes a very strong person to admit they need help. This goes for everything from addiction, to being abused. You are taking charge. That takes guts. Knowing who to talk to is important. there are crisis numbers in every community. Program it in your phone. It will be there when we need it. Most of us are not counselors and therapists. we don't know what to say. Help is a phone call away.

Signs include feeling helpless, change in behavior, withdrawal from things you once liked, talking about taking your own life, looking for ways to do it, feeling trapped or being a burden. There is no single cause. Substance abuse, depression, loss of employment, debt, legal problems, mental disorders, physical conditions and disease like cancer, a major love loss and history of abuse and trauma. There are dozens of websites with this information.

In this case the three of us didn't say anything and should have. We thought she was talking out of her ass. As a result we spent the day with a counselor. She reassured us we did nothing wrong however I know we did. We ignored a major sign and told no one. We didn't take action. We didn't get involved. This could have been avoided. She needed someone to listen. She needed someone to help. Something could have been done. There are courses out there. Use a search engine and you can find them.

We all have it in us to help. In this case the talking about it as a way of reaching out and it was met with "stop talking like that" when it was a golden opportunity to get her talk about her problems which can ease the thoughts of suicide. It was an opportunity to find someone more qualified to deal with it. We shut it down. this is why having that local number in your phone can help. It can save a life. Instead it played out in tragedy. Search out these resources. You never know when you will need them. 911 should have been called, management, anyone.

I have learned a lot over the years and I am sharing this with you as a learning tool. the ripples are far reaching and go deep. It is sad, devastating, and a mixed bag of emotions from anger, shame, guilty as I have felt these personally in all cases. I will reiterate the same thing get that number in your phone. I now act on it and you can hate my guts all you want when I alert someone of a potential suicide. A person jokes about it, I tell them why it isn't funny and immediately offer help. I don't ever want to feel that way again. The feeling of knowing something could have been done but wasn't.

In all 3 cases, some or all would be here today had I known what to do and how to act. I tried to help but got nowhere. two were before cell phones. Now there is no excuse. We have them with us at all times like our wallets and purses. With that number saved in your contacts, it can and will make a difference. Games and social media can wait. Taking the time to help is what matters when it comes to someone you care about. End the stigmatism.

While we are the subject of substance abuse, I have had opportunities in my life where I drank more than I should have. Mom had a lot of problems and I know I held her in a good light. She had a spell where she drank excessively. I thank Jerry and the other loser boyfriends for that. Ron was a drunken loser, and Jerry was an abusive, controlling son of a bitch. I would drink too.

Mom could not always handle her alcohol and drank excessively to the point where her true hostile, frustrated, unhappy feelings would come out. Hurtful and abusive things would come out. Even physical confrontation were of the norm. Bills like rent suffered and an eviction was the result.

I could not listen to another drunken sob story and if someone starts spewing their sorrows when they drink, I am out of there. I won't listen to it. Call a therapist and piss off. You see the tough guy at the bar that can't handle their alcohol and wants to fight everyone by the end of the night like Ron for example. The abusive loser.

I can't listen to that shit. I have slept in cars, on beaches, at friends houses and even in stranger's bedrooms to escape it. I have dealt with blackouts, abuse, name calling, blaming, threats of violence, violence, promiscuity from those who abuse alcohol. I can't stand a violent drunk and Ron is lucky I didn't own fire arms at the time.

Whenever I go out and start to see the signs of the type of drunken behavior, I remove myself from the situation. I suggest you do too. You put yourself in the line of fire if you don't. It is all about the safe place. It isn't about running away from the problem, it is removing yourself from it.

CHAPTER 25

• • • • • • • ● • • • • • • •

This is the end of the line for now. I really haven't written anything else. We write the story of our lives every day. I will continue to push for my happy ending and so should you. I can put forth what I have learned from being in Hell and hopefully it will help someone else through theirs.

I did think about killing myself but I quickly decided it would let them win and that isn't going to happen. Ever. I don't like to lose and to die a loser is not an option for me although my enemies have told me I will die one no matter what. I really don't give a rat's ass what they think and nor should you care what yours think either. Let me tell you there is nothing more satisfying than success. You are not a loser and I hope you will run into one of those jerks another day and be doing better than they are. If you get your dream and they don't, you've won.

I have seen what it does to family and friends that are left behind wondering why and punishing themselves for not seeing it sooner or helping. It is the cowards way out and you finish the biggest loser. It is the wrong permanent solution to a temporary problem. There never is an excuse for killing yourself.

The love you lost will be replaced with another. The overwhelming debt you have can be paid off or other avenues can be sought. You will rebuild. If you lose your job, you can retrain and/ or find another. Everything can be replaced, you cannot. The rude, vile, trash who torment you can be removed as well. If you can't come to a peaceful resolve, remove yourself from the problem. It doesn't matter if they are family or not. Move or seek help in doing so. For every problem you face, there is a way of handling it properly. If you are overwhelmed, ask for help. When you screw up, own it. Don't make excuses. I hate excuses.

There is a solution to pretty much every problem life throws at you. Suicide is never an option. If you are ever overwhelmed and there is a risk you will harm yourself or others, seek help immediately. Google Suicide Prevention or contact your local mental health unit and the help will be there at your finger tips and I strongly suggest you act on getting it.

In my case, I was getting the Hell out of a bad situation and never going back. There was nothing there for me and that was bringing me down. There is a large list of people I don't care to see or talk to again family members included. They served their purpose and in a lot of cases rather negatively. There are others I couldn't care less about mentioning and didn't bother telling you about because I didn't want to waste the ink.

We have all had the two-faced friends who pretend to be a friend to see what they can get from you. That type of shallow existence doesn't need recognition. I had a few of them. If it is a one way street, get rid of them. You are nobody's doormat. You don't owe them a damn thing. Friendship doesn't come with a price.

I did apologize to Jane through social media and threw the other bitches under the bus and wished her well. My idea of an apology is the admission and remorse for doing someone wrong. The fact I never got a response is ok with me. I have done my part and if they can't accept that I am truly sorry, there is nothing I can do further except make sure I don't repeat the error.

I find it amusing when someone I can't stand or who has wronged me like the bitches try and friend me through social media. The insanity definition resonates in my head. Doing the same thing over again and expecting a different result. I did however have an online chat with Rachel and gave her multiple opportunities to apologize and take responsibility for throwing me under the bus and acknowledge the fact she played an active and willing role in the incident.

All I got was excuses, useless information and pity trips. I called her on it and asked if her conscience could justify her actions or if it was merely swept under the carpet and then if she continued to pretend to be Jane's friend like the two-faced, lying bitch that she is. Then I deleted and blocked her ass after 30 seconds of silence. It says everything. All of them have made the list.

I couldn't resist posting "It's amazing how someone from your past that you can't stand tries to add you as a "friend" on social media when you haven't spoken to them in years or even bothered to look for them yourself. There is a reason for it. I also have to wonder if they have amnesia or suffered a blow to the head. If so, the more severe the head trauma, the better."

Here's a tip: If I haven't sought you out, it's because I no longer have use for you or want you in my life. Your purpose has been served. If I kept you, you are special.

Take a mental inventory of the people in your life. Write them down if you need to into 3 columns. Positive, Neutral and Negative. Another easy way to do this is by using a traffic light. For each person think of whether they are positively effecting your life, make it better, offer valuable advice, are there when you need them and so on. If you can answer "yes", write them under the positive side or Green Light spot. These are the people worth hanging onto. They are positive and should be kept in full contact but don't overdo it. They are here to help but not make your decisions for you. Don't be too needy or tell them too much, you may shift them to the other zones.

If you have someone who is only around when they want something, mistreats you and makes you feel like a second class citizen or is abusive to you in any way, they go on the Negative column or Red Light. Who likes getting stuck in traffic? These people are out to stop you from achieving your goals and dreams. Family members included.

These people are who you will sever all ties with immediately or distance yourself as much as possible. Unfortunately it may mean letting go of a few friends or relatives in the process especially if they are closer to the negative influence than you are to them. An example is a niece or nephew if your sibling is disrespectful to you. If you can be in the same room, keep it short and civil and then hang with someone else. If you have to deal with them at work/ school or at family events- Poker Face. No personal information under any circumstances. Siblings who withhold visitation of their children as a means of punishing you for not getting their way. Pathetic. Let them. It is on them, not you.

Kelly has always done things to go against me just because she can. If I were in a competition, she would support my competitor. I know if I were to open a business, she would support another of the same and promote them. It's really pathetic and shows nothing but jealousy since she is unemployed and can't hold a job or participate in the events I did. These actions really show what type of person they are: Poison. Poisonous people will do anything to destroy your happiness and accomplishments through sabotage, trash mouthing, being rude and disrespectful towards you, trash your dreams and do whatever it takes to make your life miserable. She had no problem running her mouth to those who bullied me to give them more material to use against me. Any second chance she has had is done. Red Light! You are better off without them. They are everywhere whether at work or in your own family. Everywhere. Be careful.

Poison is intended to kill. To drive you to suicide, depression, financial hardship and any other type of misery there is. They can drive you to a nervous breakdown. Not sure what a nervous breakdown is? Check it out with any credible medical based site. It is also knows as a Mental Breakdown. Some symptoms include outbursts, depression, insomnia, mood swings, suicidal thoughts, withdrawal from loved ones and loss of interest in favorable talks such as hobbies, lack of concentration. Should you feel these or know someone going through this get professional help immediately.

We use poison to kill rats and other pests. Ever have that nosy bitch at work who has to know everyone's business and loves running to the boss to snitch? The line is always the same. "I don't want to be the bad guy/ person but..." Yeah, right! That is your very intention you passive aggressive lying snake. To get someone suspended or fired, you pathetic.

Telling on someone is only permitted when they are going to hurt themselves or others. No exceptions. Bob took an extra 5 minutes on his lunch is none of your business. That's the boss's job to catch him not yours. When a snitch needs help for getting ill and has financial hardship, let Karma run its course. They are rude, condescending, conniving, backstabbing and basically belligerent at work to pretty much anyone who crosses their path.

When they get sick or have a traumatic event in their life, they expect help and sympathy. My first reaction is "Are you kidding me?!" I find it extremely difficult to be the better person and help them. In fact I don't. Fuck you and the horse you rode in on. I will not help someone who disrespects me and causes me grief. Hell No! We all have it in us, I am just more vocal about it. Some may feel like not doing it but give in and be the better person. I will not. The better person is a doormat. Disrespect is never to be rewarded under any circumstances. They intend to give others financial hardship by snitching, let them suffer the same. When nobody is there for them, they will know the lying, antagonistic waste of skin they are. Karma is a bitch and so are paybacks.

Also stand up for yourself. When you feel like crap you can bet our ass they don't. They feel good. They won. They bullied or mistreated you. I found over the years the best weapon to use is the truth. Most people can't handle it. It is my weapon of choice. Everyone has insecurities and weaknesses. I find whatever hurts the most and use it. Let them have it. If their husband ran off with someone else, tell them their husband deserved better than the soulless, selfish, shallow bitch she is. Let is sting. Now you are just pure evil. Polish your horns and smile especially if they crack like an egg. The truth hurts, doesn't it? Be careful. Some may get violent. Be assertive in these cases. You will know who you can do it to when the time arises.

Always be honest. If you don't want to hurt the other person's feelings, use an empathetic tone and start off with a compliment. For example, if the soup was over seasoned with pepper, tell them you really liked it but it had a little too much pepper. It's easy. Honest people have integrity. Candy coating is for kids especially when it is someone you can't stand. Tell it like it is. The respect you've wanted will come. Your enemies and bullies will stop because you are now an asshole or a bitch. Pin the label on and wear it with pride. You have your dignity. Wear it well.

There are the Neutral or Yellow Light people when you just aren't sure which column they belong in as they are both positive at times and negative. These are the ones to watch and the ones you shouldn't trust as much or at all. A Yellow Light is a Caution light. The transition between Green and Red. It changes quickly. True colors will shine through. Be careful around these ones. They may be just pretending and gathering information for the negative influences to be used against you at a later time. This goes for acquaintances such as co-workers as well. Give as little information as possible. Life is great Life is fine. The less they actually know the better. People talk and I really don't think you want your dirty laundry and problems to be conversation in the break room or at the water cooler when you aren't around.

Another good way to see if they are genuine is to stop talking to them for a while. If they don't make the effort to contact you or even enquire about you through mutual friends or acquaintances, they are either just acquaintances or negative people. You can figure that one out for yourself.

Sometimes you just work together and exchange pleasantries just to keep some harmony in the workplace. We are all nice to clients and customers we can't stand. This goes for co-workers too. Letting them know what we think of them will poison the workplace and/ or relations that could cost you your job or a rather important client. Keep them in the Neutral or Yellow Light Zones. Robotic state/ poker face relations. Keep the conversations and contact with them casual and professional. Do not let them in on anything too personal or give them anything they can use against you. Play by the rules.

The fact is it is a round world, everything comes around like the old saying "What comes around goes around." Treat others with disrespect, they will do the same to you. I will do it at your lowest point and will refuse to help when you need it. In Ron or Jerry's case, if they needed a kidney I would get tested to see if I was a match. If I were, I would have no problem telling them I was a match and how screwed they were because they would not be getting one. It sucks to be you!

241

You are born alone and die alone. The rest are here for the ride to either make it better or worse. Lose the dead weight. A good friend gave me the analogy of trying to swim with dumbbells. Thanks Dylan. Speaking of Dylan, he found happiness and has a partner who truly understands him. He isn't selfish. He was just holding out for what he wants. He got it and I wish him the very best. A friend I want to keep for life.

A negative person will always pull you down. Let them go and put them where they truly Belong. Red Light. You can't swim with dumbbells for very long. You either have to let them go or let them sink you. I waited too long in some cases and didn't have much of a choice in others. I can assure you I won't let it happen again.

I take inventory on a regular basis. Especially do this on social media. Be careful what you post and who you allow to see it. Social media should be treated as Yellow Light area at all times. Never bash anyone or post negative remarks about them. Do a generalization of the behavior if you must. Once you post anything and it is seen, it is out there forever. Copy, paste and share, right? Does it have the potential to be damaging against you or change how people feel about you? If yes, Don't Post It! Jokes are fine, however know your audience or make it clear some of your material could be offensive. They can stop following you but still be friends. Watch who you have on your "friends list" and what they can see. If you don't know them or trust them, don't add them. Your personal information can be used against you. Be smart and be safe.

On a personal note, most can't tell I have nerve damage to the right side of my face unless I mention it. The chances are that whatever you are self conscious about, they can't tell either. So don't mention it. Sometimes we are too self conscious about our looks and imperfections for our own good.

Another thing, forget about embarrassing things and mistakes you've done, they don't matter. If someone keeps reminding you of them, you need to cut ties with them. Red light. Forgive those who have wronged you too. If you can't forgive them, forgive yourself for being in the situation. You learned the lesson and what to watch for. Let it go. If you let it, it will torment you for the rest of your life or could turn to anxiety, depression and substance abuse. Who wants that? The only one it hurts is you. Let the hurt go. Today is a new day or a new page ready to be written the way you want. Reruns are boring on TV. Why have them constantly in your head of tings from the past? If you think the person who wronged you thinks about it all time, forget about it. You aren't even a thought. They don't care about you. Stop being a victim and feeling sorry for yourself. It's depressing. Move on.

Accept the fact you can't please everyone and concentrate on yourself. Spending your life trying to please everyone else and neglecting yourself makes you a servant. Do what you want to make things better for you. Saying "yes" and doing everyone favors makes you a doormat especially when you get mad at yourself for doing it. If you don't want to do it, don't do it. Say "No." It's ok. You aren't a servant. You don't have to say the right thing all the time. Be honest. if they can't take the honesty, respect your decision and they resent you, red light! It's easy.

Stop worrying about the future and take it as it comes. The future is about setting goals and accomplishments. Set achievable goals and accomplish them. Do what is right for yourself. I want you to do yourself a big favor. I want you to take care of that wonderful, talented, beautiful person you see in the mirror every day. Don't ever let anyone else decide what is best for them. You decide that.

If you don't love that person staring back at you, nobody else will or will ever be able to give them what you can. Treat that person like a diamond and cherish them until the end. Give that person the best you can. Only you can. That is who you have to rely on and never let them down. Make your life count and have no regrets. Mistakes happen, learn from them and don't repeat them. Don't dwell on them. That's life. Live it. Learn from it. Listen to and follow your intuition. It is never wrong. Enjoy it and write the best story you can.

Justin Williamson

ABOUT THE AUTHOR

· · · · · · ● · · · · · · · ·

Wyatt was born and raised in Southwestern Ontario and currently lives in Windsor, Ontario. He is a certified chef for the coast guard and a Golf & Country Club. His background includes business management, union steward, and hotel/ restuarant management. He runs a small business on the side Walkerville Candles & Gifts which can also be purchased on Amazon. He is currently in a relationship for the last 18 years. His hobbies include scuba diving, cycling, working out and his family at home which includes 2 dogs and 2 cats.

CPSIA information can be obtained
at www.ICGtesting.com
Printed in the USA
LVHW081116181219
640914LV00006B/21/P

9 781643 671314